THE CHRONICLES OF FAERIE

THE SUMMER KING

ACHILL
ISLAND

Saddle Head

Dirk (Boo

Europe's
Highest Sea Cliffs

Achill Head

Carrickakin

Croaghaun Doo
2,192 ft.

Moyteoge Head

Keem Bay

Achill Island

IRELAND

Claremorris

Castlebar

Castlerea

Westport

Tara

Clew
Bay

Dublin

Bray

River Shannon

Kildare

Irish Sea

Tullamore

Atlant
Ocear

Atlantic Ocean

0   1

Scale of

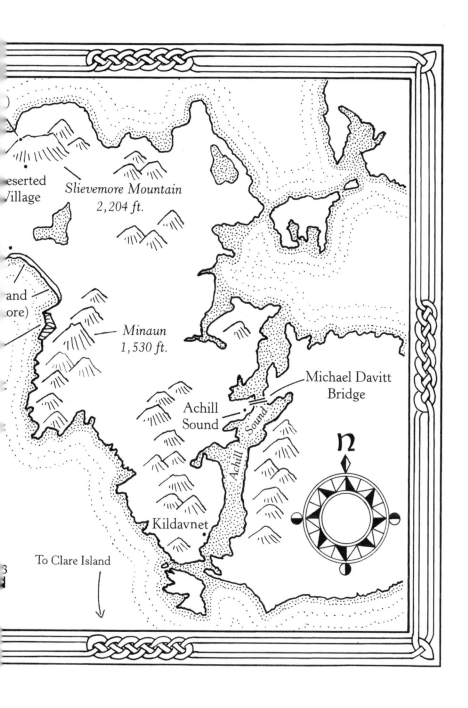

)

eserted
Village

Slievemore Mountain
2,204 ft.

and
ore)

Minaun
1,530 ft.

Michael Davitt
Bridge

Achill
Sound

Achill Sound

n

Kildavnet

To Clare Island

Also by O.R. Melling

The Druid's Tune

The Singing Stone

My Blue Country

Other books in The Chronicles of Faerie series

The Hunter's Moon

Adult Fiction

Falling Out of Time

THE CHRONICLES OF FAERIE
THE SUMMER KING

O. R. MELLING

Amulet Books • New York

Library of Congress Cataloging-in-Publication Data
has been applied for.

ISBN 10: 0-8109-5969-0
ISBN 13: 978-08109-5969-9

Copyright © 2006 O.R. Melling

Designed by Jay Colvin

Published in 2006 by Amulet Books, an imprint of Harry N. Abrams, Inc.

Printed and bound in U.S.A.
10 9 8 7 6 5 4 3 2 1

HNA ▉▉▉▉▉
harry n. abrams, inc.
a subsidiary of La Martinière Groupe

115 West 18th Street
New York, NY 10011
www.hnabooks.com

Permissions
Verse from Runrig song on page 52 "Faileas Air An Airigh" words & music by Calum
& Rory MacDonald © 2003, Chrysalis Music Ltd. Used by permission. All rights
reserved.

Verse on page 55 is from the poem "Connemara," from *The Collected Poems of Oliver
St. John Gogarty:* Constable, 1951.

The lines on page 130 are from "The First Elegy" copyright © 1982 by Stephen
Mitchell, from *The Selected Poetry of Rainer Maria Rilke,* translated by Stephen
Mitchell. Used by permission of Random House, Inc.

The poem on pages 124 and 140 and extracts from "The Colloquy of Fintan and the
Old Hawk of Eacaill" in Chapters Eleven and Twelve are taken from *Achill Island:
Archaeology-History-Folklore* by Theresa McDonald (IAS Publications, Tullamore,
Ireland, 1997), reprinted with the kind permission of the author.

In addition to the above, there are two traditional Irish-language songs on pages 160
and 195–196 as listed in the glossary.

The lines on page 334 are from " the Stolen Child" by W. B. Yeats.

All other poems and songs written by the author.

For Findabhair,
this was always yours

Acknowledgments

Many thanks to Georgie Whelan, mum and supporter extraordinaire; Patricia Burns, sister and fellow climber on Achill; Sheila Pratschke and the wonderful staff of the Tyrone Guthrie Centre at Annaghmakerrig; John Duff and Brian Levy (for a bed in New York!); Marcus McCabe and Kate Mullaney of the Ark; Brenda Sutton, Weird-Sister on the Web; Sandy Burns for the poker game; Michael Scott for writerly advice and friendship, as always; Piers Dillon-Scott (Webmaster); Dr. Nena Hardie, intrepid fellow traveler to Orkney and the Western Isles; Professor Dáibhí ó Cróinín for help with the Irish (any errors are mine); Joe Murray, computer guardian angel; the Arts Council of Ireland and Cultural Relations Committee for travel grants; agents Lynn and David Bennett of the Transatlantic Literary Agency Inc.; all at Abrams, especially my editor, Susan Van Metre, and Jason Wells and Samantha Sizemore. Last but not least, *Na Daoine Maithe*, for their generous permission and assistance. *Go raibh míle maith agaibh!*

Oɴe

It was a cold wind that blew from the left hand of the moon. A cold wind that woke the one who slept on the mountain. Ancient eyes looked out at the still stars and the slumbering sea. With a slow spread of wings, the great bird rose from his eyrie and flew over the water. His shadow sailed the dark-blue waves as his eyes searched the horizon for signs of the harbinger.

She came on a white horse that stepped upon the moon's trail crossing the water. As above, so below. She was pale and beautiful and luminous as the stars.

Over the distance of sea and sky, time and tide, he called to her.

"I sing of the ruined nest on Eagle Mountain."

Her hair flowed around her like quicksilver. Her voice was melodious.

"The Midsummer Fire must burn in the West."

His anger was swift and furious. As the golden wings beat the air, his cries shattered the night. When at last he grew calm, a sigh issued from his throat.

"Would you free the king?"

She had already turned the head of her steed. She was already disappearing over the rim of the sea. Her voice lingered on the wind that stirred the waters.

"Light may lie hidden inside a dark thing."

She woke with a start, and the images of the dream splintered around her. For one dizzying second she was utterly lost. Where was she? *Who* was she? The answer seemed impossible: a fragile creature swallowed by a giant bird flying over the ocean.

Then Laurel Blackburn remembered.

The low drone of the airplane was almost a purr. The lights had been dimmed in the cabin to help the passengers sleep. Rain spattered against the small window on her left. It was night outside. Far below, the dark waves of the Atlantic heaved in slow motion. The yellow speck of a lone ship traversed the vast waters.

Not fully awake, Laurel turned without thinking to speak with her twin. She recoiled instantly. A stranger sat in the seat beside her. She closed her eyes as the pain knifed through her. Her thoughts went back to the flight the two of them had taken the previous year. She could almost catch the scent of lilac in the air, her sister's favorite perfume.

There sat Honor beside her, scribbling in her journal, glass bangles clinking, all excitement and chat. She had been more than happy to give Laurel the window seat, as flying made her nervous. In some ways each twin mirrored the other, with fair hair, hazel-green eyes, and finely honed features, but it wasn't difficult to tell them apart. Honor was the free spirit in her long flowing skirt, embroidered top, and seashell belt. Her hair fell loosely over her shoulders and she had four piercings in each ear to hold all the silver stars and moons. She had a shy and wistful smile, and her voice was low and soft-spoken. Laurel was the stronger personality, forthright and outgoing. She dressed in a simpler though more stylish fashion, usually designer label jeans with a cotton shirt and jacket. Her hair was also long, but she preferred to wear it up.

"We could go hill-walking in the Wicklow Mountains," Honor suggested, biting the end of her pen. "That would suit both of us. You'd get lots of exercise and I could go exploring."

"Exploring?"

Laurel raised an eyebrow at the euphemism for her sister's real wish.

"Don't start," her twin warned. "I don't make fun of your obsessions."

"Sports and fitness are not obsessions."

"Hmm."

Their differences were obvious even as babies. When Honor didn't get what she wanted, she burst into tears. Laurel would open her mouth and yell. Before they reached school-age, Honor had pestered her parents to teach her how to read and was soon begging for a library card. Laurel had no interest in books. She was always outdoors, on Rollerblades or bicycle in good weather, and ice-skates or toboggan as soon as the snow arrived. She would do her best to drag her twin with her.

Come out and play! I've made a snow fort! You can read later.

Let's go! The pool's only open for three more hours. Finish your book when we get home!

No one was surprised that Honor's grades were high from the start while Laurel barely passed. The only things that Laurel liked about primary school were recess and Phys Ed. High school proved more of the same, but along with being captain of the girl's basketball team, Laurel discovered the world of boys. Honor, on the other hand, retreated into books and study and soon gained a reputation for being a loner. Her sister did what she could to encourage a social life.

Jason's friend Eddie is really nice. Kind of a nerd like you, but seriously cute when he takes off his glasses. Hang out with us. A movie, a pizza, that's all I ask. Please please please.

I'll go on one condition: you study with me every night.

You can't mean it!

Half an hour, Monday to Thursday.

Oh all right, if it'll keep you and the 'rents happy.

By graduation, Honor was at the top of her class, and Laurel had scraped a solid pass thanks to her twin's tutoring. As a reward, their parents gave them a summer vacation in Ireland visiting their grandparents. Neither had been there since they were four years old when their father brought them over to meet his family. At seventeen, both were thrilled to set off on their own.

Laurel stared bleakly out the airplane window. She was now eighteen. It was almost a year and a day since she and Honor had made that trip.

If only they hadn't gone.

She leaned forward to rummage in the handbag tucked under the seat in front of her. The snacks and soda her mother had packed were still unopened. She pulled out a diary made of handcrafted paper. Honor's journal. Her twin loved to write.

I'm words, you're action, she used to say. *Two halves of a whole.*

Laurel turned the pages, smiling at the forest of exclamation marks, brackets, smiley faces, and hearts. There were magazine cut-outs from *The Lord of the Rings* movies and photos of the two of them horsing around. The writing scrawled across the pages in feathery strokes. Some entries were short and breathless, others detailed and even illustrated. Only a few were dated. Honor had a rich fantasy life. She loved myth and legend, liked to chart her dreams, and was adept at creating imaginary worlds. It was all very alien to the pragmatic Laurel.

Give me the facts, ma'am, just the facts.

Of course they had fights. What sisters didn't? And especially two with such contrary natures. But only a twin can know how close a twin can be.

Laurel turned on the overhead light. The white pages of the journal shone dimly.

⌐ ⌐

That dream again. It's so beautiful. The shining lady on a horse and the huge golden eagle. I always wake up with a kind of thrill. It's like a premonition—no, a promise!—that something wonderful is going to happen. But it also makes me feel sad and restless and sort of worried, as if the wonderful thing could be awful, too. Weird.

The entries made in Ireland were the ones that concerned Laurel the most. Scattered and disjointed, they meandered through the early days of that doomed vacation.

*"Up the airy mountain and down the rushy glen
We daren't go a-hunting for fear of little men."*

Hah! I'm not afraid of little men. In fact, I am a-hunting one! I'm sure I spotted him scrambling up the side of the cliff as if he was strolling on the sidewalk!!! I knew Bray Head would be a good place to start. Under hill and under mountain, isn't that the saying?

You have to keep a sharp lookout for them, that's the trick. They move so fast, at the corner of your eye, and they hide all the time. You have to keep looking sideways in a sort of lazy, casual, I-don't-care-if-I-see-you-or-not kind of a way. That's when you spot them.

He says he doesn't climb up cliffs and that I have an overactive imagination. I don't think so, mister!!!
I'm getting lots of exercise climbing Bray Head. Is it a

small mountain or a big hill??? Didn't huff and puff half as much today as yesterday. (I'll be as fit as El before she knows it, hah!) I love going up there. There are different paths that lead to the top, but I've already picked my favorite. When the sun shines through the ivy and the leaves of the bushes, it's like going through a green tunnel. There's a tree blasted by lightning that looks like an old witch pointing at the sky. When you stop to look back, the Irish Sea stands up behind you like a blue wall.

Today I discovered what's been biting my legs—not bugs, but plants!!! Nettles!!! They look so innocent, like wild mint or something, but they sting like a swarm of bees. (I'm never wearing shorts up there again.) The roly-poly man pointed them out, and he also showed me this other weed that grows close by which cures the stings. The dock leaf. You scrunch it up and rub the green juice onto your leg where the nettle scratched. Works great. I said it was cool that the good and bad plants grew together. He said something strange that keeps ringing in my head: "A bright thing can nurse a dark heart, even as light may lie hidden inside a dark creature." So what's that supposed to mean and what's it got to do with nettles?!

When she first came upon these notes, Laurel was sure they belonged to her sister's fantasies.

The doorway to his house could be anywhere. I'm determined to find it!!! He's so sneaky though. He always appears behind me, no matter how much I watch out for him. He's not exactly a nice little guy. Sometimes he smells like he doesn't wash too often. And he's always drinking out of the bottle tucked into his belt. I'm pretty sure he was drunk today. His face was redder than usual and he kept hiccuping. And what's with all the big words, most of them used wrongly I might add? I think he's trying to impress me, which is kind of creepy. And that funny thing he does with his eyes. I wouldn't trust him as far as I can throw him. Then every once in a while he says something really pro-found in a deep voice and he looks like something totally different, something very old and scary.

Dispersed among these entries were passages about Laurel and their grandparents.

El came climbing with me today. I'm so glad. We've done hardly anything together since we got here, what with me going off on my own and her hanging around with Ian. What's that about, eh? Hardly her type. Angry young man on a motorcycle. You wouldn't catch that boy in a team sport. Gotta admit he's hot though. Mr. Tall, Dark, and Handsome. Anyway, I think she was feeling guilty. Me too. We took a picnic with us, up Bray Head, ham sambos, donuts, and Cokes.

There was a gang of hang gliders jumping off the cliffs! It was so amazing to watch. Irish guys are not shy. They just came right over and started talking to us, asking our names and where were we from and were we twins. (If I had a dollar for every time, I mean what do people think we are— clones???)

When they heard our accents, they started calling us "Yanks"—everyone calls us that here!—and tried to talk us into joining their club. It only takes a week of lessons and omigod you're up in the air! No way. Not in a million years. I'm not afraid of flying, boys, only crashing and dying! El's thinking about it, of course. I could see her doing it. No sign of the roly-poly man the whole time we were up there. I didn't expect him to show. I told him El's not a believer when he asked me about her.

Each time Laurel read the journal, her suspicions increased. Maybe this wasn't a story after all? Maybe her sister really was meeting someone on Bray Head?

I am so excited I can hardly breathe! I could die!!! The roly-poly man is going to introduce me to the Court. Omigod. OMIGOD. This is all my hopes and dreams come true!!! They have asked to see me! Yes, me! He hinted at something big, something they want me to do, but he wouldn't say what. The Boss will tell me. (I could hear the capital letters when he said that!!!) I know what this means. It's in all the tales. A mission. Some kind of special task. Something they can't do them-selves, so they need me to do it. Yes! Yes! Whatever it is, YES!

At this point Laurel always shuddered. Were they some kind of cult? Were they "grooming" her twin for some sinister purpose? They seemed to be deliberately stringing her along, keeping her off balance.

I think I've found the doorway. It's got to be somewhere

along that ledge jutting out from the cliff. Not easy to reach, but not impossible. I was on the ledge when the roly-poly man showed up. He started yelling and cursing really loud. What an old grump. But I was actually quite afraid. There was no one else around. I kept mumbling apologies as I scrambled back up. He calmed down after a few gulps from his bottle. Then he declared that they were not sure I was the right person for the job! I thought he was getting back at me for finding the door, when he added that they thought I wasn't strong enough. And to make matters worse, he even said they would rather ask Laurel!!! How am I supposed to feel about that?

Then came the most baffling entries. Laurel's vague memories of her twin looking flushed and happy only confused her all the more.

His name is Midir. Let me write that again. Midir. Midir. Midir. One more time. Midir.

If I say he is gorgeous, that is a major understatement. Golden-red hair that falls to his shoulders. Eyes that really and truly shine like stars. Tall and beautiful. Oh so beautiful. He kept giving me these long deep looks. I was all tongue-tied and dumb as usual, but he didn't seem to notice. He smiled this amazing smile and said he had not been told I was beautiful. (Ooh lah lah!!! Somersaulting stomach.) He invited me to a party tonight. Can't wait. Wow, is this the most amazing summer of my life or what?

Can't write much. No energy. Way too tired and kind of

wrecked. I had soooooo much fun. I can't begin to describe it. Everything was bright and sparkly. There was a fabulous feast with totally yummy things, but Midir kept telling me not to eat or drink. He said if I did, I might never get back. For a minute I thought—maybe I don't care? But then I realized, nah, I couldn't stay there. Not without El. I wouldn't go anywhere forever without her.

An agonizing pang always came with that last sentence. And in its wake, a plague of questions. Were these people real or imaginary? Honor didn't go out at night. Or did she? Was she sneaking out when everyone was asleep? It was hardly the sort of thing her meeker twin did, but what if she was being influenced by others?

Complications with Midir. He doesn't want me to take the mission. Says he couldn't bear any harm coming to me. He kept going on about "perilous matters" and that he would "rather seek another to do it," yadda yadda. You know what? I think he's falling in love with me. HOW GREAT IS THAT???!!!

If only I could tell El about it.

—∞　∞—

If only, Laurel repeated in her mind. How often had she said those two little words?

If only.

Still no word from Midir. I miss him so much. I don't know what to do with myself. I tried reading, but couldn't concentrate. TV's no good either. There was a plan to go to Powerscourt today, with the grands, but it's postponed till tomorrow because El has gone off with Ian. (Hmph.) Test-driving a new bike. She's obviously a good influence on him. He actually managed to smile at me and it didn't break his face!

I know what I'll do. I'll go climb the Head. It's like a magnet, drawing me to it . . .

Ah, who am I kidding? I'm going up there to mooch around. Desperate times call for desperate measures. I'll huff and I'll puff on the roly-poly man's door and make him tell me what's going on!

And that was the last entry. There was nothing more to read after that, for nothing more could be written.

Honor died that day.

Two

Though I have the gift of prophecy
And understand all mysteries
If I have not love
I am nothing.

Laurel stood between her grandparents at the front of the little chapel. The old-fashioned pews were of polished oak, with carved railings and red velvet cushions. The stained glass windows reflected colored light. The pale-gold pipes of the organ spired to the rafters.

Love is patient
Love is kind
It bears all things.

The memorial service was arranged by her grandparents for the anniversary of Honor's death. Laurel knew her twin would have approved. She could see her sister leaning against the pew, admiring the angelic figures in the high, arched windows.

"There are stories here," she would have whispered, more loudly than intended.

"Yeah," Laurel would have hissed back. "It's called religion."

Blessed are they who mourn
For they shall be comforted.

The words fell gently around her like soft Irish rain, but she was not comforted. Unlike her twin, Laurel did not believe in anything beyond physical reality; certainly not an afterlife. The only mystery she had ever accepted was the invisible bond between herself and her sister. They always knew where the other was and, even apart, they could sense each other's feelings. There was the time when Honor was being bullied in the playground and Laurel ran six streets over from her hockey practice to send the culprits packing. "I heard her calling in my head," was what she told her parents. And when she, in turn, fractured her arm on a skiing trip, Honor at home had cried out in pain, nursing the mirrored limb as if it too were broken.

Love never fails.

The minister's look was sympathetic.

Love is as strong as death.

—⌒ ⌒—

Laurel linked arms with her grandmother and grandfather. She was glad she could be there with them. When she arrived at Dublin Airport, she had seen immediately how much they had aged in the past year, how much they had suffered from having a grandchild die in their care. He, once tall and dignified, stooped over his cane, while she clutched his arm like a frail bird.

Laurel had dropped her luggage to embrace them.

"Thank you," Nannaflor said through her tears. "We thought you would never come back."

"It wasn't your fault. You did nothing wrong. You've got to accept that."

"Have you?" asked Granda gently.

After the service, the congregation gathered in the church hall for tea and sandwiches. They were a small community in a small seaside town, and they all knew each other. The murmur of conversation mingled with the friendly rattle of china. Neat little quarters of ham and cheese were served along with raisin scones and slices of rhubarb pie. Most of the people were friends of Laurel's grandparents, and many had known her father when he was a boy. Some shook her hand in silent sympathy. Others wrapped their arms around her.

"Your daddy used to pinch the apples from our orchard. Make sure you tell him the Kilrudderys were asking for him."

"You're from Niagara Falls, aren't you? You wouldn't happen to know my cousin, Heather Brown? I believe she's living somewhere over there. Florida, I think it is."

"Come visit us. Don't be a stranger."

Laurel drifted through the soft-spoken company, doing her best to be polite. Though she wouldn't admit it to herself, her eyes kept searching the crowd.

When he came up behind her and caught her by the arm, she wasn't really surprised.

"Let's scarper. I'm being nibbled to death by a hundred little ducks."

Before she could object, he had pulled her out of the hall and into the street. The road was quiet and secluded, with old chestnut trees and a grassy verge. Parked in front of the church was a dark-blue motorcycle with shiny chrome fittings.

"Do you mind!" she said angrily, breaking away from him.

"At last," he said, "a show of spirit!"

Ian Gray was the minister's son and the bane of the congregation. As gossip went, he had always been in trouble; fighting at school, running away, even robbing the collection boxes. In recent times he had apparently calmed down, working as a courier to finance his passion for bikes, but he remained sullen and hostile to his father's parish.

The biker's gear he was wearing accented his height—Rayven jacket, leather pants, and tall narrow boots. A silver stud pierced his eyebrow. He looked older than his nineteen years, with sharp angular features and a shock of black hair that fell over his forehead. The intensity of his eyes, an icy blue, made her look away.

She stared instead at his motorcycle.

It was the latest Fireblade, a high-powered sportsbike with a reputation for speed and agility. The decals on the tank were fiery wings. Beneath them curled words that she guessed were Irish, though she didn't know what they said.

Póg mo thóin.

"You got the bike."

He looked pleased.

"You remember."

He reached out to draw her toward him, but she backed away.

"Stop it!"

Anger flashed across his face, followed by a hard grin that was almost a snarl.

"At least you're still in there. You look like a shadow of your former self."

"It's none of your business what I look like," she retorted.

"No?"

His lip curled as he looked her over, slowly and deliberately. Though she tried not to, Laurel couldn't help but reflect on what he saw, how much her appearance had altered from the last time they met. In place of her lean and athletic build, she appeared thin and fragile. Her face was pale without makeup, her hair lank and straggling over her shoulders. She had taken to wearing her sister's clothing: today, a long denim skirt and bulky pink sweater. Even in June she felt the chill of the damp

Irish air, and she folded her arms to stop herself from shivering.

"Little girl lost," he said. "You look more like her now."

"Don't talk about her! I can't stand it!"

Laurel's voice broke.

His anger dissipated, and his tone took on a softer edge.

"Do you still blame me? It's not my fault . . . We couldn't have known—"

"I don't want to talk about it! Leave me alone!"

She spoke harshly, to push him away, yet she didn't go herself. It was as if she were caught there.

All his emotions simmered in his face: dismay, hurt, fury. Then he went cold. He leaned against his bike, took out a pack of cigarettes, and offered them to her.

"You know I don't smoke. And I thought you quit."

He shrugged, lit one for himself.

"People change," he said, inhaling.

"You haven't."

His look was veiled behind the cloud of smoke. She knew she was being unfair. The first time they met, he was only five years old, while she and Honor were four. Nannaflor had brought the twins to the minister's house so they could play with his son. When Ian pulled Honor's hair and made her scream, Laurel thumped him so hard he ran off crying. That was their only encounter as children. Last year, the three met again as teenagers. Though Honor had shown little interest in the tall young man who arrived at the door, Laurel was immediately attracted. He made a joke about "losing his honor over Honor," and challenged her to a duel. She couldn't help but laugh.

And then there was the motorcycle. She had always wanted to ride one and when she told him so, he was quick to offer her a ride. They roared off into the Wicklow Mountains, through the Sally Gap, and over the bogs. He drove aggressively, swerving past cars and trucks, and leaning into the curves. The road was a gray streak, the landscape a green blur. Pressing against his back, her arms around him, she had loved the rush of wind and speed.

Then he took her clubbing in Dublin. She was surprised when he said he loved to dance, and more surprised that he was good. He moved like his bike, sleek and powerful.

The first time they kissed, she got a mild shock, like static electricity. He had felt it too. They both recoiled at the same time.

"Shall we try that again?" he said.

And then the fatal day. She was supposed to visit Powerscourt Gardens with Honor and her grandparents, but had canceled it at Ian's request. He was test-driving the new Fireblade he hoped to buy, and wanted her to come with him. She couldn't resist.

They were at the showroom when it struck her, like a great soft blow. She doubled over, clutched her stomach.

He moved to help her.

"What's wrong? Are you all right?"

"We've got to get back to Bray!"

"What?"

"Now!"

And when they arrived at her grandparents' house and discovered the terrible news, he had tried to hold her and she had pushed him away. Lost in her own horror, oblivious to his anguished look, she had screamed hysterically.

"I should've been with *her*, not you!"

Now standing before him, faltering under the weight of those memories and the catastrophe that was her sister's death, she repeated the words.

"I should've been with her, not you."

She didn't see him flinch, didn't see the hurt that was swiftly smothered by rage. All she saw was the sharp intake of breath as he drew on his cigarette, and the deliberate aim of smoke in her direction.

A spark of her old self ignited.

"Do you enjoy being a jerk?"

He returned her gaze coolly.

"If I wasn't bad, how else would the rest of you know you were good?"

Once again he drew on his cigarette, but before he could exhale she made her move.

Perhaps it was a burst of pent-up emotion, so many strong feelings held down for too long. Or maybe it was the old image of him bullying Honor. She didn't intend to be violent, but her push was strong enough to knock him and the bike over. Turning to leave, she heard him coughing out smoke and swearing vociferously behind her.

In the hall, she found her grandparents with the minister.

"I'd like to go now," she told them quietly.

He was gone by the time they came out, but she could hear the motorcycle howling in the distance. She felt a perverse surge of gratitude toward him. He had awakened something in her. She had arrived in Ireland with a purpose, a plan, though unsure and anxious about carrying it out. Now the fire had been kindled. She was ready to do what she had come here to do.

THREE

Later that day, Laurel set out for Bray Head. It was early evening, still bright and sunny with the long June hours. Though she could feel her jet lag slowing her down, she was too uneasy to rest.

The sea front was bustling with a summer festival. The air rang with a medley of musics from a carousel of golden horses, a folk group on the bandstand, and drummers on the boardwalk beating lambegs and bodhráns. Clowns on stilts strode through the crowds, while children with painted faces played chase below them. As the Ferris wheel twirled overhead, screams echoed downward like the cry of the seagulls.

Laurel walked along the promenade, a little dazed by the din. On her right, green lawns accommodated the festival rides and stalls. Behind them was a Victorian terrace of hotels, bed-and-breakfasts, and noisy pubs with canopies over open-air seating. On her left, beyond the wrought-iron balustrade and a stony strand, shone the Irish Sea. The tide was out. Ripples stirred the glassy surface that mirrored the silvery blue of the sky. Children paddled in the shallows or built castles in the wet sand by the water's edge. But Laurel noticed little of this, for her attention rested on the small mountain ahead of her.

It rose up at the end of the boardwalk like a hump-backed giant tumbling into the sea. Though cloaked in heather and gorse, its uneven slopes showed bare patches of rock that shone white in the sunlight. On the summit stood a concrete cross.

Like a tombstone, she thought.

She had dreaded returning to this place. There were cruel reminders everywhere. Circling the peak were hang gliders soaring like giant butterflies. Were they the young men she and Honor had flirted with on the day of their picnic? The same shocked witnesses who had raised the alarm and reported what happened?

I saw her climbing onto the ledge. She was moving slowly, carefully, but then she lost her balance.

The winds were strong that day. Gusts were coming from every which way.

I heard her cry out, saw her waving her arms before she fell.

There are signs and warnings all over the Head, but people still take chances. They assume it's safe because it's only a hill, but it can be dangerous.

There was no one near her. No one to help her.

I saw her hit the water. It was awful. I'll never forget it. A boat went out, but not soon enough.

By the time we got to her, it was too late. She was already gone.

Laurel's feet dragged, as if reluctant to continue, but she forced herself onward. The iron railings along the promenade became a low stone wall where people sat, eating their ice creams. The boardwalk itself tapered away into a tarmac road that curved upward to the Head. She knew where she was going. There were passages in her twin's journal that she knew by heart, and they were her guide.

There are lots of holly bushes up here. "The gentle tree" they call it. Hardly any berries, though. The birds eat them. The same birds that are doing all the cheeping and peeping, I bet. The air is thick and sweet. It's like an earthy perfume, lush and green. I love being here with the sea and the sky and the mountain. It makes me feel part of something so much bigger than myself.

Laurel did not share Honor's love of nature. The pungent leaf mold caught at her throat, making her cough. The dense press of greenery was suffocating. Twigs cracked underfoot like brittle bones, and gnarled roots kept tripping her. The wind made a mournful sound in the ragged branches of the Scots pine.

It wasn't long before she discovered the tract of nettles that had attacked her sister. Though Laurel's jeans protected her legs, the weeds stung her hands as she pushed her way through them. She didn't stop to look for the dock leaves Honor had mentioned, but took some comfort from the shared experience. She imagined her twin forging ahead and yelping in panic as she tried to spot the hornets she thought were biting her.

The higher Laurel climbed, the harder it got. The brambles grew thicker, the briars thornier, and the path so steep her legs ached. She began to feel uneasy. A stray thought crossed her mind. *The mountain's working against me.* Though she told herself not to be ridiculous, she kept looking behind her. The shadows seemed to deepen in the undergrowth. The air had grown chill.

Then someone burst out of the bushes and onto the path! She cringed instinctively, but the runner veered past her and up the hill. An athlete in shorts and sneakers, with red hair tied in a pony tail, he had barely even noticed her. She tried to laugh at herself, but she was shaking.

As Laurel approached the peak, she heard the hang gliders calling to each other high in the air. She hunched over in case they saw her. She didn't want to meet them. They were not the people she was looking for.

Now the path brought her through a spinney of tangled trees. Many were shattered and blackened by lightning. With a pang, she found the one Honor had described as a witch pointing upward.

At last she came to the edge of the mountain where it sheered into the sea. White gulls wheeled in the air, screeching at each other. She could see the strand far below, the tiny people on the promenade, and the Ferris wheel twirling like a toy in the wind. But she was more interested in what lay only a few feet down. There a narrow shelf jutted out from the cliff, like a brow frowning over the rock face.

Laurel was overcome with the knowledge that this was where Honor had spent her last moments alive. She could see her twin sitting in the sun, journal on her lap, writing a story about meeting "them." But what madness made her climb onto the ledge? If only Laurel had been there, she could have, *would have* stopped her.

On a sudden impulse, Laurel lowered herself over the cliff edge. Ignoring her own protests, as if driven against her will, she inched her away along the shelf, slowly, carefully. Her sister believed it led to a doorway. Was there an opening somewhere along the ridge? A high cave in the mountainside? Where she pressed against the rock face, the stone was surprisingly cold despite the sunshine. She could hear the sea crashing below her, but didn't look down. Though she had a head for heights, she felt dizzy. What was she doing? This was crazy! A gust of wind blew around the corner. The sudden buffet nearly threw her off balance. She teetered on the edge of terror. A chilling thought slid into her mind. This is where Honor fell. Would she follow her? Was that why she had come here?

No.

As quickly as she had decided to do it, Laurel changed her mind. Battling a wave of despair, she retreated to the point where she had started. Only then did she discover, with a shock, that she was not alone.

He was carrying a load of dried sticks in his arms: a

short, stout, red-faced man. His ginger hair sprouted out from all angles—curly locks that fell to his shoulders, bushy beard, and tufts that grew from his ears and nostrils. He was just under five feet, more stocky than plump. His woolen trousers were tucked into rubber boots and he wore a tatty vest over a grimy red shirt. A patched top hat was perched on his head. Something about him made her think of a red badger. The eyes, dark like two blackberries, squinted down at her.

"Ye shouldn't be at that," he said. His voice was gravelly. "Ye might fall, and then where would ye be?"

She felt a shiver of fear. Honor had made him sound cute and funny, yet this little man seemed neither. There was something vaguely unpleasant about him. She was struck by a terrifying suspicion. The gliders might not have seen him from the air. He could have crouched down. Did he push Honor? Would he push *her*?

He dropped the sticks and reached out his hand.

"Come up outa dat, before ye catch your death."

He must have come from the spinney. That would explain the sticks. But she didn't see or hear anything when she went through it. Had he been hiding? Watching her? Her alarm was growing. She had to get off the ledge. She wished someone would come, but it was a secluded spot, and there was no sign of other hikers. There was nothing else to do but grab his hand.

His grip was sweaty, but with one strong pull he yanked her up and onto firm ground.

The first thing she noticed was his smell, like moldy

earth. She stepped away quickly, from him and the cliff edge.

"The roly-poly man," she said.

"Is that moniker here to stay, then?"

He frowned, and in that moment she saw something older, darker, and bloodred. Something displeased. But the impression passed quickly, like a flare. Still, it left her uneasy for though he appeared to be harmless, in her heart she knew he wasn't.

"Not to worry," he said, with a quick laugh. "Call me what ye want to, just don't call me early in the morning." His voice took on an ingratiating wheedle. "And isn't it a grand thing ye got here at last? We almost gave up the ghost, and us after sendin' ye messages all year long. Do ye not mind your dreams at'all?"

She stared him, confused.

"What? What are you talking about?"

Her own voice sounded strange to her, hollow and robotic, like someone in shock. But hadn't she come looking for him? Didn't she hope he would show up?

"I . . . I . . . don't understand," she stammered.

"Ye mean ye don't know the story?"

Only then did Laurel admit to herself that she didn't really know why she was there. She had been acting on instinct—so unlike her—even worse, on compulsion. She felt as if she were sliding toward a chasm. She needed to grasp onto something, anything, to keep from falling in.

"It's because of you," she burst out. "It's your fault she died!"

Yes, that was it. That was why she had come. To confront him.

The blackberry eyes stared back at her without blinking.

"Is it now? And why, then, does the guilt be hangin' off ye like a cloak? It's not me ye blame but yourself, I'm thinkin'."

The chasm was drawing nearer. She dug in her heels. She wouldn't let him trick her with words.

"I should've protected her from you."

He was quick to reply. "I didn't harm a hair on her head. 'Twas herself came after me, though I did me best to hide. 'Twas *ye*, not her, we wanted."

Laurel was at the brink, peering into the abyss. She stepped back again. Tried a different tack.

"Are you some kind of cult? Drugs? Religion?"

His gaze was implacable.

"Ye know very well that's not the case, and ye know what your sister was at."

"She didn't give you a name," Laurel said quickly. The pressure was excruciating, the force of something she couldn't accept. "Whenever she mentions you, it's always vague."

"She knew the rules." His tone was matter-of-fact but Laurel heard the challenge. "'Tis bad luck to say too much about us."

He rummaged in the pockets of his vest and pulled out a little brown bottle. Unstoppering the cork, he took a long swig, then regarded her sideways.

They had reached the crux of the matter.

"Go'wan, grasp the nettle," he prompted. "I dare ye to say it. The F word. And I don't mean a curse."

"Fairies." She nearly choked. "Honor believed in fairies."

For the first time she truly met his eyes. Red pinpricks of light glinted inside the dark irises. There was no emotion there that she could recognize, no sympathy or concern or even judgment. His look was utterly alien and disinterested. In that gaze, she caught a glimpse of an impossible reality, ancient and unknowable. Anywhere else she might have been able to dismiss it, but not here, not on the side of a lonely mountain that fell into the sea.

Laurel began to back away. She felt her thoughts unraveling, her mind threatening to unhinge. Her words came out strangled.

"I . . . can't . . . do . . . this."

"Don't be afeard! Your sister needs ye! We need ye!"

His shouts trailed behind her as she stumbled back down Bray Head. Crashing through brush and briar, she grabbed at trees to keep from falling. Nettles stung her, brambles scraped her, but still she ran, like a deer fleeing before the hunter.

At last she broke from the greenery onto the stone steps that led to the sea front. But she almost barged into a familiar figure.

Ian did not react immediately, but stood gazing at his hands.

Still distraught, Laurel was about to accuse him of following her when she saw what he was holding. It was a large black bird, a crow or a raven. The dark wings were limp and ragged. Blood spattered the feathers, a livid red against the glossy black. Its neck had been wrung.

Ian looked up, eyes burning with shame.

As Laurel took in the stillness of the broken body, a primal rage tore through her. She stood helpless in the face of death.

"*Murderer.*"

He jerked back as the word struck him.

Then she brushed past and raced down the steps, toward the beach. Her need to escape was overwhelming, as if her very survival depended on it. When she reached the seashore, she kicked off her shoes and ran into the water. The shock of cold knocked the breath out of her, but she plunged in regardless. When she dove, seeking solace in the depths, she kept her eyes open though the salt sea stung.

Laurel knew it was her own mind torturing her, yet she continued to stare at what she saw. There in the blue-green shadows of the water, caught in laocoön strands of seaweed, was Honor's body, deathly white and beautiful.

The image drove her to the surface, gasping for air.

Back on the beach, shuddering with cold, she pulled on her shoes. The icy water had condensed her thoughts to the clarity of crystal. She knew why she had returned to Ireland. The truth was simple, if absurd and insane.

She had come to save Honor.

Four

The day was warm and sunny. Laurel rested in the back garden of her grandparents' house. It was a green leafy place surrounded by old stone walls covered with ivy, clematis, and sweet-scented honeysuckle. A cobbled path wound through flower beds spilling over with color. Bees hummed in the bright blossoms. At the end of the garden was a small orchard of crabapple trees. The terrace where Laurel sat was a chessboard of blue and gray flagstones. The tables and chairs were a lacy wrought-iron, painted white.

She had played in this garden as a child, the summer her father brought the twins to Ireland. Eyes half-closed, she gazed down the path that disappeared into the trees as the veil of her memory fluttered.

There they were, two little fair-haired girls running and giggling. They were playing hide-and-seek in the rhododendron, scattering the red petals over the grass. Honor wore a light sundress. Laurel was in jeans and a T-shirt, with a baseball cap turned backward on her head. Their game changed in an instant when they spotted something flitting through the air. Something tiny and winged. With squeals of laughter, they chased it to the bottom of the garden where it settled in a patch of blue-bells.

Their shouts and laughter broke off. A breathless silence. Holding each other's hands, they bent down to look.

"It's a fairy," Honor whispered.

"No it's not! It's a butterfly!"

Now Laurel strained to capture the image, but all she could recall was the faint impression of white wings veined with gold, lambent in the sunlight. Why couldn't she remember anything else? A sliver of doubt entered her mind.

She had not slept well the night before and had risen early that morning, disturbed and restless. Though she blamed her jet lag, she knew it was something else. Over the past year, she had grown accustomed to wandering through her days like a ghost, pale and insubstantial, not really there. But her experience on Bray Head had torn her out of her malaise. She felt as if she had emerged from a fog only to find herself standing on the edge of a precipice. Her terror made sense, a rational reaction to an irrational situation. Yet whatever the little man might say he was—and she didn't believe him for a minute—at least he existed. She needed to find him again, but did she have the courage?

"Give us a hand, pet," her grandfather said, pulling Laurel out of her reverie.

Granda carried a wooden tray rattling with cutlery,

crystal, and china. Behind him came Nannaflor, bearing the food. A white linen tablecloth lay folded in front of her, waiting to be spread. As Laurel shook the cloth into the air, it fluttered like wings.

The summer meal was light and delicious: cherry tomatoes in a nest of crisp lettuce with cucumber and green onions, chunks of old cheddar, pink rolls of ham, slices of smoked salmon, artichoke hearts in olive oil, and a round loaf of brown soda bread. For dessert, there were fresh strawberries with cream, and to drink, cold lemonade and a pot of strong tea.

When everything was laid out, Nannaflor grew flustered. Two bright spots appeared on her cheeks.

"By the way," she announced, her voice rising slightly. "I've invited Ian for lunch."

Laurel and her grandfather both looked sour.

"It's always pleasant to have company," Nannaflor added briskly, "and he's a good lad, no matter what may be said of him, and if people can't speak well of each other, they shouldn't speak at all."

Laurel and Granda remained silent.

Not long after, Ian arrived, wearing a freshly ironed shirt and blue jeans. Though he had combed back his hair, it insisted on falling into his face. He handed a bunch of flowers to Nannaflor and kissed her on the cheek.

"Is that a cut?" she said, brushing his hair aside anxiously. "Were you in an accident?"

"It's okay," he assured her. "I came off the bike, but it wasn't moving."

Laurel felt a pang of guilt as she spotted the red weal above his eye.

"I should take a closer look at it," Nannaflor pressed him. "My bag's in the hall."

"No, please don't." He laughed. "Honestly, I'm fine. Let's eat. You've put on a great spread as usual."

"Oh, it's not much," she said, delighted.

Laurel was surprised by the obvious affection between them. Ian's tone was warm and respectful when he spoke to Nannaflor, and she seemed to dote on him.

"There's plenty of cheese and salad," she said, heaping food onto his plate. "I know you won't take meat or fish."

Despite the friendly talk between the two, it was an awkward meal. Laurel only picked at her food. Since Honor's death, she ate very little, as nothing seemed to have any taste. Though she had muttered a quick hello to Ian when he arrived, she made a point of sitting away from him. He, in turn, ignored her, aside from an occasional sullen glance. It soon became obvious that he and Granda were also estranged. After a brief handshake on greeting, neither spoke to the other throughout lunch.

When they were finished eating, Ian insisted on clearing the dishes away and brought them into the house.

While he was gone, Nannaflor chided her husband. "You could at least be civil." Then she turned to Laurel with a sigh. "I think your grandfather is jealous of the attention I pay him."

"Now, Florence, you know that isn't so." Granda

shook his head. "He's trouble and always has been. And though he is the son of my dearest friends—and a favorite of yours—I've come across his like before and I don't trust him."

"People can change," Nannaflor argued. "Where's your faith?"

An uncomfortable silence fell over the table and grew worse as Ian's absence lengthened.

"What's taking him so long?" said Granda, suspiciously.

Nannaflor looked hurt.

"He's not robbing you, William."

When Ian returned at last, with a box of chocolates to add to dessert, Nannaflor threw her husband a triumphant glance.

Later, after their guest was gone, Laurel went to the kitchen to wash the dishes. Her grandmother joined her.

"I was hoping you and Ian . . ."

"I'm sorry, Nanna, it's not possible."

That night at supper, they heard the news. They had only sat down to eat when Nannaflor was called to the telephone. Moments later she returned, upset.

"It was Daisy. She's in a dreadful state. Ian has left. Packed up and gone. Just a note to say he's off to England, and nothing else. No explanation, no forwarding address. She's brokenhearted, poor thing. I offered to go over but she won't cancel the choir. I'll go immediately after. Alasdair wants to call the guards, but as I've pointed out to them, he's nineteen and can't be held prisoner. Best to leave him be for now and pray he'll keep in touch."

She sat down at the table and stared at her plate.

Granda frowned. There was an edge to his voice.

"Perhaps it's just as well. He's been the odd one out from the day he was born; a colicky baby, a troublesome child, and now a surly and disagreeable young man. He'll probably be happier away from here and, God knows, we'll all get a bit of peace without him."

Laurel was taken aback by her grandfather's severity. She knew him to be a kindly, soft-spoken man.

He himself looked immediately ashamed and added in a gentler tone to his wife, "You were the only one who got any good out of him. He minded his manners for you."

She smiled faintly in response.

"I delivered him and I've tended him all his young life. He has always been angry, as much with himself as anyone else. I did what I could for him, but I'm not a psychologist and they refused my advice to send him to one. I, too, believe in the power of prayer, but I think the Good Lord expects us to use the resources He provides as well."

"Perhaps he'll make a new life for himself," Granda suggested, "and return one day like the Prodigal Son."

"We can hope for that," she agreed, but she let out a deep sigh. "You know, after I coached him in maths and science, he did so well in the Leaving Certificate. And he talked of going to the veterinary college once he worked off the loan for his bike. Now it's more likely he'll take up drink and drugs and live on the streets of London with the rest of the homeless there."

She began to cry quietly. Her husband reached out to hold her hand.

Laurel had to quash a stab of jealousy at the depth of her grandmother's feelings for Ian. And she was angry too. Didn't Nannaflor have enough pain in her life? Searching for a way to ease the situation, she decided to raise the question that was haunting her.

"You're a scientist, Nanna, yet you believe in life after death, don't you?"

Nannaflor looked surprised, but her eyes lit up. As she dished out the Shepherd's Pie, she tackled the subject with enthusiasm.

"The great Einstein himself believed in the existence of God and the life divine, and saw no need to seek proof for either. Science handles the practicalities of the body. Faith deals with the needs of the soul. As a doctor, I work by the scientific method. As a Methodist, I believe in our continuance after death, whether it be in heaven or hell."

Laurel toyed with the food on her plate and took her time before pressing further.

"But . . . do you think a person who has died could stay around for a while? Or maybe go somewhere else besides heaven or hell?"

Her grandfather started and gave her a keen look.

Nannaflor was sympathetic but firm. "It's not unusual to dream that a loved one who has died is near, and I think God may allow them to visit us this way, but I would have no time for the occult or the notion of ghosts."

After supper, when Nannaflor left to visit Ian's mother, Laurel sought out her grandfather in the library.

Dusk was falling outside the bay window that overlooked the back garden. The evening had grown cool. A small fire burned in the grate. The marble mantelpiece held photographs of the family, ornaments, and an ormolu clock. Firelight flickered over the leather furniture and the shelves of books lining the walls. In the far corner of the room was an antique desk with a computer, printer, and fax machine. Her grandfather was searching through the drawers, perplexed.

"Have you lost something?" she asked him. "Can I help?"

"What, my dear? No, I don't think so." His brow furrowed as he cast a cold eye over his collection of books. "It could be anywhere. I use it as a bookmark. A gift from an old friend." He sighed, shook his head. "I'm growing more addled by the day. It's retirement, you know. A man should never stop working. His mind seizes up."

"Dad says you're still writing papers."

She was proud of her grandfather, a professor and well-known expert on folklore.

"True. But I'm beginning to think it's just an excuse to get out of the house and into the college library."

He came over to her and put his arm around her shoulder.

"Were you looking for me?"

"I wanted to ask you something," she said, a little shy.

He invited her to sit in one of the armchairs by the fire, while he took the other.

"You didn't join in the conversation at supper," she began.

A smile twitched at the edges of his mouth.

"The days are gone when Florence and I fought long and hard over such issues. Indeed, I believe we married so we could continue the arguments at our convenience."

Laurel smiled back.

"I respect your grandmother's beliefs and I, too, am a member of the church, but the Good Book itself tells us that in our Father's house are many mansions."

Granda stood up to pace the floor, slippers padding softly over the carpet. His hand brushed along the spines of his books.

"Our great poet, Mr. Yeats, spoke of 'the rise of the soul against the intellect.'"

He pulled out an ancient volume and brought it over to her. Printed in 1815, the hardback was frayed with age, the pages as brown as autumn leaves. *The Secret Commonwealth of Elves, Fauns, and Fairies.* Inside, a young hand had scrawled the words: WILLIAM THOMAS BLACKBURN, DECEMBER 1952.

"This was mine as a schoolboy. I almost know it by heart. The author, the Reverend Robert Kirk, was a minister of Aberfoyle who was 'taken' by the fairies in the seventeenth century. He swore that he had direct experience of Faerie, and that when he died he would return to that magical land."

As her grandfather took down more books, little heaps formed around Laurel, on the arms of the chair, in her lap, and spilling over the floor. The titles alone were enchanting. *The Fairy Faith in Celtic Countries. The Crock of Gold. A Midsummer Night's Dream.* Some were old and smelled of must. Others were new with lavish illustrations on glossy paper. *Faeries* by Brian Froud and Alan Lee. Michael Scott's *Irish Myths and Legends.* Joseph Campbell's *The Masks of God.*

"Here is Professor Tolkien's essay 'On Fairy Tales.' I like this line." Granda read out loud, "'Behind the fantasy, real will and powers exist independent of the minds and purposes of men.'"

Laurel handled the books reverently. *What the Bees Know* by P. L. Travers. Lady Wilde's *Ancient Legends of Ireland.* Dr. James Hollis's *Tracking the Gods.* She felt a little lost, as if she were wandering in a foreign land where the language and customs were strange to her.

"This was the kind of stuff Honor loved," she murmured.

Her grandfather watched her closely. When he spoke again, she could see he was choosing his words carefully.

"For the ancient Irish, Faerie was the place where they went after death. There are those who believe to this day that we can still go there, if we wish."

Laurel caught her breath. Her heart beat rapidly.

"What do you believe, Granda?"

Old eyes gazed into young and didn't turn away, but she saw a struggle there and a sudden reluctance to speak. She could only assume it was out of concern for her, or perhaps a fear of ridicule.

"Please tell me," she persisted.

"I believe," he began, then frowned, stopped, and tried again. "I believe there is more to creation than either science or religion allows. I believe that a death in one world means a birth in another. And, most of all, I believe that Faerie is one of the rooms in our Father's house."

He had no sooner spoken than Laurel felt the other question rise with such force that she had to stop herself from shouting it.

"Can people come back from Faerie? Can they return to this world?"

Her grandfather blanched. She saw his anguish and knew what it meant, his fear for her, and his guilt and regret for leading her to this point.

"I'm the one who brought up the subject, Granda, not you. Please tell me what you know," she urged. "That's all I ask."

They were both suffering, but it was obvious she was determined to see it through.

Though his voice sounded sluggish, her grandfather did his best to respond.

"There are various tales of those who have tried to retrieve their loved ones from the other world. Orpheus.

Tam Lin. The first was not successful. The second was. Then there's the story of Catkin. He was a kitten that went to Fairyland to rescue a child who was stolen when he was minding her. The outcome in that story was a compromise. It was agreed she would spend part of her time in this world and part in the next."

Laurel could hardly breathe. His words mesmerized her. They were exactly what she wanted to hear. And for that very reason she doubted them. Not so long ago, she would have dismissed them as nonsense or a cruel fantasy. But the shock of her sister's death had cracked the monolith of her disbelief. *There is a crack in everything. That's how the light gets in.* Wasn't that from one of Honor's favorite songs?

Laurel rubbed her forehead. Too many conflicting thoughts.

Granda squeezed her shoulder.

"Have a look through the books," he said gently. "I think you'll enjoy them."

He left her alone curled up in the armchair. The ormolu clock ticked on the mantelpiece. The fire settled into a labyrinth of red embers. A hush fell over the big house. The only sound was the soft fall of rain outside. Poring over the books, Laurel was soon enthralled. There were tales of demon lovers, stolen brides, shapeshifters, and enchanted beasts. Some of the stories were so beautiful they filled her with a strange longing. Others told terrifying accounts of tithes and curses inflicted on humans. A few were so sad she almost cried.

At the bottom of the pile was a journal with dried flowers pressed between the pages. The delicate scent of bluebells, harebells, foxgloves, and daisies tickled her nose. A little shiver ran up her spine when a handwritten note listed these flowers as fairy favorites. Did it belong to her grandfather? She touched the dried primroses. Yellow, blue, pink, purple—they looked like colored wafers, tempting to taste. Absently she slipped one into her mouth even as she read that eating primroses allowed one to see fairies.

"Hello," said the little man.

He was sitting in the chair opposite her, legs crossed, feet above the floor. His appearance had changed from the last time she saw him. He was much tidier. The coppery hair and beard were combed, and the dark-red suit looked new despite its antiquated style. He even sported a waistcoat stiff with gold embroidery. His shoes were of black patent leather with silver buckles. On his head perched a tricorner hat, which also had a shiny buckle. Puffing on a blackthorn pipe, he sent smoke rings toward her that smelled sweet and grassy.

Many of the stories had described folk like him. Before she could stop herself, she asked him outright.

"Are you a leprechaun?"

"Would ye go 'way outa dat," he said, and chuckled.

Laurel laughed too, surprised at herself and a little embarrassed. The books were obviously influencing her. In fact, she felt groggy from reading so much. Specks of light floated in the air around her. The room was very warm. She must have dozed off. That explained why she hadn't heard him come in.

"I'm a cluricaun."

He stared at her boldly, as if daring her to object. Glints of red light shone in his eyes.

"Of the *Fir Dhearga*. 'The Red People' in your lingo. We're the more cheerful branch of the family. Leprechauns don't have the diplomas to deal with your kind. Too cross and cranky, and short on the oul gray matter. This is a tricky situation. I've been sent by the High King himself to confab with ye."

"High King?" Laurel frowned. Her head ached. She felt dizzy. "Isn't Ireland a republic? I didn't think it had monarchs."

The room was definitely too stuffy. Perhaps if she got up and opened a window? But she couldn't move. Her body felt heavy, like a lump of lead. An inkling of terror crept through her. This wasn't right. There was an outdoor smell in the room, wet soil and leaves and the night perfume of columbine. Her eyelids began to close. She forced them open. Though the fire was nearly out, red shadows were dancing over the bookshelves. The little man's silhouette rose up behind him, large and vaguely menacing.

She opened her mouth to yell for help, but instead she yawned.

"Ye've got to fight it," he said, and his tone was urgent. "The solace of sleep. 'Tis your human nature. It wants ye to nod off so ye can tell yourself this is all a dream."

He leaned toward her, eyes dark and glittering.

"'Tis no dream, *girseach*, and ye've got to accept that. We can't be about our business till ye do. Can I give ye a little hint o' help? Something to get ye around that wall of logic that bricks in your brain?"

Laurel tried to speak, but couldn't. Waves of fatigue were washing over her. Her head kept dropping onto her chest. She was overwhelmed by the desire to have a little nap. Maybe lie down on the carpet in front of the fire? The alternative was too bizarre: to continue talking with this little man who looked like one of Santa's elves.

His tone was suddenly matter-of-fact.

"Look, stick to the essentials and never mind the existentials. Forget all that palaver about fantasy or reality. *Act as if ye believe and see what happens.* Is that too much to ask?"

It wasn't. In fact, the suggestion was so simple and pragmatic it appealed to her instantly. No need to wrestle with the bigger issues. Take it a step at a time. And Laurel so wanted to believe. She knew the stakes. Either there were more things than she had ever dreamed of, or there was nothing beyond her own experience and philosophy. And if the latter were true, there was no hope for her. She would never, ever see her sister again.

"I'll try." Her tongue felt thick and furry. She had to force the words out. "I'll act . . . as if . . . I believe."

She had no sooner uttered the words than she began to feel better. The room came back into focus. Energy returned to her limbs. The little man himself looked more solid and even normal, as he rubbed his hands gleefully.

Laurel sat up straight, her mind clear. There was only one thing she wanted to know.

"Was my sister stolen by the fairies?"

The cluricaun was quick to answer.

"No, she's not with us, more's the pity. She's caught in a quare place."

"What do you mean?!"

Laurel's heart was beating so fast she thought she might faint.

The little man sighed, even as the turf ash sighed in the fire.

"Your sister's fallen through a crack, a tear in the fabric of Faerie. It's a story that belongs to a bigger tale, like most things."

He drew on his pipe. Laurel held her breath.

"These are dark days for the Realm," he declared momentously. "'Twas only a short while ago we lost our High King. Not the new one who sent me to ye, mind, but the old one. The First King."

"What happened to him?" she asked, trying not to be impatient.

"'Twould take a book to tell ye. I could be here all night with tales about the fairies. The story in a nutshell? He lost his heart to a human girl and that was the end of him."

"*Dead?*"

The cluricaun nodded.

"Dead to our world, alive in yours. But there's no time to be talkin' about metempsychosis. There's too much to do and it should've been done yesterday."

"It's okay, I understand. My grandfather explained it earlier. But I didn't realize it went both ways, that fairies could die and come here!"

"Well, they can," he told her, "but it's never happened to the High King before! The place is in rag order because of it. Ruptions and ructures and *ruaille-buaille.* Your sister's not the only one missin'. But I'll tell ye this. If things aren't set right and soon, bedad, they'll only get worse. And if Faerie is doomed, ye know what that means."

After all she had read, Laurel did. Disaster for both worlds. As the two were linked, the existence of each depended on the other. Faerie needed humanity to protect and believe in it, while the Earthworld was nourished by the land of hopes and dreams. She recognized the chief theme in her grandfather's books: the Rescue of Fairyland. And in all the tales, it was a mortal who did the job.

Outside, the wind whistled round the corners of the house. The ivy trailing over the window tapped against the panes. The cluricaun put more turf on the fire, and continued.

"Midsummer's Eve is nearly upon us. It's a high feast celebrated by the fairy folk and those of your kind who remember the old ways. 'Tis a special night, but all the more so in the seventh year. For every seven years, on the day that's in it, the isle of Hy Brasil appears in the West.

"This magical island is the home of the Summer King who rules the fairies of the western seas. He's the one who lights the Midsummer Fire on Purple Mountain. It's the beacon that triggers the others to burn until the last, the heart-fire, is set ablaze on the Hill of Tara by the High King himself. Thus is forged the *Fáinne na Gréine*, the Ring of the Sun, a fiery chain that pours light and power into Faerie."

The cluricaun stopped to catch his breath.

"Here's where the plot thickens," he warned.

Rummaging through his pockets, he produced his little bottle and took a slug.

"This is the seventh year, when Hy Brasil rises in the West and the Ring of the Sun must be forged. But there's no Summer King to light the Midsummer Fire."

"He's one of the missing!"

The cluricaun blinked and a sly look crossed his face, but Laurel didn't notice. She was feeling a bit dazed. After all the fairy tales she had read that evening, here was one just as weird and wonderful, and somehow it involved both her and her sister!

"The mission Honor wrote about in her journal . . ." she said slowly.

"Now you're gettin' it," he said.

She could see he was waiting with bated breath. His pipe had gone out and though he clutched the bottle, he didn't take a drink.

"You want me to light the fire?"

He shook his head. "Only the Summer King has the spark to do it." He paused a moment. "We want ye to find him."

A heavy silence fell over them. The ticking of the

clock on the mantel sounded ominously loud, like the toll of a bell. The fire was a heap of gray ashes.

Laurel was thinking hard. She couldn't put her finger on it, but there was something wrong with the cluricaun's story. Something didn't add up. Still, though her instincts warred against her, it made no difference. There was only one thing she cared about.

"If the fire is lit and the Ring of the Sun is forged, will that save Honor?"

The little man nodded so vigorously his hat spun around.

"*Go cinnte!* Once Faerie is fixed and the cracks are mended, she'll be right as rain."

It was as if a sunburst exploded in Laurel's brain. She felt giddy and lightheaded. Just like that, her deepest dream and greatest hope presented on a silver platter! She ignored the faint alarm at the back of her mind. There could only be one response to such an offer.

"I'll do it!"

FIVE

Leaving Dublin behind, the train sped across the midlands on its way into the West. The landscape was flat, sprawling with the monotony of suburban estates and the rectangular boxes of factories and offices. Building cranes swayed on the horizon. Plastic bags flapped in the trees. From time to time a field peeped out through the urban blight, like green eyes wincing.

The train was sleek and shiny, with newly upholstered seats facing each other over narrow tables. The driver used the intercom with zeal, roaring out messages and announcing the stations in Irish and English.

Kildare. Cill Dara. *The Church of the Oak Tree.*

Laurel had placed her knapsack on the empty seat beside her. The car was not too crowded, a few families with children, some young people with backpacks, and several tourists with big suitcases blocking the aisle. People played cards, read newspapers, and to her surprise, drank. Beer cans and wine bottles were conspicuous on all sides. Cell phones were also an Irish custom apparently, as everyone was talking on them. Laurel reached for the one she had bought in Bray. Honor used to text her constantly, even if they were only in separate rooms. She put it back in her pocket and stared out the window.

The train was passing green fields hedged with bushes of yellow whin. She turned on her iPod and listened for a while to the Peatbog Faeries, then switched to Runrig, a group from the Outer Hebrides. Their sound was strange to her ears, wild and anarchic. The Scots Gaelic words and rhythms were like waves pounding cold shores. It was not her music, but Honor's. She had replaced her own collection with her sister's.

Togaidh sinn ar fonn an ard,
Togaidh sinn ar fonn an ard,
'S ged 'tha mi fada bhuat,
Cha dhealaich sinn a'chaoidh.

Laurel was doing her best not to be overwhelmed by the task ahead.

"Ye must go to Achill Island on the western seaboard. 'Tis off the coast of Achill that the isle of Hy Brasil appears. Begin your search there. Be of good courage and keep your wits about ye. The fire must be lit by sunset on Midsummer's Eve." He cocked his head and blinked at her. "That's Friday week."

"What?" she had gasped. "So soon? There's hardly any time!"

"Well didn't ye waste most of it gettin' here? Ye've only yourself to blame for the last-minute element."

She would have argued with him, but she knew there was no point. Six days were all she had, and that was that.

One of those days was spent convincing Nannaflor to let her go.

"You want to travel around a strange country on your own?"

Her grandmother had tried to talk her out of it, but Granda was supportive.

"You were the same age, Florence, when you went off to England—a strange country—all on your own."

"I went there to study, William. That's hardly the same thing. And it was a safer world back then."

It was Laurel's destination that clinched the matter. As soon as she mentioned Achill, all protests ended. Her grandfather had grown up on the island and though the big family home was long gone, he and Nannaflor owned a little cottage by the sea where the two of them spent vacations. Their "love nest" they called it.

While she was surprised by the coincidence, Laurel was more than happy that it saved the day. She packed her bags that night.

The next morning, her grandfather drove her to Dublin to catch the train.

On their way into the city, Granda gave her final instructions for the cottage and the old car that went with it. He kept hesitating, as if he wanted to say more but couldn't find the words. When they reached the station he spoke up at last.

"Achill is like nowhere else on earth. A special place.

Your grandmother and I would have liked to bring you there ourselves. Are you certain you want to go alone? Isn't there any way I can help you?"

The look he gave her was so wise and kind, she almost told him of her mission. But it was all too fragile and illusory, like the stuff of dreams. She was afraid it would disappear if she expressed it out loud.

"I'll be fine, Granda. I need to do this alone. You mustn't worry about me. I promise to call."

On the train, she battled with second thoughts and doubts. Was it a wild-goose chase? Another desperate way to hold on to her sister? Was she deluding herself? Going crazy? She had seen her face in the mirror that morning, pale and haunted. And yet, at the same time, she was feeling more alive than she had in ages. However faint, there was hope ahead. *Act as if you believe and see what happens.* She repeated the line like a mantra.

Even as Laurel whispered the words to herself, the train passed a field covered with dandelions. The downy tufts were dislodged by the draft and sucked into the open windows. The car was deluged with feathery seeds, floating and dancing and drifting like snow. Children clambered on the seats to catch them, crying out with delight. The passengers smiled at each other. Laurel, too, felt the thrill. Magic was alive in the world.

Tullamore. Túlach Mhór. *The Great Hill.*

Three men clambered onto the train, shabbily dressed in torn jeans and old sweaters. They were short and stocky, with bulbous noses and bulging eyes. After loading their table with cans of Guinness, they took out their instruments—a fiddle, a tin whistle, and a bodhrán drum—and played as if their lives depended upon it. When they lit up cigarettes, it wasn't long before the driver yelled over the intercom.

"GET RID OF THEM SMOKES OR YOU'LL BE PUT OFF AT THE NEXT STOP!"

This was met with hoots and jeers as the cigarettes went flying out the window. Chastened, the three struck up a gentle ballad. A hush fell over the car as everyone listened.

There's something sleeping in my breast,
That wakens only in the West,
There's something in the core of me,
That needs the West to set it free.

Indeed the train was now traveling into the West. The passengers clapped as it crossed the Shannon River, a natural border recognized by all. The river was wide, cold, and dark blue. The countryside beyond it looked different. Stone walls replaced hedges in a lonely vista where towns were a rare sight. Horses, sheep, and cattle dotted the fields.

Castlerea. Caisleán Riabhach. *The Brindled Castle*

It was at Castlerea that an elderly lady got on and sat down opposite Laurel. She was tall and stately, dressed in an old-fashioned manner, with a trouser suit of forest-green and a white ruffled blouse. Her high-heeled boots had pointed toes that curled slightly at the tips. She wore gold jewelry, a big brooch shaped like a serpent swallowing its tail, and earrings to match. Her steely gray hair was pulled back in a bun, revealing a strong forehead, narrow cheekbones, and a sharp narrow nose. Her eyes were dark and dramatic.

An old actress, Laurel mused, or maybe a music teacher. *How about a witch?* The stray thought surprised her; the kind of thing Honor would have whispered if she were there.

The woman had a carpetbag with wooden handles and a small suitcase on wheels.

"I beg your pardon," she said to Laurel, as she tucked her luggage under their table. Her voice was deep and measured.

Laurel murmured a polite greeting and looked away, hoping to avoid conversation.

The old lady didn't seem to mind. She took out a cell phone and began texting messages with long deft fingers. When the phone rang with the hoot of an owl, she threw Laurel an apologetic look before answering.

"Yes, I'm on the train. Claremorris? Better still. There's a chance we'll make it yet. Don't rush now. Drive carefully."

Laurel continued to gaze out the window. In the distance rose a range of mountains scarved with blue mist. There something caught her eye. At first she assumed it was a trick of light in a cloud formation, but then the image was suddenly shockingly clear.

A female figure. A giantess, to be visible at such a distance. In radiant garments, with streaming hair, she was running across the hilltops, trailing light behind her like wings. She was only there for a second, but it was a moment as perfect as a pearl.

Laurel gasped in wonder. So did the old woman. Startled, they looked at each other.

"You saw her?"

Immediately wary, Laurel didn't respond.

The old lady glanced at the flag on her knapsack.

"Ah," she said, "another good neighbor from across the water." She lowered her voice. "Grania Harte is my name, but everyone calls me Granny. I am a fairy doctress. You may speak freely with me."

Laurel remained silent. Her first instinct was to flee, change seats or even cars.

The old woman frowned as she studied Laurel's features.

"You are not a believer," Granny said at last. Her voice echoed surprise, but also sympathy. "And yet you have the Sight."

"The . . . the what?"

"The Second Sight. The ability to see beyond the veil. It must be difficult for you. A curse, perhaps, instead of a blessing?"

Her kindly understanding disarmed Laurel.

"I'm getting used to it," she said tentatively. "Do you know a lot about . . . Faerie?"

Granny smiled. "No one can know 'a lot' about the

Faraway Country, not even its own inhabitants, save perhaps the High King. With the fairies you'll always get
more than you bargained for. But I have earned in my day
the title of Wise Woman. I know some of the old ways
and can work spells and cures."

Laurel could almost hear Honor crow. *Like I said, a
witch.*

"Who was she?" Laurel asked, and her eyes strayed
to the horizon.

Granny spoke with awe.

"The White Lady. An ancient being of the Old
Magic that came before the creation of our world and
even Faerie itself."

Laurel was suffering a mixture of fascination and
horror. It was like turning over a rock. What else might
show up? And did she really want to see these things? She
took some comfort from the fact that the old lady reminded her of Nannaflor, self-assured and plain-speaking.
That made it easier to hear what she said.

"The nature of Faerie is complex and elusive."
Granny cupped her hands in an effort to explain. "Think
of our reality as an island surrounded by an infinite
ocean. Faerie is all around us, lapping against our shores,
a world of the imagination, ever creating and re-creating
itself. Yet what it becomes and how it evolves is affected
by its relationship with us, even as our world can be
influenced by it.

"The territories and denizens closer to us belong to
the New Magic ruled by the High King. But the farther

out you go, or the further in perhaps, the more intangible and mysterious things become. The Old Ones are the primal beings who existed before everything else, or at least everything we know of. From time to time they enter the worlds, and may even intervene for the good of all."

Granny looked toward the mountains.

"She is on the move for some great purpose."

A thrill ran through Laurel that was also a shiver; joy edged with a trace of fear. She knew in her heart that the White Lady had gone into the West for her. But she wasn't ready to admit this to Granny nor to speak of her mission.

The snack trolley came trundling down the aisle and stopped beside them.

"Tea, sticky bun, crisps?" asked the attendant.

He was a tall young man in a disheveled uniform with the shirttails hanging out. His long red hair was tied back in a ponytail. Silver rings pierced his ears, eyebrows, and lip.

Ignoring his flirtatious grin, Laurel purchased a bottle of mineral water.

He slipped a Danish pastry, wrapped in plastic, onto the table.

"Something sweet for a sweetie," he said with a wink.

Before she could react, he had moved down the aisle, whistling to himself.

Granny threw him a suspicious look, then grimaced at the bun.

"Don't eat that, my dear, it's all artificial ingredients. They don't serve proper food on the trains anymore."

From her carpetbag, she produced a lunch that made Laurel gape. First came a flask filled with hot chocolate, then a little basket of wheaten farls, and a pot of red jam and another of clotted cream. She even had knives and linen napkins.

"Would you care to join me for a bite?"

Though she meant to decline, Laurel found herself sipping the rich chocolate and nibbling on a farl. The jam tasted of fresh strawberries. Even as she murmured her thanks, it occurred to her that the old lady was trying to gain her confidence. But Laurel was not someone who trusted people easily, especially with matters so private and bizarre.

"It's an amazing coincidence we've met," was all she said.

"Good heavens, there's no such thing as coincidence!" Granny protested. "Whenever that word is used it simply means we don't know the full story. A web of circumstances has me sitting here beside you, including a sick brother, a lost ticket, and a missed train. I even had a porter insist that I take this very carriage! Something is afoot. We were meant to meet and *they* arranged it."

Silence fell between them again, resonant with unspoken questions and answers.

"It's because of Faerie that I am traveling today," the old woman continued. "I'm on my way to Shannon Airport, hopefully to catch a plane despite the delays. I'm going to New York with my nephew, Dara, to join his American sweetheart and her Irish cousin who lives there. We are all Companions of Faerie." Granny paused a moment, emphasizing the importance of what came next. "We are meeting with Finvarra, the former High King, he who died and was born again, as a mortal."

Laurel was now hanging on every word.

"We are gathering because of Faerie. We have heard nothing since Finvarra came among us and not one of has been invited to return to the Realm. We are concerned that no word has come from Midir, the new High King. And yet, in truth, this is typical of the fairy folk. They are always about their own business, and only call us when it suits them."

"You mean they use us at their convenience."

The bitterness in Laurel's voice took Granny aback, but she replied honestly.

"Yes, I suppose you could put it that way." Her shrug was light. "They are not like us, the *Daoine Sídhe*. They have their own way of doing things. And they consider their existence more important than ours. Yet I would not want to live in a world without fairies."

Granny was about to say more when her cell phone rang. Excusing herself, she answered it.

"Excellent! I should be there shortly. On schedule? Oh dear. Then we're down to the wire. We'll just have to do our best. Here's some good news. I've made a new friend, another Companion perhaps. Yes. I'll tell you about her when we meet."

Granny was tucking the phone back into her carpetbag, when Laurel blurted out the words: "I'm on a mission.

Faerie is in trouble. Maybe that's why there's been no contact."

In a rush of words, she told of the cluricaun, the lost Summer King, and the Midsummer Fire that had to be lit on Hy Brasil. She didn't speak of Honor's death or her hope of saving her sister. That was her own concern and too personal to reveal.

But she had said enough.

The old woman's face had gone deathly pale. She covered her mouth with a trembling hand. Her voice was barely audible.

"I know this king. I know this story."

And now her features were alive with panic.

"What is your name, child?"

"Laurel Blackburn."

"Blackburn!" Her eyes widened. "I know this name."

The train let out a high-pitched whistle, signaling its approach to the next station.

Claremorris. Clár Chlainne Mhuiris. *The Plains of the Clan Maurice.*

"We're out of time!" Granny looked stricken. "This is all my fault! I'm losing my touch! Too old and doddery! They crossed our paths so I would help you. We should have spoken sooner!"

Her anxiety was contagious. Laurel was already regretting that she had taken so long to let down her guard.

As the train pulled into the station, it passed a young man pacing the platform. When he spotted Granny, his face flooded with relief and he ran to catch up with their car.

Visibly distraught, Granny was struggling in the aisle with her suitcase. She spoke hurriedly to Laurel.

"It's an old story, a tragic tale. It belongs to a time when I was Queen in Faerie. You must be careful! Have they warned you of the dangers? Have they given you weapons and charms of protection?"

Laurel moved to help her with her luggage. Only now did she see in Granny the frailties of an old lady.

"Dangers?" she repeated, a little stunned. "Weapons?"

"Oh my dear girl." Granny's expression was pained. "You are dealing with Faerie. The Perilous Realm."

The train jolted to a stop. Passengers hurried off as new ones embarked. The doors would soon close. Granny had to go.

"I'll be okay," Laurel assured her, though she had no idea if it was true.

She watched as the old woman was helped out of the car and hugged by her nephew. He had dark-brown hair and a handsome face. The two stood on the platform talking animatedly. Now the young man glanced over at Laurel where she sat in the window. He looked concerned, and was about to call out to her, but he was left behind as the train pulled away.

Laurel sat dazed, clutching her knapsack. Granny's words circled in her brain like birds of ill omen. *Danger. Weapons. The Perilous Realm.* The cluricaun had said nothing about such things, had given her no warnings.

And the old woman knew the Summer King! *A tragic tale.* If only Laurel had opened up sooner. If only she had heard the story.

The train was heading north on the last leg of its journey that ended at Westport. Clouds scudded across the sky in the evening sun. Shafts of light fell on the hillsides where horned cattle were silhouetted like mythical beasts. Now rain spattered sideways against the window. As the train curved around a steep corner, she caught sight of the coastal mountains ahead. The sun still shone there, beyond the veil of gray.

Castlebar. Caisleán an Bharraigh. *The Castle of the Proud.*

The eerie beauty of the landscape did nothing to ease Laurel's foreboding. She couldn't shake the feeling that she was journeying into enemy territory.

When the train arrived at the last stop, her fears proved true.

Six

He grabbed her the moment she stepped off the train. She caught only a glimpse of a tall figure behind her and a dark wide-brimmed hat. Sharp nails dug into her arms as she was propelled forward. The station was a blur of details imprinted with shock: wooden benches on the platform, an old stone building, flower boxes in the windows, a passageway that led to the street. There was no time to struggle or cry out. She was pushed into the Left Luggage storeroom beyond the passageway.

Laurel was stunned by the speed and violence of the attack. She backed away from her captor as he slammed the door shut. Gaunt and ragged, he seemed to tower over her. His capacious black coat was sleek and oily like feathers. The broad fedora shadowed most of his face. He had kept his head lowered, but when he looked up, her heart stopped.

He wasn't human.

His skin was dark with a violet tinge, his features hard as if carved from ebony. The neck was thick, the nose hooked like a beak. But it was the eyes that truly terrified her. Pure black and rimmed with gold coronas, they burned with a feral intensity.

Laurel felt weak. There was something very wrong here. He was grinding his teeth as if from some inner torment. For an incomprehensible second she thought of Ian.

"What do you want?" she demanded shakily.

She clenched her fists against the terror as her mind raced with wild plans of escape. From the corner of her eye, she scanned the room. It was dimly lit, with only one dusty window close to the ceiling. Metal shelves and lockers lined the walls, stacked with boxes, baggage, and cleaning supplies. Was there anything she could use as a weapon? Just behind her was a wooden counter with paper and pens; beside it, a swivel chair with a big ginger tabby curled up asleep. Where was the person in charge? The sounds outside were muffled and distant. No voices. She had got off the last train. Everyone had gone home.

No one would hear her scream.

The creature opened its mouth. Laurel shuddered at the flash of incarnadine red.

"*Aaarrcckkk.* Listen!"

His voice was harsh and guttural, grating on the nerves as well as the ears. When he spoke, he lifted his arms from his sides, like a bird flapping its wings. He cocked his head this way and that, as if trying to get a better look at her.

A bird-man, she realized. Yes, that's what he was.

She would have to fight him. A sudden charge to catch him off guard? Quick knee to the groin? But his

coat looked heavy, like padded armor, and would probably soften any blows.

"*Corrraawwkkks.* No help king!"

An idea struck her, a desperate bid. She inched back
toward the counter as he continued to shriek at her.

"Go home! *Aaaarcckkkk!* You go? Yes?"

"No!" she cried suddenly.

And she lunged for the big tom asleep on the chair.

"Time for work," she told the cat.

Then she flung him at her captor.

In the furor of feathers and fur, screeches and yowls,
Laurel pushed past the bird-man and out the door.

She stood dazed a moment in the blaze of a red sunset. Behind her came the whirr of wings as a great raven
took to the air, cawing loudly. A glance into the storeroom showed it was empty. On the threshold stood the
tabby, black feather in its mouth, eyes blinking with
satisfaction.

Laurel was trembling all over, but fought to stay
calm.

"Good boy," she said, leaning down to scratch the
tom's head.

He purred like an engine.

Now she glanced at her watch. She had a short walk to
catch the bus for Achill. Her grandfather had told her
where and when it arrived. If she didn't hurry she would
miss it! Dashing through the passageway, she ran for the
town center. Her knapsack felt like a bag of bricks, slowing her down. As she raced down the hill toward the bus

stop, she caught sight of her bus up the road, disappearing around the corner.

She stood on the sidewalk, devastated. Things were going from bad to worse. Only now as she caught her breath did she face the horror of the attack at the station. Though the cluricaun had said nothing about an enemy, it was obvious that someone or something didn't want her to find the king. Granny's warnings of danger were true. Laurel braced herself against a wave of fear. She was stranded and defenseless in a foreign country.

The urge to return to her grandparents in Bray was overwhelming, but it wasn't an option. To give up on the mission was to give up on her twin. As she debated what to do next, a different kind of bus pulled up in front of her.

A vintage vehicle, it was painted deep purple with the word WINGS emblazoned in gold on the side. Her first thought was that the cluricaun had come to her rescue. Then the doors hissed opened and a cloud of incense wafted toward her, followed by a blast of folk music and the driver's greeting.

"Sawr ye miss yon bus. We's gangin' north if yer goin' tha' way. I'm Sandy. 'Op on if ye like."

The hippie girl leaned on the big steering wheel of the bus. Pentangles dangled from her ears, half-hidden by a mane of dark hair. A necklace of crystals hung around her neck. She wore a tie-dyed T-shirt over a patchwork skirt that fell to sandaled feet. Her toenails, like her fingernails, were painted in bright colors. Her arms were tattooed with zoomorphic designs.

After a moment's hesitation, in which she reflected she had no alternative, Laurel climbed onboard.

There were at least fifteen people living on the bus, a jolly crew of young and old, including several toddlers and a baby. Most of the seats had been removed and replaced with rugs and cushions. There were built-in bunks and hammocks for sleeping, and a kitchen in the back. The windows were draped with beaded curtains. Glass chimes and mobiles dangled from the roof. Books, toys, and musical instruments were scattered everywhere.

When Laurel introduced herself, names like Pip, Lavender, and Sinbad were called out in turn, their accents echoing various parts of Britain. As she made her way to a seat by the window, a group of musicians struck up a song.

> *Oh fair-haired lady, will you go,*
> *Beyond the land of mortal woe?*
> *To the kingdom of the light,*
> *Beyond the stars, beyond the night.*
>
> *Taste the golden honeyed mead,*
> *Eat the cakes of sweetened seed,*
> *Life itself grows pale and sere,*
> *After you have lingered there.*

The sweet strains of the hammer dulcimer mingled with the mandolin. Against the lighter notes beat the understream of a bodhrán drum. Laurel rested her head against the window. The music and the steady pulse of the engine soothed her nerves. She rubbed her arms where the bird-man had clawed her. The dark side of Faerie. Would she meet it again? How would she protect herself? What should she do? What *could* she do?

Outside, the hills rose steeply like the great waves of a green ocean. As the road climbed higher, the way grew rougher. Sometimes the dips were so abrupt she felt her stomach drop. The mountains she had seen from the train were drawing closer.

A young man named Fionn came to sit beside her. His long fair hair fell in fine strands to his shoulders, his eyes were gray. Unlike the other passengers, he had the soft lilt of an Irish accent. Though he wore jeans and a T-shirt and appeared otherwise normal, Laurel sensed something unusual about him. She found herself wondering if he had fairy blood.

"Where are you going?" he asked her.

"Achill Island."

"The Isle of the Eagle," he said with a nod, and at her puzzled look, explained. "It's said the name comes from the Latin word *aquila*, meaning eagle. The King of the Birds used to be plentiful on Achill, both white-tailed and golden eagles, but now they're extinct in Ireland." A shadow crossed his face. "Hunted out of existence."

"You know a lot about birds?"

"I like to read them," he answered. When she raised

an eyebrow, he smiled. "They are messengers of the gods. If you can interpret the patterns of their flight, you can learn many secrets."

Laurel wasn't sure if he was serious or not. She indicated the black birds circling the sky.

"So what are they saying?"

A mischievous look crossed his face.

To see one raven is ill luck, 'tis true
But it's certain misfortune to set eyes upon two
And meeting with more—that's a terror!

Then he laughed. "I'm speaking in riddles. You may have heard of a 'murder' of crows? According to some, the collective term for a raven is a 'terror.'"

Laurel shuddered involuntarily as she thought of the bird-man. She was considering telling Fionn about him, when their conversation was interrupted by one of the children.

"Sandy wants to know where you're going," she said to Laurel, handing her a map.

"You mean she'll drive me there?!"

The kindness of strangers.

"Well, we'd hardly drop you off in the middle of nowhere," said Fionn. "It's not on the way."

He unfolded the map. It was hand-drawn and crinkled with age. The place-names were written in gold ink, and fantastical beasts marked the four corners.

"It's beautiful," she murmured.

"Thank you. I copied it from a map in a monastery on the Continent."

"Were you a monk?"

"In one of my lives."

Laurel didn't know what to say. There was a time when she would have dismissed such remarks—and the one who made them—as ludicrous. Now she wasn't so sure.

He touched the map reverently.

"Here lies *Loch Béal Séad*. The Lake of the Jeweled Mouth. This is *Leitir Bhreac*. The Speckled Hill. This, *Inisbófin*. The Isle of the White Cow. And here is the place I mentioned. *Trian Láir*, roughly translated to 'the Middle of Nowhere.'"

"It really exists!" she said, astonished.

There was a ripple of laughter around them.

Outside, the night had grown darker. The landscape was lost in shadow; lonely fields of scutch grass, bog, and stone. She caught her reflection in the window opposite and was startled by what she saw. The face looking back at her was more like Honor's, fey and dreamy-eyed. Who was she becoming as she journeyed through a strange countryside to an even stranger future?

Fionn regarded her solemnly.

"There is a great sorrow upon you," he murmured, "and you so young."

She looked away.

He tapped the map lightly.

"Be sure to avoid this place now. The coldest spot in all Ireland."

Laurel bent her head to see where he pointed. She read the name out loud.

"Birr."

Her laughter slipped out before she could catch it, even as the others joined in. It was an old gag but a good one, and he had got her fair and square. It was the first time she had laughed since Honor died.

"Fionn Mílscothach!" Sandy called back. "Thar's ole honey-tongue workin' 'is magic."

Pulling over to the side of the road, she got one of the men to take her place. She invited Laurel and Fionn to join her in the back of the bus where they sat at a booth in the little kitchen. Someone brought them a pot of fennel tea.

Sandy asked to see Laurel's hand and gazed a moment at her palm.

"Ye mun take care where ye go in th' night," she said gravely. Then she offered to do a card reading.

Laurel's first inclination was to politely decline. She remembered the time Honor dragged her to a New Age convention in exchange for a camping trip. Utterly cynical, Laurel had cast a cold eye on the crystal-gazers, aura seers, and rainbow therapists. When her twin consulted a fortune-teller about her love life, Laurel quickly spotted the sleight of hand. Laying the gilded deck facedown on the table, the man had made a sly motion with his finger, pointing to a certain card. Oblivious to the subliminal suggestion, Honor duly chose it.

The King of Hearts.

"You'll marry a royal with red hair, rich and handsome," the fortune-teller pronounced fulsomely.

Honor had looked all flushed and happy.

Laurel had snorted.

"I can't believe you believe that."

Sandy's deck was similarly gilded but the cards were frayed and obviously very old.

"Th' Gypsy Oracle," she explained. "Maw greatgrandmother's cards. 'Alf Romany, 'alf Welsh. Ah've th' gift o' the Seeght thro' hur."

"Born at Stonehenge," Fionn whispered to Laurel, in case she had any doubts about Sandy's credentials.

Laurel had already decided to hear the reading, reflecting wryly to herself that *"act as if you believe"* was beginning to apply to more things than expected.

The four suits of Sandy's deck were unique: clubs had been replaced with triple spirals, spades were stone daggers, diamonds were crystals of amethyst, and hearts were made of gold. The distinctive features of the kings and queens expressed the nature of their suits. The royal hearts appeared passionate and full of laughter. The spiral couple were lofty and serene. The amethyst pair showed strength and willfulness, while the king and queen of daggers were cold and aloof.

As instructed, Laurel chose seven cards at random and laid them facedown.

Turning them over one by one, Sandy's eyes widened. "Weel done! They's nut ah small un. A pa'rful spread!"

Laurel gazed down at the kings, queens, and aces. A good hand for poker, but what else could it mean?

"Th' Queen o' Hearts," Sandy began. "Yon fair-haired woman be ye. She tha' acts fur love. Thar'in lies her power. Then cooms th'Ace o' Hearts." Her eyes darkened. "'Tis the severed heart. Yer heart be wounded as Fionn say. An' this be the cause. Th'Ace o' th' Dagger. The knife tha' cuts th' thread o' life. It wur Death as had broken yer heart."

Laurel's face paled. She had been ready to hear nonsense, or at the best something vague, but this was too close to the mark.

Sandy stopped when she saw her distress. Fionn looked sympathetic.

"Please go on," said Laurel.

She would hear what had to be heard. Like the bus ride itself, the journey was beyond her control She was already on the way, there was no turning back.

"Now th' King o' Daggers," Sandy continued softly. "He be th' Dark Knife. The flaysome bane o' light. 'Ware him, for he be yer enemy. Thar beside him, th' King o' Spirals. The Hidden Lord. The Enchanter. He stands in th' shadow o' the Dark One, his prisoner perchance."

Everyone on the bus had grown quiet. Only the engine rumbled and roared, as if they were deep in the belly of a beast that prowled the dark roads.

Sandy touched the last two cards with awe.

"Th' Ace o' Spirals. Th' eyes o' th' White Goddess. All reversals an' fresh ortherings an' pa'rful transformations. Th' Wheel o' Fate. Then cooms at th' end, outa th' vortex, th' last king, th' last card. The King o' Hearts. Burnin' wi' light an' red-gold fire, th' power tha' binds th' worlds together. Love is all."

The young woman stopped speaking. Pale and exhausted, she closed her eyes, absently rubbing the center of her forehead. When she opened them again, she smiled at Laurel, but there was confusion in her look. Even as she uttered the final prophecy, it was evident that she didn't understand her own words.

"A bright thing may lie hidden inside the dark."

Laurel shook her head, dazed. The phrase sounded vaguely familiar. Given her mission, some of the reading made sense, while other parts hinted of possibilities to come. She felt overwhelmed by the weight of mystery.

Sandy stood up and made a general announcement.

"Thar be great doin's here, folks. We mun aid th' queen. We mun bring 'er to 'er destination. We mun bring 'er to 'er destiny."

Then she resumed her place at the wheel.

The bus moved swiftly through the dark landscape, over long winding roads dimly lit by the moon. When they crossed the Michael Davitt Bridge, they left the Irish mainland behind and arrived on Achill.

Even in the dark, Laurel could see this was different country from the Ireland she knew. Here was a place on the edge of the world. A great craggy island dropped into the ocean. Except for a few sheltered areas, the land was treeless, its vegetation stunted by harsh winds and salt air. Small white houses huddled on the hillsides like gulls come to land. The smell of turf smoke and wild thyme drifted through the windows. They were now in sight of the Atlantic, glimmering in the night. On their left rose the Cliffs of Minaun. On their right brooded Slievemore, the Great Mountain.

Laurel joined Sandy at the front of the bus to give her directions. She kept watch for the boreen that led to her grandparents' seaside cottage. When they passed the village of Keel, she knew they were near.

"There it is, just ahead!"

Sandy drew up the bus near the verge. The air brakes hissed. Two stone pillars marked the little road that ran down to the dunes bordering the seashore.

"We canna go dahn thar," she said. "We'd ne'er get aht agin. Hahsiver, we'll bide an' watch whar ye go till we see th' lights go on in yer hahs."

"How can I thank you?" Laurel said shyly, as everyone crowded around to say their good-byes.

Fionn kissed her hand in a courtly manner.

"Think of us when you enter the Kingdom."

The moment she stepped into the cool night air, Laurel felt the loneliness settle over her. The hippie bus had been warm and homey. Trudging down the lane, with her knapsack on her back, she felt the shadows press against her. Fields of marram grass spread out on either side. Above glittered an immensity of stars undimmed by the spill of urban light. All around whispered the sound of the sea.

The lane ended at her grandparents' cottage. Long and low, it stood pale in the moonlight, its curtains drawn like lidded eyes. The roof was thatched and there was a square front porch. A path lined with white pebbles led to the door where two stone vases stood guard. As she reached behind the left-hand vase to get the key, she wished that her grandparents were inside to greet her. Her Granda would be filling the kettle for tea as Nannaflor took fresh scones from the oven.

No key.

Had she got the instructions wrong? A search behind the vase on the right was also proving fruitless, when she heard the bus start up at the top of the road. She was surprised they were leaving before she got in the house. Then she saw the light spilling out the window. Her heart stopped. An intruder! The raven-man? Before she could move, the porch door jerked open and there he stood.

Laurel could only gape.

"I guess you'd better come in," said Ian.

SEVEΠ

"What are you doing here?!"
Laurel followed him into the cottage and saw immediately that he was camping out in secret. The place was cold and damp. No fires had been lit, either in the fireplace or the solid-fuel stove that fed the central heating. He had just finished his meal. A teapot stood on the table beside a loaf of bread, cheese, and a jar of olives. There was also a book and a flashlight.

Ian didn't answer her question. He cleared away his dishes and began to wash them at the sink, his back toward her. It was obvious he was thrown by her arrival. His movements were awkward and nervous.

She was unsettled herself, tired from traveling and still shaken from thinking he was the raven-man. Dropping her knapsack on the floor, she sank into the couch.

The cottage smelled faintly of turf smoke. The one big room was both living space and kitchen, with bedroom and bathroom off to the left. The walls were hung with water-color paintings, mostly scenes of Achill. The furnishings were antique; crowded bookshelves, an oak table with high-backed chairs, and a wooden dresser with china and crystal.

The stuffed sofa and armchair were by the fireplace. The far wall was dominated by the solid-fuel stove with a black kettle on the hob. Next to the stove were the kitchen appliances, cupboards, counter, and sink. Nannaflor's touches could be seen everywhere in the dried bunches of wildflowers, pieces of pottery, and lace antimacassars.

"Do my grandparents know you're here?" she tried again, though she already knew the answer.

He froze at the sink. His shoulders clenched under his T-shirt. He dried his hands on a towel.

"Can I get you something?" he asked. "A cup of tea? Coffee?"

She was about to refuse his offer point blank when she changed her mind. Though he avoided her questions, he seemed anxious to please. His look was strained and unhappy. Her antipathy toward him eased a little. Aware of the dark night lurking outside, she admitted to herself she was glad of the company.

"A cup of coffee, thanks. Milk, no sugar."

"Would you like a biscuit?"

"Do you mean a cookie?"

"*Cookie?* Is that a real word?"

His quick grin was disarming.

"You must be hungry after your trip," he said. "I'll fix you something."

Though she hadn't thought of eating, she found herself savoring the sandwich he made. The bread was thick and fresh, the cheddar tangy, and he had sprinkled a green herb onto the tomato.

"Thyme," he told her, when she asked. "It's growing wild in the garden."

She ate at the table. He pulled up a chair beside her.

"I didn't know you were coming," he said quietly, "or I wouldn't be here. I just needed to get away."

His eyes finally met hers in a flash of startling blue. It was like a plunge into the sea. She looked away. Sipped on her coffee. This was a complication she wasn't prepared for.

"How long were you planning to stay here?"

He shrugged.

"I have no plans. I've been wandering around on the bike. I thought of going to London, but I hate cities. Nannaflor often spoke of this place. She said I was welcome to stay whenever I wanted, and she told me where the key was."

Laurel's curiosity was piqued.

"Why did you leave like that?"

He flinched at the directness of her question.

"It was always on the cards. I . . . I couldn't . . ." His voice sounded strangled. "The whole son-of-the-minister thing. The others always watching me, judging me. I'm not like them. I never have been."

Though she didn't say so, she could understand.

An awkward silence ensued. The ticking of the old clock on the mantel seemed uncommonly loud. Outside the cottage, the wind was rising to a high-pitched whine. A light rain began to fall, whispering in the thatch.

"Do you mind if I stay here tonight?" he asked

tentatively. "I'm kipping on the sofa. That leaves you the bedroom. I'll be gone in the morning."

She had already decided he could. After her experience at the station, she was happy not to spend her first night there alone. Yet she couldn't resist a throwaway remark.

"I'd hardly kick you out at this hour, even if I wanted to."

He wasn't able to hide his reaction. She caught the look of fury before he suppressed it. An image nagged at the back of her mind.

"On the cliff path in Bray, that bird . . . did you kill it?"

He was taken aback.

"No . . . no, that's not . . . It came at me out of the blue." He touched the cut on his face that was now a pale scar. "I didn't know what was going on. There was kind of a flurry, I grabbed at it and then . . ."

His voice trailed off. He seemed genuinely unsure of what happened.

Great, a psycho in the house. She made a mental note to put a chair against the door of her bedroom.

"I wouldn't kill anything deliberately," he insisted. "And I have a thing for birds. I would never hurt them."

It sounded true. She was reminded of Fionn on the bus, and asked without thinking, "Can you read the patterns in their flight?"

He gave her a funny look and snorted derisively.

"I'd never've pegged you for the hippie-dippy type."

"People change."

Her tone was sharp, but she was more annoyed at herself. By giving him a hint of her secret world, she had allowed him to mock it. She wouldn't make the same mistake again. *Tread softly because you tread on my dreams.* Wasn't that what Honor once said when Laurel made fun of her beliefs?

Another silence fell between them, but this one was volatile. All that was needed was a spark to set them off.

Ian stood up.

"It's bloody cold in here. I'll get the stove going."

She welcomed the distraction and offered to help.

"Roll up some newspaper," he said, "and bung it in with the firelighters."

He located the tongs for lifting the iron plates that lined the top of the stove. As he set the fire, he showed her what to do.

"Put small bits in at first, then when the flames get going, shovel in a load and keep feeding it. There's more turf and coal in the shed outside. If you're leaving the house for a while or going to bed, cover the fire with slack. That's the bucket of crushed coal, there. It forms a kind of cave over the flames and keeps them on a slow burn. If the fire stays lit, you'll always have hot water in the radiators, and for the sinks and bath. But there's an electric shower, too, so no panic."

Her grandfather had given her the same instructions, but she was glad to see them in action.

By the time the radiators were singing with heat and

the cottage was cozy, they were both feeling friendlier toward each other.

"Cup of tea?" Ian suggested.

Laurel shook her head. She was collapsing with exhaustion.

"I'm going to bed. It's been a long day."

It was only when she said good night that he asked the question she had hoped to avoid.

"Why are you here on your own?"

It was her turn to lower her eyes and struggle for explanations.

"I . . . it's . . . private," she mumbled, before hurrying to her room.

He would hear nothing from her about fairies and lost kings.

The bedroom was small and had an iron bed covered with a patchwork quilt. There was a dressing table with a round mirror and a washstand with porcelain jug and bowl. Pots of dried lavender tinted the air. The bookcase was stacked with children's books. *The Chronicles of Narnia. Martin Pippin in the Apple Orchard. The Midnight Folk. The Enchanted Castle. The Turf-Cutter's Donkey. The Blue Fairy Book.* The musty hardbacks had notes scrawled inside their jackets. With a mild shock, she discovered her father's name. Of course. These would have been his as a child.

A wave of pain struck her as she thought of her dad and then her mom. She had shut them out the past year, living like a ghost in their home. It must have broken their hearts all over again, as if they had lost not one but two daughters.

Mustn't think about that, Laurel told herself. Don't look back, only forward. *Act as if you believe* and all will be well.

She dragged herself into bed. The mattress felt cold and damp. She cocooned herself in the quilt, glad of the flannel pajamas her grandmother had packed. The wind whistled in the eaves above her. Rain spattered the window panes. The susurrus of the sea sounded outside.

Closing her eyes, she tried to will herself to sleep. So far, so good. Whatever surprises the day had brought—Granny, the raven-man, the hippie bus, and Ian—she had arrived in one piece and would begin her quest tomorrow.

She slipped her hand under her pillow where she had put a photograph of Honor.

Good night, sis.

It was much later when she woke. The room was dark, but she knew someone was there.

EiGHT

It was the noise that woke her. Scuffles and snuffles and scampers across the floor. Along the base of the walls. Over the dresser. A clink as the water jug rattled in its bowl. Mice? Laurel was about to jump up and turn on the light when she heard the giggles. She caught her breath. Something strange was happening. There were more giggles and then whispers. They were moving swiftly around the room. She nearly screamed when something landed on the bed with a small thump. She bit her lip, willing herself to be still. There was no squeaking. Definitely not mice. More soft bodies landed on the bed. Now they ran up her back! It was the oddest sensation. Little feet like finger tips. Giddily she realized they were playing tag and using her as a springboard to leap off the bed. She was more curious than afraid. When she peeked through her eyelashes, she glimpsed flickers of color. The logical part of her brain offered explanations, including a vivid dream brought on by the mission and headlights from a passing car refracted through raindrops on the windowpane. She dismissed these as nonsense. Whatever was happening was much more exciting.

Something stood close to her nose. She could sense it peering into her face. A sweet fragrance wafted toward her.

"Ah, poor thing," said a silvery voice. "She's sad and lonely."

"Give her a kiss," suggested another.

This led to snickers. Other voices added their encouragement. Laurel felt the press of tiny lips on hers, and tried not to smile. A feather's tickle. The taste of dewdrops.

A crowd had gathered at the edge of her pillow. Their game was suspended as they discussed her.

"Moon-colored hair and a face like a pearl."

"I wish we could steal her."

"Don't be silly. You know she is in league with the Gentry."

"Her family has always sided with the Court."

"More's the pity!"

A stroke as gentle as thistledown brushed her cheek.

Laurel couldn't help herself.

She sneezed.

In the cacophony of screeches that followed, her eyes flitted open. She had to swallow a cry. Oh the wonder of it! She was surrounded by whorls and tinsels of light— glittering golds and greens, frilly pinks and blues. A burst of miniature fireworks! And inside the lights flashed limbs, veined wings, and streaming tresses. But it was all too much. Too weird and unearthly. Terrified, she clenched her eyes shut again. She was *fairy-struck*.

Yet with the terror came a thrill of delight. Woven

through the fear of the supernatural was the thread of enchantment. The faint shimmer of a promise in the dark of night. *If such things are possible, then dreams may come true.*

She didn't want them to leave. She pretended to snore so they would settle.

They dropped out of the air and back onto the bed, like a shower of petals. The giggles started up again. A daring imp climbed onto Laurel's head.

"I'm giving her elf-locks for the fright she gave us."

"Mind you don't wake her!"

"She can't be woken. A *pisreog* was put on the biscuits and all have been eaten."

"They'll come for her soon," someone said with a sigh.

"What a shame!" cried another. "Will they harm her?"

Laurel could feel the little fingers making knots in her hair. She fought the urge to scratch. Alert now, she stopped snoring to listen. What were they talking about? It didn't sound good.

"I want to warn her!" one of them burst out.

"You can't! It's forbidden! *Tá sí sa leabhar ag an bhfiach dubh,*" came a lugubrious voice. When the others gasped in unison, it persisted. "The Fir-Fia-Caw claim her as foe."

"We must wake her then!" argued her defender. Now she recognized the voice. He was the one who had kissed her.

When a few others backed him, a quarrel broke out.

"Even if we woke her, she cannot fight them. She knows nothing of charms."

"We could tell her! If she turns her clothes inside out, puts a nail in her pocket, hangs scissors on the wall, puts a knife in the doorway – "

"—salt on the threshold. Daisy chain tea. A horseshoe on the door—"

"—a sock under the bed. A knife under her pillow—"

"—her shoes pointed away from the bed—"

"—running water. A twig of broom. St John's Wort—"

"—red thread tied round branch of rowan—"

"—a circle of white stones to keep her safe—"

"Enough! We cannot defy the Doom of Clan Egli. You know this."

Laurel was fast growing alarmed. Something called the Fir-Fia-Caw were coming for her, and they didn't sound friendly. Her newfound enemy? The raven-man? It seemed she was supposed to be unconscious, thanks to something in the cookies. But she hadn't eaten any. That meant Ian was out for the count, as he had scoffed the lot.

Then she heard it, rising like a wind in the distance, a shriek that chilled her to the bone. As soon as it died down, another followed, and then another. She buried her head under the quilt.

The fairies themselves were squealing with fright. In a flutter of wings, they fled the room. Only one lingered to whisper in Laurel's ear.

"Fare thee well, dear heart."

Her champion! Then he, too, was gone.

As if released from a spell, Laurel jumped from the bed. Adrenaline coursed through her. She had to move fast. This was no dream. The danger was real. The dreadful cries were growing louder. Drawing nearer. Whatever the Fir-Fia-Caw might be, they were coming for *her*.

She pulled off her pajamas and turned them inside out. What else did they say? *Sock under the bed. Knife under the pillow.* She threw her socks under the bed, then remembered the one about pointing her shoes outward. No good, she had to wear them! When she ran into the other room, she was brought up short.

Ian lay sprawled on the sofa. The biscuits had obviously taken affect before he went to bed. He was still dressed, and his arm dangled to the floor over the book he was reading.

She rushed to his side and started to shake him.

"Ian, wake up! Something's coming! Wake up!"

His breathing was shallow, his skin even paler than usual. An image flashed through her mind. The effigy of a knight carved on a tomb. Her anxiety was peaking. She couldn't stop to help him. She had to make the cottage safe.

A storm was brewing outside, as if stirred up by the howls of the Fir-Fia-Caw. Gusts of wind struck the house. The thatch groaned under the lash of a downpour. Thunder roared overhead, making the doors and windows shudder.

Laurel grabbed a knife from the kitchen drawer and

shoved it under the cushion behind Ian. There was another charm to do with knives—yes!—she put one at the door to the porch. And another to do with doorways. She ran to get the salt. She couldn't possibly remember every item, but the more the better. The fiendish cries spurred her on.

She turned on the taps for running water. Was there something about scissors? What else? What else! *A circle of white stones to keep her safe.* The pebbles that lined the path! She ran out the door.

The night was pitch-black and angry. A fist of rain struck her, soaking her to the skin. Wild with panic, she raced down the path, grabbing at stones.

Shrieks erupted overhead, screeching down like missiles.

When Laurel looked up, her heart froze.

The sky was alive and writhing. Ragged shapes flew toward her, great shadows from the dark side of the moon. As they drew nearer, she saw them: giant ravens with eyes that glowed silver-white like lightning. Seven there were, with razor-edged wings and curved beaks like scimitars. Carrion birds. Flesh-eaters. The Fir-Fia-Caw.

Laurel was paralyzed with terror. There was no time to return to the house! Now she scrambled to make a circle of stones around her. Her cold fingers fumbled even as the creatures began to land in the garden.

The moment the Fir-Fia-Caw touched the ground, a harrowing change took place. With savage contortions they each unraveled to a tall and almost human form.

Feathers melded together to make the black greatcoat that she remembered. As arms and legs emerged, the bird talons contracted into clawed hands. A dark layer of skin slid over the face; the beak became a sharp nose. Like a horrible budding, the broad-rimmed hat burst from the top of the head. In the final stage, the lightning-white eyes were flooded with darkness and rimmed with gold.

The first to land was the leader, to whom the next six bowed. Laurel recognized him instantly. Her attacker at the station! The madness that stamped his features set him apart from the rest. He turned his head this way and that as he scanned the area with burning eyes. She was crouched on the ground, in the act of putting the last stone in place. Her heart pounded so hard she was sure he could hear it. She had completed the circle, but it seemed so flimsy, an absurd protection against such creatures. How could she possibly be safe?

The Fir-Fia-Caw stood together, oblivious to the pouring rain, talking to each other in their croaking language. Raucous squawks trailed into mournful sighs and rattles. They wore human shape, but they were not men.

Laurel straightened up carefully, poised to run. The leader looked her way. He cocked his head sideways as if sensing her presence. Now he moved toward her. She stood deathly still, too terrified to breathe. He came so near she could have touched him. Her legs went weak, threatening to buckle, but she dared to meet his ferocious stare.

Only the shapes of the garden were mirrored in his

eyes. There was no sign of her there. The fairy charm was working! His gaze glanced off her and into the distance. Turning quickly on his heels, he signaled to the others to enter the cottage.

A new bout of horror struck her. *Ian!* He was defenseless. They would tear him apart with their claws! She couldn't stand by and do nothing. They had come for her, not him. She was about to step from the circle and challenge the creatures, when they jerked to a halt in front of the porch. The leader spat out harsh words. Laurel guessed what they meant. *Salt. Knives. Running water.* She suppressed a laugh of hysteria. The other charms were working too. The way was barred.

Did that mean they would leave?

No such luck.

The seven formed an arc in front of the house. Opening their mouths wide in a shock of bloodred, they emitted a sinister sound. The hair on the back of Laurel's neck stood up. The drone was strangely compelling. She could sense it seeping under her skin, snaking through her bloodstream and into her brain. Her limbs began to twitch. She knew what was happening. Her mind was betraying her, commanding her body to answer their call. Against her will, her right leg began to move. She struggled to stop it. Slowly but surely her foot left the ground, ready to step from the circle.

The leader's dark eyes searched the garden again. Laurel stood poised on one leg, holding herself back with agonizing effort. If she lost her balance, she was done for.

Please make them go.

The chanting broke off suddenly. Ian had lurched into the porch and opened the front door. Bracing himself between the jambs, he stood on the threshold, battered by the wind and rain. His eyes were blank.

When the Fir-Fia-Caw saw him, they exploded with rage and ear-splitting shrieks. In fitful spasms, they shriveled back to raven form. Now great wings beat the air and they flew away, disappearing into the night.

Safe at last.

Laurel staggered from the circle. Drenched, freezing, and trembling all over, she stumbled toward Ian.

He stared at her, bewildered. His hair was plastered against his face, his wet clothes clung to his body. Like a sleepwalker slowly coming awake, he tried to focus and make sense of the scene.

"Your pajamas are inside out," he said.

Then he collapsed in a heap.

Nine

Half-dragging, half-carrying him, Laurel got Ian into the house. They were both drenched and shivering, but there was something else wrong with him. The edges of his mouth had a greenish tinge and his eyelids fluttered unnaturally. Both the biscuits and the Fir-Fia-Caw chant had affected him badly. He was slipping deeper into unconsciousness. She had to act fast.

The fire in the stove was still burning beneath the cover of slack. She shoveled in several loads of coal until the heat rose up in waves. Hauling Ian closer to the warmth, she stripped off his clothes, swabbed him dry with towels, and wrapped him in blankets. She was searching the cupboards for medicine when she spied it on the windowsill above the sink: a daisy chain. Wasn't that one of the charms the fairies spoke of?

"Thank you," she whispered.

The black kettle was simmering noisily on the hob. She dropped the daisy chain into a mug and added the boiled water. Leaving the tea to brew, and Ian wrapped up by the stove, she went to change. As she didn't have a second pair of pajamas, she borrowed a nightgown from Nannaflor's dresser. Her grandmother's scent lingered in the soft folds, comforting her.

Back in the living room, she cradled Ian's head in her arm and spooned the pale-gold liquid into his mouth.

The tea trickled from his lips. Nothing happened.

"Please," she said quietly, tipping back his head and trying again. "Please drink it."

He started to cough as he swallowed. A little color seeped into his cheeks. His eyelids flitted opened.

"How do you feel?" she asked, anxiously. "Should I call a doctor?"

He stared at her, mystified. His features showed his struggle to understand.

"No. I'm okay. I . . . what happened? The last thing . . ."

"Not now," she said, relieved and exhausted. "We'll talk tomorrow."

She helped him to stand up, still bundled in the blankets, and led him to the sofa. He was too weak to protest. As she placed a cushion behind his head, he closed his eyes and sank into sleep. She stood and watched him for a while. His breathing sounded normal and he looked much better. Without thinking, she brushed the hair from his forehead, then pulled back her hand.

She was almost fainting with fatigue. The storm had died down and all was quiet outside, but she was worried that the Fir-Fia-Caw might return. She put more salt around the house and placed knives under every cushion and pillow. Then she dragged herself to bed and fell quickly asleep.

The next morning, Laurel woke late to a room flooded with sunshine. The horror of the raven-creatures seemed like a nightmare dispelled by daylight. She scrambled out of bed. She had to clean up before Ian woke. She couldn't begin to explain the odd things left about. But would he remember what happened?

She pulled on jeans, a T-shirt, and one of Honor's sweaters. Already sensitive to the Irish damp, she found Achill even colder. As she ran a brush through her hair and pulled it back in a ponytail, she glanced in the mirror. There were purple smudges under her eyes and her look was gaunt. She turned away. Her appearance didn't interest her.

She was about to leave the room when a knock came on the door.

"Breakfast's ready if you are," Ian called.

When she joined him in the living room, she was surprised to find him looking well. There was an unusually cheerful air about him. His light-blue shirt accented the color of his eyes. His skin seemed to glow. Even the silver stud in his eyebrow shone.

The table was laid with plates of scrambled eggs and toast. The aroma of freshly brewed coffee hung in the air.

"I drove down to the shop for a few things," he said.

She couldn't stop herself from tucking in. The night's encounter seemed to have given her an appetite. The eggs were delicious, cooked with butter and a hint of herbs.

"Is this a bribe or something?" she asked him.

Ian sat opposite her, eating more slowly. He paused before answering.

"It's a thank you. I don't remember much, but I've got the weird impression you saved me somehow?"

She was thinking fast. She couldn't possibly explain. Nor did she want to. Things were complicated enough without adding him to the mix.

"You were sleepwalking," she said quickly. "I found you outdoors in the rain."

His eyes narrowed. He looked unconvinced, but also uncertain.

"Did you take off my clothes?" He stared at her frankly. "I woke naked."

She felt her face go hot.

"You were soaking wet," she said, flustered. "I was afraid to disturb you. You're not supposed to wake a sleepwalker."

"What about the others?" he persisted. "Men in black coats and hats?"

She had to end this line of questioning.

"Sounds like you were hallucinating."

"I don't do drugs," he said, so forcefully she wondered if it was a lie.

And there the interrogation ended.

"I don't care what you do," she said tartly, "but you promised last night you'd leave today and I'd prefer if you did."

She saw the flash of anger in his eyes, watched it battle with disappointment and despair. A part of her sympathized with him, but there was nothing she could do. She was overburdened already, and barely coping. There was no room in her life for anything else.

"Why don't you go home?" she suggested. "Why make things harder for yourself?"

"What would you know about it?" he snapped. "You don't know anything about me or my life!"

Her temper was as quick as his.

"And I don't want to! When are you going to get that into your head?" The chair crashed behind her as she jumped to her feet. "I'm going for a walk. You'd better be gone by the time I get back, or I'm calling the police."

Breakfast abandoned, she stormed out the door.

Achill looked refreshed and invigorated after the night's storm. A cool sunshine was drying out the island. The air was so clean it tasted like champagne. Laurel strode down to the dunes and onto Trawmore, the great strand of Keel. Before her stretched two miles of sand curving toward the Cliffs of Minaun. The tide was out, and a thin mist lingered over the water. Seagulls circled in the sky with lonely cries. Looming over the strand from the north side of the island was the great mountain of Slievemore, capped with mist like a cauldron brewing. The beach itself was deserted, except for a stroller walking his dog.

Laurel wandered along the shore. Tiny birds skittered across her path, pecking in the sand. A cold wind bit through her sweater. She had left the house without her coat, but she wouldn't go back. She felt raw and shaken, all her emotions ajar. She was furious with Ian, yet she knew he wasn't really to blame. After a year spent in a state of numbed shock, she had begun to *feel*. And she didn't want to. It left her open to the unbearable anguish of her loss. The pain was always there, trying to break through, like waves pounding against the seawall; and she just barely held it back.

Now an awful thought struck her. She had accused Ian of hallucinating. Could it be true of her? Had the pain driven her to some crazy delusion?

The flat of sand before her was glazed with a film of water that reflected the sunlight. Land, sea, and sky seemed to blend together in a haze of blue. Laurel raised her hand to shield her eyes.

And that's when she saw her.

Out of the mist, crossing the water, came the White Lady upon her pale horse. Like an elusive mirage, she seemed both distant and near. Her silvery hair streamed behind her. She was riding toward the Cliffs of Minaun.

The vision lasted the length of a heartbeat, but it was enough. As Laurel raced for the cliffs, she spied the caves cut into the rock face at the edge of the sea. Dark, wet, and rimmed with moss, they were only visible because the tide was low.

She clambered over the barrier of huge stones that lay before the cliffs. Seabirds nested on the heights above her. Water sluiced through the grasses that straggled down the crags like long green hair. The smell of dank seaweed curdled the air. Though she wasn't sure what she was looking for, she began to explore every crack and crevice. None went deeper than a foot or two and all were empty.

Laurel sat down on a rock and stared out to sea. There had to be a reason the Lady rode this way. She picked up a stone and flung it glumly.

"There ye are now!" piped a voice so tiny she thought at first she was imagining it.

Something tickled her hand. A little red spider no bigger than a dot. She flicked it away.

"Ow!" it cried out.

She hunched down to get a better look. The cluricaun!

"Why are you so small? You're almost microscopic!"

"I'm the size of your opinion of me," he squeaked. "We're simpatico, ye know."

She wasn't sure what he meant, but she got the gist.

"Serves you right. Why didn't you tell me about the Fir-Fia-Caw?"

A tiny sigh issued from the tiny cluricaun.

"Ah, the Doom of Clan Egli. A bit of an oversight for which I am heartily sorry. *Mea culpa.* Sure, amn't I payin' for me sins?"

She had so many questions to ask him, but Laurel found herself fighting off a fit of giggles. She was talking to a spider!

"Will you have to stay this way for long?"

"Haven't a bog," he cheeped. "But it's all for the best right now. Keeps me incognito. Have ye found the way in?"

"What do you mean? The way into the cliffs? But where am I going?"

"That's good. Keep up the questions. They like that

game. You're in need of allies, *girseach*. Time's fleeting and the bird is on the wing. Ye can't be doin' this all on your sweeney. Find the Amethyst Cave. It's the old palace of the Summer King. If ye play your cards right, his people might give ye a hand. But they're a fishy folk, so be on your guard. Now ye can't say I didn't warn ye this time. Follow the music and—"

The cluricaun's instructions broke off with a screech as a beetle scuttled toward him. Laurel brushed it away, but a small crab took its place, pincers clicking. Suddenly the rock was crawling with insects marching in lines like an army.

"They're on to me!" the cluricaun screamed. "I'm off! Remember what I said. Ask questions all the way!"

And then he was gone.

Laurel let out a frustrated noise. She needed to ask him about the Fir-Fia-Caw, why they were against her, and what she should do about them. And what was the Doom of Clan Egli? The fairies had mentioned it too. There were so many things he hadn't told her. She was beginning to wonder how far she could trust him. Still, she agreed with his suggestion to try and gain allies. A good thing to acquire, now that she had enemies!

Her search of the cliffs resumed. After a while, she came across a fissure veiled by a little waterfall and half-choked with grass. She couldn't explore it without getting wet. As the icy shower struck her she let out a yelp, but squeezed herself through. The dousing was worth it. She had found the way in.

There was a moment of doubt as Laurel peered down the dark passageway. Where did it lead? Who or what would she meet? The rock around her pulsed with the beat of the waves striking the far side of the cliffs. The air was thick with the smell of fish and seaweed. When was the tide due? If she went in, would she have time to get out again?

Inching forward, she felt her way along the walls of wet rock. A phosphorescent lichen eased the darkness with a greenish light. When she came to stone steps leading downward, she halted. Her heart beat rapidly. She was already deep inside Minaun. How much further would she have to go? She started down.

It wasn't easy. The steps and walls were slimy with sea moss. Despite her caution, she kept slipping. She would be black and blue before the day was done. The stairway seemed endless, but there was no question of turning back. She could already hear it: the faint sounds of music and revelry below.

At last the stairs came to an end, and there stood a high arch fashioned from the stuff of the sea. Clustered like flowers on a trellis were periwinkles, purpura, cowries and conches, crusted barnacles and fans of sponge, slender razor clams, speckled starfish, and clumps of brightly colored coral. The whole structure resonated like an aeolian harp, whispering and sighing.

Surely something so beautiful could only lead to something good. What was there to fear?

Laurel stepped through.

Ten

Nothing could have prepared Laurel for the sight she now beheld. Not her grandfather's books nor her talk with Granny, not even her encounters with the cluricaun and the Fir-Fia-Caw. Indeed, no feat of the imagination, either hers or anyone else's could have been quite so fantastical, gorgeous, or extravagant. She was almost convinced she had walked into a dream.

The hall before her was as immense as a cathedral, carved out of the hollow of Minaun mountain itself. Walls of cream-colored rock met corbeled roof, all veined with glittering streaks of amethyst. Galleries a thousand feet up dripped with sea plants, while slides and waterfalls splashed down into blue pools. Flying fish leaped out of the water and through the air like silver birds. Every ledge and cranny was festooned with creatures twinkling like gems; sea urchins with ivory spines, pearled oysters and mother-of-pearled abalones, white stars of ascidian, red beadlets of anemone, blue-rayed limpets, spangled tompot blennies, and soft-bodied sea-lemons like yellow meringue.

But it was the fairies themselves who took her breath away, for these were also creatures of the sea but not as she knew them. And so different from familiar fairy images! They were not garden sprites nor winged woodland dwellers, but *boctogaí*, water fairies. *Bunadh na Farraige.* The Folk of the Sea. Amorphous and mercurial, like flowing water, they changed size and shape at will, one moment as small as a cowry shell, the next human height, and taller still. Their skin colors mirrored the waters of the world; sea-green, briny-blue, aquamarine, the deep brown of mountain rivers, the white of capped foam, the flecked gold of sunshine on the waves, the silver sheen of moonlight on the night surf. Some had webbed toes and scalloped ears, others feathery antennae and green hair like seaweed. Many had scales. They dressed in lurid hues of pink, lime-green, inky blue, and orange, and their jewelry was made of coral and shell.

The whole scene was a mad dream, luscious and bizarre. A party in a giant aquarium! Divers leaped from pool to pool, jackknifing and somersaulting in the air. Some arrowed across the cavern with the flying fish. Teams slid down slides, gripping whips of kelp. One group played with a freckled squid who kept squeezing off ink blots before disappearing underwater. The *boctogaí* squealed as they dodged the squirts, but there was always someone who got pelted with the dark sticky fluid. And behind all the laughter and chatter wound mellifluous music.

No one noticed Laurel at first, where she stood in the archway, utterly agog. Then one of the fairies spotted her and let out a cry. The music stopped. The revels ceased. A profound silence settled over the hall, broken only by the tintinnabulation of falling water. It was as if a thousand-eyed sea beast had suddenly turned to gaze at her.

Fear and wonder surged through her. She was *fairy struck*. The collective stare only worsened the sensation that she was caught in a dream. Instinctively, she checked to see if she was dressed. When she looked up again, they were all around her. She stifled a scream. One of them reached out to touch her. A clammy stroke. Her body jolted from the shock. These were beings who lived in her world but were not of it. Yet those starry eyes regarded her as if *she* were the alien.

Laurel fought the urge to flee. She was there for a reason. She had a mission. It actually helped that some of the glances cast her way were unfriendly. Cold splashes of reality. She needed to keep her wits about her. This wasn't a safe place.

An emerald-skinned lady draped in pearls addressed her.

"What are you doing here?" she asked in a melodious voice.

Laurel was about to answer when she remembered the cluricaun's instructions.

"W-w-why do you ask?"

Her own words made her flinch, she could hear how rude they sounded, but she saw immediately that she had said the right thing.

The fairy faces lit up. Some let out little cries of pleasure. She knew the rules. The game was on.

"Have you lost your way?" asked a pixie with purple hair.

Laurel hesitated, still anxious not to offend.

"Have you found it?" she countered.

A titter echoed through the hall. Some applauded, clacking seashells together like castanets. There was a frenzy of whispers. *Good sport. Well played. A clever mortal. Send in the Master Riddler.* The crowd parted to make way for a young man of amber-brown color. He wore a tunic of shells that rattled like chain mail and a mantle of seaweed. His eyes flashed with mischief, but his smile was friendly.

"Why do you always answer a question with a question?"

His voice sounded vaguely familiar. She smiled back at him.

"Do I do that?"

The outburst of laughter was unnerving. Some even hooted and hollered, while a few capered about. Then, as if by some unspoken signal, they resumed their revels. A new tune rang through the hall. Trumpeted on conches, with clams clattering like bones, it was an air as wild as a storm at sea. Everyone began to dance.

Caught by the hand, Laurel was whirled between partners till her head spun. She tried to relax, to join in their antics, but the shock waves kept hitting her. Again and again the truth would present itself, like a pearl inside an oyster: she was dancing with fairies. *Fairies!*

They brought her to a banquet table laid out with a

feast. The centerpiece was a fantasia of fruits and nuts glazed with honey. Silver platters held heaps of caviar, black and red. To her surprise, her favorite foods were also there: barbecued chicken with roast potatoes and crispy duck with fried rice. A golden cup was placed in her hand. It sparkled with something that looked like champagne. She was about to take a sip when the Master Riddler walked behind her and muttered quickly.

"Eat no food and drink no wine if you wish to see your world again."

Trembling, she realized she had almost been trapped. Didn't Granda's books warn not to touch fairy food? The table wavered before her sight. A fishy whiff wafted from the dishes. For a moment she saw a very different meal. Great tureens spilled over with plankton, algae, and moss. The cup in her hand was a conch of sea water! Other warnings rang in her mind. *They are not like us. You are dealing with Faerie, the Perilous Realm. They're a fishy folk, so be on your guard.*

Stealthily, she placed her goblet aside but of course they noticed.

"Will you not accept our hospitality?" someone shouted.

There was an edge to the voice. She was about to apologize and make some excuse when she stopped herself in time.

"May I ask for something else instead?"

The music came to a halt, but this time with a discordant clang. Her suspicion was confirmed. The game was still on. Yet it seemed to have taken a darker turn. Many of the fairies appeared tense and uneasy. Some looked hostile.

Once again, the Master Riddler stepped to the fore. He no longer smiled.

"What is it you want?"

Laurel took a deep breath. The moment had come. It was now or never. She glanced upward into the recesses of the roof. She had spied it earlier when she was dancing. High on a rocky ledge it stood, glittering and abandoned: an amethyst throne.

"Will you help me find the Summer King?"

The hall erupted. As her words rebounded from the walls—*the Summer King? the Summer King?*—it was met with a cacophony of cries and conflicting emotions: outrage, terror, fury, dismay. Gathering momentum, the swells of feeling surged higher and higher, threatening to collapse and swamp them all. Some of the fairies began to fight among themselves. Others ran away screeching. Many fled to the craggy ledges above, to peer down fearfully at the pandemonium.

Laurel was growing more anxious by the minute. Things were seriously out of control. The crowd was near to rioting. Hemmed in against the banquet table, she was a long way from the arch on the other side of the hall. And she had to get past the fairies to reach it. Some were already throwing her sullen glances. A few huddled together, whispering furtively. The malice in their eyes was plain to see. A little mob began to move toward her.

Laurel looked around quickly for a weapon. She was

about to grab her goblet when someone sidled up to her and caught her arm. The yell died in her throat as she saw who it was.

"Come with me," said the Master Riddler, under his breath.

He led her around the perimeter of the crowd. She was grateful for his help. At the corner of her eye, she could see the other group shadowing their movements.

"Don't look back," he murmured.

She trusted him, for she had finally recognized his voice. He was her champion from the previous night, the one who had kissed her!

At last they reached the shelly archway. Clasping her hand, the Master Riddler pulled her up the stairwell. They moved impossibly fast, their feet barely touching the slippery steps.

"Why are they so angry?" she gasped as they went. "What have I done?"

"All is not as it seems," he told her. "You have been schooled by the Gentry. We are spirits of another sort. We do not bow to the Court."

They climbed so quickly, Laurel could see the top of the stairs and the green light of the passageway that led out of the cavern.

"Please tell me what's going on," she begged. "Do you know what's happened to the Summer King? Do you know where he is?"

The Master Riddler didn't answer. He either wouldn't or couldn't say more.

Shouts rang out below them. Her enemies were in the stairwell and heading their way!

The Master Riddler let go of her hand.

"Make haste!" he urged. "I will try to hold them back."

"Will you be all right?"

"It is not me they are after."

She paused to kiss him on the cheek with a "thank you," then she was off.

The stairs were no longer easy to manage. Without his help, she kept slipping and sliding on the moss. As she grabbed at the walls and the steps in front of her, the jagged rock cut her hands. She was moving too fast to be careful. The angry noises behind spurred her on.

Suddenly the Master Riddler called out.

"Seek the Old Eagle of Achill."

His voice sounded strangled. Were they hurting him? His words triggered a furious howl from the mob. They sounded so near. Glancing over her shoulder, she yelped. Livid faces were charging at her!

Laurel bolted to the top step and down the passage. A sliver of light flickered ahead. She could hear the waterfall. But she could also hear the heavy breaths behind her as her enemies bore down. Heart pounding, she raced for the opening. With a triumphant cry she reached it and started to squeeze through.

The cry died in her throat.

Became a strangled screech.

Cold webbed hands had grabbed her like pincers. She

screamed and struggled, but in vain. As they pulled her back into the passageway, more arrived to swell the assault.

"Won't you let me go?" she cried.

It was too late to be clever. The game was over. She could sense their ill will, malevolent and merciless. They were all around her, pushing and pulling her back to the stairwell. The light of the fissure faded behind her. Weeping and pleading, she tried to resist, but their fingers dug cruelly into her skin. Some pinched and poked her. In her frantic struggles Laurel fell on the steps, banged her head, bit her tongue. The taste of blood was in her mouth. No matter how hard she fought, they drew her inexorably downward.

Now she realized the truth. She was about to disappear forever, into the underworld. That insight brought a surge of new strength. She had been a tomboy when she was little. She had tussled with the best, in the schoolyard, on the streets, and at the hockey rink. She was a girl who knew how to brawl. YES! Like a wild thing battling for its freedom, fighting for its life, she rose up with a roar. In a furious flurry of kicks and punches, she threw them off and sent them tumbling down the stairs.

Shrieking with rage, they rushed back.

She was waiting for them, sitting on the steps, fists up, eyes cold.

"I'm one of the fighting Irish too. Come on, I dare you."

They came to a halt. She could see the doubt assail

them, respect mingling with fear in their eyes. A few were nursing bruised limbs. Others whimpered. Some began to edge away, creeping back down the stairs. But the remainder obviously intended to fight.

As the first few charged, Laurel kicked them back with such force they bowled the others over. Their squeals were deafening. Another group set upon her. She sent them flying too. She had the advantage of the higher ground. Each time they came, she drove them back, and more would slip away and not return. In the end she was left with three, the ringleaders. They stood on the steps below her, glaring up. They were much bigger than the others. Her courage wavered.

"Okay," she said, chest heaving, heart pounding, fists back in the air. "Winner goes free."

True bullies, they rushed her together. Two pinned her legs, while the other scrambled ahead on the stairs and tried to choke her. With a last gasp of will, she twisted so violently that the ones holding her limbs crashed into each other. Then she reached up to grab the third and hauled him over her head. As she flung him at the others, she kicked out ferociously. They all went sprawling down the stairway.

It was her chance to flee. She dashed up the steps and back through the passageway. The fissure shone like a beacon ahead. With tears of relief she reached the opening and squeezed her way through, gasping at the splash of water. Then she stumbled out onto the shore, blinded by sunlight.

Her clothes were torn and dirty. She was limping from her injuries and staggering with shock. Her only thought was to get away, as far and as fast as possible. But she wasn't able. The barrier of rocks bordering the cliffs was too hard to cross, called for too much effort. She collapsed on the ground.

How long she lay there, she wasn't sure. She felt a hand on her shoulder. With a yell she struck it away and tried to rouse herself to fight.

"It's all right," said Ian. "It's me."

He was out of breath. His leather jacket looked too heavy in the sunshine. His boots and jeans were caked with sand.

"I came as fast as I could. I couldn't get the bike across the beach."

She saw the alarm in his eyes. Did she look that bad? She tried to stand up and almost fell, but he caught her in time.

"Lean on me," he insisted.

She didn't argue. She knew she couldn't make it herself.

He grasped her around the waist and led her forward. They had only gone a short way when they both saw it was impossible.

"I'll have to carry you," he said.

She opened her mouth to object, but hadn't the will. Though she was mortified, it was sweet relief to be lifted from the ground. The strain on her bruised body instantly lightened and her shock eased.

"Put your arms around my neck," he ordered, as he tread carefully over the rocks. "It will help balance me."

"I . . . I'm sorry about this," she mumbled.

"I'm sure you are," he said, with a grin.

She rested her head against his shoulder. The black leather was warm and soothing. She closed her eyes. He smelled of soap and aftershave. A nice smell.

Once they cleared the rocks and were on the strand, Ian picked up speed.

"You're light as a feather," was his only comment, "don't you eat?"

As they approached the dunes near her grandparents' cottage, she insisted that he put her down. His motorcycle stood in the marram grass. Dark-blue and silver glinting in the sunlight, it waited like a patient horse for its master. His helmet lay on the ground where he had apparently flung it.

"If you sit on the bike," he suggested, "I can push you to the door."

Laurel agreed. Though she was beginning to recover, she still felt weak. As he helped her onto the saddle, her mind raced. She was more than grateful that he had come to her rescue, especially since she had thrown him out, but what would she say to him? What *could* she say?

"Do I look like hell?"

ELEVEN

As soon as she was in the house, Laurel went to shower. Peeling off her clothes, she inspected with horror the many cuts and bruises that covered her body. This was not fun and games with the fairies. And yet, the experience had steadied her. She was no longer struggling with mystical impossibilities. Faerie was as real as her own world, and though it had proved indeed to be "the Perilous Realm," she now knew she could handle it.

She changed into baggy trousers that wouldn't rub against her wounds, and another sweater of Honor's. Wrapping her wet hair in a towel, she checked herself in the mirror. Despite her ordeal she looked quite good. There was color in her cheeks and her eyes were clear.

In the living room, she found a mug of soup left out on the table. Tomato, plain and fortifying. She had heard Ian leave when she was still in the bathroom. Sipping the warm soup, she wished she had got the chance to thank him.

When she heard the motorcycle roar back up the road, she hurried to comb her hair.

And when he came in the door, she felt suddenly shy.

"Thanks for your help," she said. "I really appreciate it."

He raised an eyebrow at the warmth of her tone, but said nothing as he dumped a shopping bag on the table. He started to take out various items—bandages, ointment, a packet of paper stitches. Then he removed his jacket and hung it on a chair.

"Sit down," he said. "I want to look at that gash on your forehead."

His voice was neutral, as if he were handling her carefully.

She didn't think to argue. Her head was throbbing, and she was glad he was there. She winced as he dabbed the cut with antiseptic. Then he applied a strip of stitches. His fingers felt rough against her skin.

When he was finished, he tipped up her chin till their eyes met.

"Are you going to tell me what happened?"

"I was climbing over the rocks and I fell."

He frowned.

"Liar."

The word struck her like a dart. He watched her closely.

"Oh yeah?" she countered, but her voice faltered. She was still shaken by her ordeal. She tried to stand up, to get past him. "Look, I can't do this right now. I've got to lie down."

He blocked her path.

"What is it with you?" he said, exasperated. "You're acting so weird."

"Oh, and you're Mr. Normal All-Irish Boy?"

He was about to snap back but seemed to think better of it. Instead, he shook his head.

"You're something else."

They had reached an impasse. She sat down again, too weak to oppose him. He took the chair near her and stretched out his legs. His manner was deliberately casual.

"Are you involved in some kind of cult?" he asked.

Laurel's eyes widened. Her own early suspicions of what the fairies might be! She was too surprised to dissemble.

"What makes you say that?"

"Men in black. Scissors and knives. I don't remember much from last night but I'm pretty sure I was in some kind of danger. And I've been in enough fights to know your injuries didn't come from a 'fall.' What are you hiding? Who attacked you?"

Her bravado was beginning to crack. He was forcing her to face the truth. First the Fir-Fia-Caw and now the *boctogaí*. Two attacks, and she had only begun her search for the king! The quest was dangerous, deadly dangerous, and she was all alone.

"Tell me," he insisted.

Laurel let out a sigh. She searched his face for something that might encourage her to confide in him. The black hair fell over his forehead, obscuring the stud in his eyebrow. Though the pale blue eyes were calm, his features looked tense, tormented. He had shown he could be kind, but most of the time he was at war with the world. Hardly someone who could hear her story.

"You wouldn't believe it," she said hopelessly.

"Try me."

In the silence that fell between them, two breaths were held.

"Okay," she said, finally. "First you have to answer a question with complete and total honesty, no matter how crazy or stupid it sounds. Do you agree?"

He looked bemused.

"I don't make promises, but I'll do my best to be straight with you."

Laurel rushed out the words before she could stop herself.

"Do you believe in fairies?"

She expected him to laugh or sneer or accuse her of mocking him. She would not have been surprised if he had flown into a temper and stormed out of the room. What she couldn't have foreseen was the way in which he was so caught off guard that he looked like someone else altogether. Someone younger and happier.

"Are you kidding me?"

"Yes or no?"

It was almost funny then. He looked abashed. His voice fell, low and embarrassed.

"Yeah. When I was a kid. In a big way. If I was really pissed off, with school or home, or if I had just got in a fight, I would go off on my own. Up Bray Head, or along the cliff path, into the mountains. I was always looking for a way out. A way in. To their world. I was always looking for them."

He glared at her defiantly, daring her to laugh.

Instead she asked softly, "Did you ever find them?"

His mouth thinned. He was about to retort sharply when she stopped him.

"Now I can tell you."

Without mentioning Honor, she spoke of the cluricaun, the missing king and the Midsummer Fire, the old woman on the train, then the attacks of the Fir-Fia-Caw the night before and the sea fairies that morning. Even as she detailed the events, she could see the struggle in his features, disbelief and cynicism battling with astonishment and wonder.

"I'm not the sort of person who makes this stuff up," she finished. "You know that."

He didn't respond right away. Though he looked a little stunned, she could see he was thinking.

"Why are they against you?" he said, at last. "Sounds like the king's disappearance is more than a case of missing persons. And I'd take what the cluricaun says with a pinch of salt. All leprechauns are tricksters. You can bet there's more going on than what he's told you."

She almost cried with relief. He hadn't even asked for proof!

"My feelings exactly. Granny spoke of a tragic tale. The Doom of Clan Egli? Something sad and terrible happened to the Summer King."

"Find the missing story, find the missing king," he agreed.

That's when she told him the Master Riddler's message.

His face brightened. "The Old Eagle of Achill? That explains it! Do you know how I found you? I wouldn't have seen you from the road, you know. I was driving away when I spotted it—a great golden eagle, flying over Minaun. I couldn't believe my eyes."

"Could it be the one?"

"It must be! The golden eagle's extinct in Ireland. They're trying to bring it back, but nothing that big has been seen here for centuries. I thought I was imagining it. I drove the bike back to the dunes and pulled over to have a look." He shook his head. "There was no sign of it, but that's when I spotted you. I knew something was wrong. You were staggering around like a drunk."

"Maybe *he* was the reason the White Lady was there," she said, thinking about it. "It must be the same eagle."

"Makes sense," said Ian. "We should look for it."

She heard the "we" and was both glad and uneasy. Did she really want him involved? She could use some help. Midsummer's Eve was only three days away, and she needed an ally, especially someone who could fight. On the other hand, he was so moody and unpredictable, and there were other complications she didn't want to think about.

"Are you going to tell anyone you're here?" she asked him. "I'm calling my grandparents today. I don't want to lie to them."

His features shut like a door.

"That's my business," he said coolly.

"I promised to call. They trust me."

"Then I'll go."

He was pulling on his jacket when she changed her mind.

"Okay, I won't mention you. It's your life."

"Then you want me to help you?"

She nodded.

"Say 'please.'"

It was her turn to be angry but he flashed a grin.

"I'm winding you up, eejit. "

"*Eejit?* Is that a real word?"

They were back on even keel.

"We've got to find the eagle," she concluded, "and fast. Time is running out. You're the expert on birds. Where's the best place to look? Back on Minaun?" She flinched at the thought.

"I don't think so. It's too open. They like to build their nests in secret and inaccessible places. The more isolated the better. There's a stack of guidebooks here. We should take a look at them."

"Will you do that? I want to check out the car. We'll need it to get around."

"We've got the bike."

"Hmm," was all she said.

Her grandfather had given her the car keys and a list of instructions concerning the old Triumph Herald parked in the shed. It was love at first sight. The little green car had silver headlights like big round eyes. The humped shape of the hood tapered back to elegant wings. Laurel checked the tires, saw they needed air, then lifted the hood to look at the engine. An old blanket had been tucked around it to keep out the damp. She checked the spark plugs, topped up the brake and clutch fluid in the master cylinders, removed the dipstick to gauge the oil. The engine was a mechanic's dream. You could see everything in a glance. Time to warm it up. She knew the car had to be coaxed into action, and then at no more than forty miles an hour.

The vintage interior made her sigh with joy—silver-gray seats of soft leather, ivory-colored roof cloth, and a wooden dashboard with an antique radio. It had a standard stick shift but she didn't mind, as she drove one at her family's cottage. She pulled out the choke and started the engine. After a few tries, it caught at last and purred like a cat at the fireside. Easing the car out of the shed, Laurel let the engine run for a while.

"That's it, old girl, I'll be gentle."

Turning on the radio, she tuned into *Raidió na Gaeltachta*, the Irish-language station. The strange words rang in the air, like colored marbles pinging off each other. They had a pleasant sound. She considered taking some lessons when she returned to Bray. Then a tremor ran through her. She caught her breath. It was the first time she had thought of doing anything new or rewarding since Honor's death. A stab of guilt shot through her. Was she forgetting her twin? But no, this mission was for her . . . wasn't it?

Ian came striding out the cottage and jumped into the passenger seat. He carried a pile of maps and guidebooks.

"I think I've got what we need!" he said, then stopped when he heard the radio. *"An bhfuil Gaeilge agat?"* he asked, surprised.

"What?"

"Oh, I thought, since you're listening . . ."

"You speak Irish?!"

"Yeah, I have a thing for it. I went to Coláiste Ráithín, the Irish-language secondary school in Bray." He let out a short laugh. "Well, I went for the girls. It's the only mixed school in town. But then I found I liked the language, and I was good at it. My best subject."

"Besides girls?" she said wryly.

He shrugged. "Didn't do too bad there either."

He stared at her, a challenge.

She returned his gaze.

Both looked away.

"Right," she said, "what did you find?"

He started flipping through the thickest guidebook.

"Something good. It's in the chapter on prehistoric Achill. Listen.

It is old thou art, O Bird of Eacaill,
Tell me the cause of your wanderings,
I possess, without denial,
The gift of speaking in the bird language."

"Our eagle?" she said, excited.

"There's more." He turned the pages. "A section in a fifteenth-century manuscript called *The Book of Fermoy*. It's entitled 'The Colloquy of Fintan and the Old Hawk of Eacaill.' Eacaill is an ancient version of Achill," he added.

"As if I couldn't guess."

"Jesus, you're sensitive."

"As opposed to you being insensitive?"

He made a noise. "Do you want to row, or do you want to hear what I found?"

It was like butting heads with a mirror. They glared at each other a moment, then nodded a truce.

"Here's the colloquy," he said, returning to the guide-book. "The word must mean 'dialogue.' There's a kind of play for two voices. Someone called Fintan and then the bird."

She watched him as he scanned the lines. He looked thoughtful and scholarly like a young poet or professor. Obviously he had "a thing" for books as well. She remembered the one on the floor by the sofa, and he had more in his knapsack. He was so different from the boys she knew. A lot more complicated.

"Here we go!" he said suddenly. "This is Fintan talking. *O Bird from Achill of the hunters. I have been seeking you for aeons.*"

"Sounds right," she said, leaning over his shoulder. She read out the bird's reply. "*I was never a night in the west of Achill that I could not get by my skill all I devour of fish, of game, of venison.*"

Ian unfolded a large map of the island, which showed the contours of the land.

"*The west of Achill,*" he repeated, poring over it. "Look at those cliffs, all facing west from Saddle Head to Carrickakin. And here we are, the highest peak in the ridge. Croaghaun." He tapped the paper where it detailed the peak at 2,192 feet. Now he picked up the guidebook and riffled through it. "Dead on! In ancient days, Croaghaun was called Eagle Mountain."

Laurel stared through the windshield. There it was, directly ahead of her on the far side of the island, the great ridge that Ian spoke of, rising to the dark summit of Croaghaun.

"If we were any closer, we'd be sitting on it," she murmured.

"Wait a minute, slow down." He perused the guidebook again. "Yeah, should've known. Things were too good. *The highest cliffs in Europe. A sheer drop to the sea.* It's impossible."

"Nothing's impossible," she said.

He looked up, startled.

"You can't—"

She cut him off.

"I must."

Twelve

The argument was well under way as Laurel drove the Triumph Herald to the garage to put air in the tires and gas in the tank.

"Are you out of you mind?" he demanded. "If the nest is up there, you can bet it's on the highest part of the cliffs. That's a fall into the sea of over two thousand feet. You're going to risk your life to find a mythical bird?

"It's not mythical. You've seen it. And what else can I do? He's the only lead I've got."

"Why are you doing this anyway? How did you get mixed up in it? You're not the sort—" Ian stopped suddenly. He studied her face as she drove. "Does this have something to do with your sister? You didn't say—"

"I don't want to talk about it," she said shortly. Her expression was pained. "I can't."

He frowned, but didn't press her.

She appreciated his tact.

The silence between them grew friendly.

"It'll be all right," she assured him, after a while. "I've done some rock climbing and rappelling. I've got a head for heights."

"It's still crazy," he objected, but in a milder tone. "Are you sure there isn't another way? What about the cluricaun?"

"We've already agreed he's not to be trusted. Besides, we don't know for sure if I'll have to go on the cliffs. Maybe once we get up there, the eagle'll find *me*."

"I wouldn't bet on it," Ian muttered.

After the garage, they drove to Achill Sound to shop in the department store. Ian looked happier when she bought climbing boots, rope, a proper harness, and other expert equipment. He bought hiking boots for himself and a pair of binoculars. They stopped for tea in a coffee shop. She was still picking through her salad when he gave her money to pay the bill and told her he would meet her outside. By the time she went looking for him, she found him in a craft shop down the street.

Ian handed her a knitted sweater of a deep blue wool with pearly flecks.

"Do you like it?"

"Yeah, great colors."

"Try it on."

She pulled the sweater over her head, freeing her hair to spill onto her shoulders.

"Looks good," he said, admiring her.

She got a little flustered, and was about to take it off.

"Keep it. It's yours. Let's go."

She hesitated, remembering his reputation for stealing, and glanced uncertainly at the register.

He caught her look. His eyes narrowed.

"It's paid for! I thought you'd wear it. Yanks are always whingeing about the cold."

She flinched at the insult, but didn't respond.

Neither spoke in the car on their way back to the cottage. He stared out the window, thin-lipped and sullen. She kept her eyes on the road.

As soon as they arrived at the house, Laurel escaped into the bedroom to change into a track suit more appropriate for climbing. She put the sweater Ian bought her into a drawer. Her hands were shaking. She was close to tears. She should never have let him stay. He upset her too easily.

She could hear him banging around in the kitchen. When she returned to the living room, he was closing his knapsack.

"Are you going?"

"Of course," he said shortly, without looking at her.

She was caught between relief and regret, and was even more confused when he sat down on the sofa to read his book. But when she started to make a sandwich to take on the hike, she discovered the misunderstanding.

"I've got enough for both of us," he said, glancing up from his book.

"What? I thought—"

Then she registered that he was wearing his new hiking boots.

He frowned as he grasped her meaning.

"You think I'd let you go up there alone because I'm pissed off at you? You really don't know me, do you?"

Before he could lose his temper again, she threw up her hands.

"I surrender! I'm sorry! Shoot me!"

She had said the right thing. Amusement flickered in his features.

"I really am sorry," she said, in a quieter voice. "About the sweater, I mean."

"Apology accepted. Are you ready to go?"

"Almost." She regarded him curiously. "What are you reading?"

"Rilke. German poet. Do you know him?"

It was her turn to be amused.

"I'm not a big reader." Her tone was wry. "You're looking at the dumb twin."

He raised an eyebrow at her remark, then turned a few pages and read out loud.

For beauty is nothing
but the beginning of terror, which we still are just
    able to endure,
and we are so awed because it serenely disdains
to annihilate us. Every angel is terrifying.

"That's beautiful," she said, amazed. "And it describes exactly how I felt among the fairies!"

"Maybe you're not so dumb after all."

She smiled and finished her packing. Along with the climbing equipment, she took rain gear, a water bottle, matches, a daisy chain, a small bag of salt, and a handful of white stones. Finding a tin of nails under the kitchen sink, she slipped one into her pocket and offered another to Ian.

"Charms against the Fir-Fia-Caw," she explained. "We need to be prepared for an attack."

"I've got my own charm," he said, and showed her the switchblade he carried in his back pocket.

She didn't ask questions, but felt comforted all the same.

It was late afternoon by the time they left the cottage to set out for Croaghaun.

"It would be faster if we took the bike," he suggested.

"We've got too much stuff," she disagreed, "and it might rain. Time's not a problem. It'll be light for hours yet."

She saw his lips press together as he made a deliberate effort not to argue.

"You can drive if you want," she offered.

Though he revved the Triumph's engine, making her wince, and drove faster than she would have liked, she managed to keep her mouth shut. Like him, she didn't want to fight anymore.

They drove to the village of Dooagh where a small road took them to the foot of the ridge that rose up to Croaghaun's peak. Having studied the map, they had decided not to climb the steepest side but to follow the old sheep farmer's trail up the eastern slope. It was a gentler incline that led directly to the cliffs. The precipice they sought ran for over two miles along the Atlantic. The eagle's eyrie could be anywhere along it.

After leaving the car at the end of the road, they set off on the trail. The massive ridge rose up before them, treeless and cloaked with bog. Over to the left, a great coomb scooped out the mountainside, its bare rock shining white in the sunlight. On their right, the western face of Slievemore Mountain cast its shadow toward them.

They hadn't walked far when they came to the ruins of a cluster of stone houses.

"It's a booley village," Ian told her. "The islanders used to take their animals into the hills for the summer. They'd camp out in these stone huts—men, women, and children. Everyone stayed up all night, sang, told stories, watched the stars. It must have been great *craic*."

"How do you know this stuff?" she asked, admiringly.

"I'm a bloody genius." When she threw him a look, he grinned. "I read it in the guidebook."

"You shouldn't read so much, you'll get a brain tumor."

The climb was more like a stroll at first. They were wandering through a vast empty landscape carpeted with heather. Behind them, Dooagh and Keel were like cubes of sugar sprinkled on the coastline. The strand of Trawmore curved like a lunula toward the Cliffs of Minaun.

At one point they heard the flutter of bird wings. Ian reached for his binoculars. He frowned as his gaze swept the sky.

"An ouzel, maybe," he muttered.

"Any ravens?" Laurel asked, anxiously.

He swore.

"Three of them. Over Slievemore."

"Keep an eye on them," she said, fingering the nail in her pocket.

Eventually the way grew steeper, and they had to stop occasionally to catch their breath. They kept a close watch on Slievemore. It looked different from high up. Instead of the dark face that always glowered over the island, the northern flank was bright with sunshine and plunged joyfully into the sea. Two deep coves bit into its side, with half-moons of sandy shore. But though plenty of seagulls wheeled in the sky, there was no further sign of the ravens.

When they stopped for a rest, Ian offered her the food he had brought: thick slices of bread and cheese, a flask of hot tea, mandarin oranges, and chocolate bars. The long climb had given her an appetite.

"I feel like you're looking after me," she said, with a little laugh.

"Maybe you need some looking after."

She concentrated on her sandwich.

The hike began to take its toll on their patience. Though they had been climbing for over an hour, they had yet to reach the top of the ridge. Every time they thought they were near, another height would appear beyond them. Hill was heaped upon hill.

Then they came upon a strange place. Grotesque

shapes loomed around them, sculpted from the bog by rainwater running off the mountain. Some of the hulking figures looked faintly human, others monstrous. The ground was pocked with brown pools. The air was gloomy.

Laurel stood at the edge of a pool and peered into the murky depths.

"Don't stand too near!" Ian said suddenly.

"What?" she said, moving back with alarm.

"Kelpies, water spirits, like Jenny Greenteeth. They clutch you by the ankles, drag you in and drown you."

She looked at him aghast, then caught the wicked grin.

"Very funny," she said. He dodged her slap. "The guidebook again?"

"Nope. Bedtime stories. It's an Irish tradition to scare your kids to death before they go to sleep."

They were both laughing as they hurried away. And not long after, they reached the top.

The ground sheered away below them in a breathtaking plummet to the sea. They were so high up, the waves struck the foot of the cliffs with only the faintest of sounds.

They began their trek along the two-mile precipice, in search of the eagle's eyrie. It was like walking on top of the world. There was a faint track in the grasses, worn by sheep. In some places the cliff plunged down in a straight fall of rock; in others, it sloped gradually, bearded with heather and grass. The two walked in silence. As they scanned the crags for any sign of a nest, they also watched

the sky for eagles and ravens. Nothing. Then they discovered the gorge.

As if from some cataclysmic event, a huge part of
the rock face had split from the mountain, creating a
narrow gorge a few feet wide that dropped to a channel
below. The sea surged through the narrow passage,
exploding on the rocks. It was a somber and lonely spot.
If the Old Eagle of Achill was to be found, this was
surely the place.

It took only a glance into the chasm to set Ian arguing
once more against a descent. They both ended up shouting, as much from tension as the need to be heard above
the wind.

"You have some crazy urge to be a hero!" he yelled.
"It's a bloody death wish!"

"I don't care what it is! One of us has to do this and
I'm the best for the job. I'm the athlete. You're the one
who reads poetry!"

By his furious silence, she knew she had won that
round. But then he began to insist that he would go with
her.

"You can't. You've got to watch the ropes, and stand
guard in case the Fir-Fia-Caw come. Please, I need you to
do this. "

Grudgingly, he agreed.

"It's not as severe as it looks," she said, fastening her
harness. "I've got plenty to hold onto."

Now she took out the rest of the climbing gear and
placed it professionally, attaching the ropes to the ground

and clipping them to her harness. Lowering one line into the gorge, she handed Ian the other. By the time she had tested the ropes, and he had checked them again, he looked a little less worried.

Laurel took a deep breath to calm herself. She was doing her best to hide her anxiety.

Something clicked in Ian's features.

"You'd do anything for your sister, wouldn't you?"

"I'd walk into the fires of hell for her."

There was nothing he could say to that.

"Good luck, then."

"Thanks. Watch my back, eh?"

The descent was unnerving. She had to get used to being in the gorge. The wind whistled around her. The waves crashed below. She was caught in the teeth of the rock, miles above the sea. Her breaths came in quick rasps, as much from tension as the icy air. But with each step she took, she found her strength on the mountain. It was exhilarating.

Slowly, cautiously, she lowered herself deep into the crevice. There were plenty of holds to grip on to. Occasionally she came upon a grassy ramp that she could scramble across. Sometimes a smooth slab of stone would stop her short. These she had to rappel, clinging onto the rope till she found purchase beyond.

From time to time Ian shouted to her and she called back to reassure him. If she craned her neck, she could still see him, peering down anxiously. There was no question of her returning yet. Though she had passed many nests tucked into the rock, none were large enough to house an eagle.

She wasn't sure when she started to feel different. A strange gloom seemed to creep from the shadows and into her mind. The solitude of the mountain began to weigh on her. The lonesome cry of the seabirds made her want to cry too. She thought of Honor and how she had died, falling off a cliff into the sea. The terror she must have felt as . . .

Stop it.

Then she caught sight of something that wasn't visible from the top of the precipice. She gaped in astonishment. Where the sides of the gorge ended to face the open sea there were pillars hewn in the rock, with a broken lintel overhead. The arch was definitely not a natural formation. Amidst the cracks in the stone were carved inscriptions. The writing looked vaguely like the traceries of bird print. A shattered ledge ran toward the archway and continued beyond it. The remains of an old road?

Tugging on the rope, she yelled up to Ian and pointed to the arch; then she realized he couldn't see it from where he stood. Her words were muffled by the wind. When he shouted down, she couldn't hear him either. But she had decided what to do. Moving sideways, she climbed onto the road. She had to be careful. There were many gaps in the path. If she lost her footing, the ropes themselves would pull her backward and smash her against the rock.

As Laurel neared the arch, she felt suddenly afraid. A

cold wind blew through the opening. The hair on the back of her neck stood up. Though she could see nothing but the blue of the sky, she was sure someone or something was on the other side. Watching her.

"Who's there?" she called out, her voice quavering.

Was it the Old Eagle? Or one of the Fir-Fia-Caw? She reached for the nail in her pocket. Her heart stopped. It wasn't there! She must have lost it on the climb. And she had left the other charms in her knapsack above! She was defenseless. For a moment she thought of turning back. She tugged on the rope for reassurance, as she couldn't see Ian. The line felt loose. She was about to call up to him when she changed her mind. Fear wasn't going to stop her now. This had to be the eagle's domain.

When Laurel stepped through the arch she was struck by a blast of icy air, and found herself standing on a shelf above the ocean. Her head spun before the infinity of sky and water. She suddenly knew that no one had ever stood here before. Looking upward, she spied the great cleft in the rock overhead, like the mouth of a cave. The eagle's eyrie!

She had just pulled on the rope to signal to Ian when the ground crumbled beneath her. Worn by time and wind and rain, unaccustomed to holding the weight of a human, the shelf collapsed.

Falling was oneiric and unreal. A blur of wind, cliff, and terror. The rope whined as it raced through her harness. Her arms and legs seemed to float. The world was moving strangely around her. Thoughts moved strangely

through her mind. How flimsy life was. The puff of a thistledown. A planet bobbing in the ocean of the universe. A
person bobbing in the air. She was both light and heavy.
Dropping like a stone. Flying like a bird. And even as she
grasped that her life was ending, she saw Honor falling
beside her.

Was the screaming coming from someone else? She
felt the protest in every part of her body. No! Unfair! It
wasn't her time! She had a mission!

When the beating of wings came overhead, it seemed
at first to belong to the dream of falling. But the talons
clutched her with violent force. A curved beak slashed at
her ropes, severing them like threads. And now she
surged upward in a rush of wind and wings. Up, up, past
the rock face. Everything was askew. The sea was rushing
away, out from under her, and she was falling upward
into the sky. Now the mouth of a cave hurtled toward her,
opening wide.

Inside, she was dropped lightly onto a floor of soft
moss. Stunned by the nature and speed of her rescue,
Laurel could only stare around her speechless. She was in
a huge nest. It was woven of branches and lined with
grasses, but was also adorned with rich fabrics. A canopy
glimmered overhead with the iridescent eyes of peacock
feathers. Even as she realized that the eyrie was a royal
bower, it wavered in her sight and everything changed. For
a fleeting second, she stood in the hall of a shining palace
with high windows and balconies overlooking the sea.

Yet the splendor of both nest and hall was dwarfed by

the great golden eagle that alighted before her. He was so magnificent she quivered in his presence. *For beauty is nothing but the beginning of terror.* He exuded radiance. Before he closed them, his wings spanned as grand and glorious as an archangel's. When the tawny head inclined toward her, she flinched at the sight of the hooked beak; but it was his eyes that caught her, shadowed with an age and wisdom beyond her comprehension. *Every angel is terrifying.*

Instinctively she bowed to him. Then she repeated the words from the guidebook.

It is old thou art, O Bird of Achill,
Tell me the cause of your wanderings,
I possess without denial,
The gift of speaking in the bird language.

He cocked his head sideways and stared at her a while, eyes unblinking. She wondered if he understood her. Wondered also, for a second, if he intended to eat her. Then he spoke.

His voice was musical; birdsong translated into human speech. She strained to listen as the words took shape inside a stream of sound.

"You are not speaking the language of birds. Fortunately I can converse in passable English. I do not suppose you have any Irish?"

"I . . . sorry . . . no."

"Pity. 'Tis a language more suited to my tongue."

"I intend to learn it," she added, wishing to please him.

"You are courteous for a wingless one. And you have great courage. Few have dared that descent. Why have you come to my eyrie? Speak and I will hear you."

She knew that she had been granted an audience with a king. It was up to her to state her case and request a boon.

The wind ruffled the canopy overhead. The sea murmured outside. The westering sun illumined the cave with an orange glow.

Laurel spoke simply, describing her search for the Summer King and the need to light the Midsummer Fire. As was her way, she didn't mention Honor's death or her private hope of saving her sister. But she did tell of her disastrous visit to the sea fairies and the attacks by her enemy, the Fir-Fia-Caw.

"I've come to ask for your help with my mission," she finished.

The great eagle regarded her solemnly.

"I am of the Old Ones, the Five Ancients of Ireland, they who came before your kind and Faerie: the Salmon of Assaroe; the Old Woman of Beare; Blackfoot the Elk of Ben Gulban; the White Lady; and myself, Laheen, King of the Birds, Lord over Clan Egli," he paused, his eyes darkening, "and the Fir-Fia-Caw."

Thirteen

Laurel's heart stopped when she heard the name of her enemy. She had come for help and fallen into a trap! A stray thought struck her. When she fell, the rope didn't pull her back against the rock face. That meant no one was holding it. They must have got Ian! Panicked, she looked around her. Miles above the ocean, on a lonely coastline, there could be no escape.

Yet the eagle didn't move to harm her.

"Long have your people lived on Achill," he said. "A noble line. You are welcome here."

"But . . . the Fir-Fia-Caw . . . they attacked me."

"All is not as it seems. Let me tell you the cause of my wanderings."

Once again Laheen opened his great golden wings, and a feathery light surrounded Laurel. What followed after, she could never be sure of. Did she fly through time to see events unfold? Or were memories sent swirling into her mind, like leaves caught in an eddy of wind? Laheen's voice was always there so that words and images flowed together like a story. Here at last was the missing tale of the Summer King and the Doom of Clan Egli.

I am of the Firstborn from the Dawn Before Time. Behold Eagle Mountain where I made my eyrie. Behold the Temple of the Birds which I did fashion for my Queen and her children.

There stood the sea-swept cliffs of Croaghaun, but not as Laurel knew them. Emerging from the mountain like its very soul was an immense and shining ziggurat. Tier upon tier of pillars and pathways rose into the sky. Clouds sailed through the tall columns carved of white quartz veined with gold.

Behold the Golden Age of Clan Egli. See my people, bounteous, multitudinous, living, glorious.

The Temple resounded with the song of countless birds, as well as fabulous winged creatures of myth and folklore. Some perched on the marbled ledges, preening their feathers. Others wheeled through the air in arabesques of flight. None fought or preyed upon each other, for this place was a haven, sacred to all.

Laurel found herself inside the Temple on a shelf so high it made her feel faint. Near her sat two old ladies, knitting and gossiping together like sisters. Both had bright eyes, beaked noses, and shrill, chattering voices. One wore her hair in a long gray braid the same hue as her skin. The other had a black plait that also matched her coloring. Feathered shawls draped their bony shoulders. Laurel was uneasy to see them teetering so precariously above the earth, their feet in midair. Then she blinked, and there stood a thin-legged crane and a shaggy black cormorant!

Now she glanced upward. Enthroned on the loftiest perch of all were two great golden eagles. The King and Queen of Clan Egli. Laurel recognized Laheen instantly.

Behold my beloved Ular, she who came from Faerie to be my wife.

The queen's image wavered. One moment there stood a glorious eagle; the next, a beautiful tawny-skinned woman with golden hair and eyes like coins. A jeweled gown flowed to her feet, a crown graced her forehead. Her face was grave and kind. Laurel sensed that she was something much older than a fairy, though he who stood beside her was older still. And while the Queen shape-shifted in form, Laheen did not, for he was an Ancient of Days, a spirit who came before Faerie and the Earthworld.

Ular raised an elegant arm and blew kisses to her children. Only now did Laurel catch sight of the Fir-Fia-Caw, the great raven-creatures with eyes that flashed like lightning. Here and there on every level they flew, black and glossy, cold and aloof. The Temple guard.

"What?" said Laurel under her breath, as the first sliver of doubt entered her mind.

But the vision was already fading in the golden light of the sunset.

And the story changed.

The Sídhe, whom you call fairies, came into being when Faerie was already old but your world was young. Where light mingled with the elements of earth, fire, air, and water, there they were born.

It was the birth of the sea fairies she witnessed.

By the shape of the land, Laurel knew she was looking at the early days of the world. Achill itself was not an island, nor yet was Ireland, for both belonged to one vast continent. Humanity was nowhere to be seen.

It was a midsummer's night. The warm sky rained falling stars. A tempest of wind tossed the waters. Sea spray exploded in the air. Wherever the starlight fell upon the surf's foam, they began to emerge. Lithe and sinuous. Wet and luminous. Some crawled to shore like jeweled insects struggling out of their cocoons to lie exhausted on the rocks, shimmering faintly. Others leaped up from the depths of the cold water, like flying fish or gamboling dolphins. Still others rode the white-capped waves, giving cry to the ecstatic joy of their existence. And the tallest and fastest and most beautiful of these was he who would be the Summer King.

Laurel caught her breath when she saw him, he was so exquisite, but her next impression was that he shone too brightly. He seemed incandescent, white-hot and fiery.

Once the sea fairies came to shore, all sparkling like fireworks, they rushed into Minaun Mountain. There they hollowed out the Amethyst Cave for their abode, and set a throne on high for their sovereign. But the king lingered outside to look upon the world. As he surveyed the island that was his domain, his eyes rested on Eagle Mountain and the Temple of the Birds, long established there. In that glance Laurel saw a new birthing: one of discontent.

*The Summer King ruled over the Folk of the Sea, but
he himself was drawn to fire.*

It was a stormy night. Lightning streaked across the
sky. The sea roiled. On the rocky shore of the embayment,
the outline of a tall figure could be seen, dark against the
shadows. Arms raised to the sky, hands sparking with fire,
he was singing and chanting—enchanting—working New
Magic still young in the world.

Out beyond the bay, volcanic upheavals at the bottom of the ocean spewed up steam and boiling foam.
Then slowly it rose up out of the water, like a shining sea
serpent: the isle of Hy Brasil.

*The Summer King abandoned his palace on Achill and
made his home on the island he had called into being. It was
a fair flowering place; yet a bright thing may nurse darkness
at its heart.*

Laurel caught glimpses of green hills and woods,
white waterfalls and streams, and dwellings of bronze
that shone in the sun. Overlooking all, on the slopes of
Purple Mountain were the glittering towers of the
Amethyst Palace.

She also caught sight of the king on his battlements,
glaring toward Eagle Mountain.

*The Summer King brooded over the Temple of the Birds.
The West was his kingdom and he did not want to share it.
In his heart he declared war on Clan Egli and plotted its
doom. Many ages would pass before he could act, but those
who live forever need not hurry.*

She knew she was now viewing more recent times, for

though Achill was not yet an island, Ireland was. And there was Hy Brasil off the western coast, and the Summer King standing by a great pyre on Purple Mountain. The sun was setting in a red-gold sky. As the king extended his hand toward the pyre, he let fly a spark that set it aflame. Once the bonfire burned, it signaled to the others on hills and mountains girding the mainland. Then, on the broad summit of the sacred Hill of Tara, with a flash of light from the star on his forehead, the High King lit the final fire. For as one was the beginning, the other was the end in that circle of power.

As she felt the sudden surge of energy, Laurel knew this was the *Fáinne na Gréine*. The Ring of the Sun.

The Sídhe-Folk were pleased with the Summer King's gift, for it made them stronger. And though they were one of the youngest races in Faerie, they became the most powerful. Thus the High King of the Sídhe became High King over all. But power always comes at a price, though they did not see it. I saw, being an Old One, and yet I could not interfere, for it is not the place of Old Magic to counter the new.

Laurel, too, saw something. In the moment when the circle was forged, the Summer King stepped into the fire and then staggered out again. A sense of foreboding came over her.

Many times was forged the Ring of the Sun before another race came to walk upon the Earth, one whose heart and soul would be linked with Faerie.

It was strange and unsettling for Laurel to observe the early humans struggling to survive. With a mild shock she realized she was looking at her Irish ancestors. She was also surprised to see the two races meet and the people bowing to the fairies as if they were gods. Then the first little boats of skin and wood set out from Achill for Hy Brasil.

They brought offerings to appease the Summer King, but he was not pleased. He removed his island to the Land Below the Waves. Yet every seven years he would raise it again so that the Ring of the Sun might burn at Midsummer. And though the king hated the new race on the Earth, he did nothing to harm them, for he saw that they would further his aims.

At first the weapons of the human hunters were crude, made of stone, wood, and bone. But in time new technologies developed and with them, greater skill and accuracy. Spears and darts turned to bows and arrows, then increasingly more complicated and deadly guns. With growing horror, Laurel watched as the men shot, trapped, and poisoned eagles all over Ireland. There was no doubt that both hunter and farmer were bent on eradicating the great bird. And though she turned away from the sight of hatchlings poisoned in their nests, she could not shut out the cries of all the eagles on their way to extinction.

The slaughter of the eagles in Ireland weakened Clan Egli, for the fates of Faerie and the Earthworld were now entwined and what happened in one world could affect the other. The Summer King knew the days of waiting were over. His time had come.

Bonfires burned on every hilltop. The *Fáinne na*

Gréine had been forged once again. Now the Summer King stepped into the Midsummer Fire and did not step out again. There was a single fiery moment in which he contained all the power that surged through the Ring of the Sun. Then, like a volcano erupting, like a mushroom cloud rising, he unleashed its force upon Eagle Mountain.

It was like watching the fall of Atlantis.

The first blast shook the foundations of the Temple. Ledges cracked and broke. Pillars toppled into the sea. Streams of fire reddened the air. Hot winds gusted. Everywhere Laurel looked, birds and winged beings were set ablaze. The second blast hit the mountain itself. With a mighty crack like thunder, the rock face severed to create a deep gorge. Chunks of cliff slid into the ocean. Too late, screeching hosts of the Fir-Fia-Caw swarmed in dark clouds to attack Hy Brasil. But their valor was hopeless, and they were seared to ashes as they crossed the water.

Laurel couldn't watch any longer. She turned away.

I sing of the ruined nest on Eagle Mountain.

And she was back in the eyrie overlooking the Atlantic.

Laheen's golden voice rang with a sorrow beyond measure.

"Many millions of years did not spoil it, but the Summer King did. So much was lost: the Temple broken, the Fir-Fia-Caw massacred, Clan Egli dispersed."

Laurel's mind was reeling. She could barely grasp what she had seen and heard.

"I don't understand," she said, barely audible. "My mission is to find this king. To light the fire again!"

The old eagle inclined his tawny head toward her.

"The Summer King is not lost. He is here on Achill, imprisoned in Slievemore, the Great Mountain. The last of the Fir-Fia-Caw are his guards and jailers. For though the Summer King won the battle that day, he did not win the war. The *Sidhe*-Folk themselves rose up against him and he was captured and bound. In keeping with the covenant between the two worlds, a mortal was called to do the deed."

Darkness was descending over Laurel's thoughts. The full import of Laheen's words threatened to unhinge her. She was on the wrong side. She was doing the wrong thing. She had been sent to free an ancient evil. Her quest, her mission, was all wrong.

She felt as if the eagle hadn't saved her, that she was still falling downward into the cold sea. She choked on the taste of bitter salt tears. The treachery of the fairies! They had sent her to do what they could not or would not do themselves. Their dirty work. A crime against justice. And the reward, oh God, the reward they offered, something for which she would sell her very soul.

"The fire must be lit!" came her strangled cry.

In a flow of hoarse words broken by sobs, she confessed to Laheen why she had taken the mission. *My sister, my twin, is dead.* It was the first time she spoke the unspeakable words. The first time she said them aloud to herself and another. *She is gone. I'll never see her again. She is gone.*

Now the grief tore through her like a jagged knife. And there in the eagle's nest, beyond the world, above the sea, that part of her in chains was finally set free. She broke down and wept.

The great eagle did not move at first. Then something floated through the air and down toward Laurel. A golden plume. As the feather sailed past, it stroked her cheek with the gentle touch of an angel. Warmth and light and sweet scent soothed her. She caught the feather, held it against her heart.

"Dear child, I know your pain."

Laheen's golden gaze shimmered with tears.

"In the hour before he destroyed the Temple, the Summer King slew my mate."

FourTeen

Laurel had not recovered from Laheen's new revelation when he surprised her again.

"Despite these dark truths, *mo chara,* I do not stand against you or your mission. You were well chosen for the task as you act out of love."

"But . . . if the king is evil . . ."

"It is not a question of good or evil. The Ring of the Sun must be forged. If it is not, two worlds will suffer: Faerie, which needs the power to heal itself, and the Earth, whose soul is nourished by the land of hopes and dreams."

The golden eagle looked out from his nest and across the ocean enameled with the hues of sunset.

"The *Sídhe*-Folk are caught in their dilemma. They acknowledge Clan Egli's right to the prisoner, yet they need the Summer King to light the fire. But as long as he is bound, he cannot do so. As it has always been since the two races met, a human must act to save the day."

Laurel nodded. The Rescue of Fairyland. Like so many of the stories in Granda's books.

"But how can I do it?" she asked in a small voice. "I don't have any special powers."

"Seek help amongst your own kind," the eagle told her. Then he let out a short squawk that she guessed was a laugh. "What is the saying amongst your people? 'Birds of a feather flock together.' There is a great human spirit that haunts this coast. The Sea Queen of the West. Win her as your ally and you will need no other."

The last rays of sunset dispersed over the sea. Dusk settled on the mountain. Before they parted, Laheen gave her final words of advice that sent a shiver through her.

"The golden feather will loose the chains of the Summer King, but you must beware. Though you free him he will see you as foe, for it was one of your kindred who defeated him. Work your will upon the king and use the feather to help you bind him. It is a truth in all the worlds: *by that which you kill are you bound.*"

It was only after the eagle set her down on the mountain path that Laurel thought of Ian. She was hurrying back toward the gorge when she heard a shout above her. He stood on the ridge, waving down.

By the time he reached her, she could see the huge relief in his features.

"Thank God you're all right!" he cried, his voice hoarse. "I thought you were dead!"

He crushed her against him.

She let him hold her for a while, glad of the solid feel of his arms. Then she sensed he might kiss her and she stepped back. Now she noticed the slashes in his anorak and the cuts on his hands.

"You're hurt! What happened?"

He, in turn, was inspecting her and only when he was convinced that she was unharmed did he answer.

"They caught me off guard. The three ravens. My own bloody fault. I didn't see them. But I got out my knife. I'm not sure what happened next. They must've knocked me out. When I came to, I was lying on the ground and there was blood and feathers nearby, but they were gone. I ran to the edge of the gorge. The ropes were hanging loose. I pulled on them . . ." She could hear the horror in his voice. "They came up so easily, sheared clean away. I kept shouting, but you didn't answer. I nearly went mad. I didn't know what to do. What happened to you?"

"I met Laheen," she said quietly. "The Old Eagle of Achill."

A gray mist was moving over the mountain. It began to drizzle. They headed back to the car in silence. Laurel wasn't ready to say more, and he didn't press her. When they reached the Triumph, Ian opened the passenger door to usher her in. She was happy that he drove. All the way home, she stared out the window at the darkness beyond. The world had changed. She felt utterly different. It was not only that she had narrowly escaped death, but she had seen things she could never have imagined. She felt lost, but not in a bad way.

Back at the cottage, the rooms were cold. Despite the

slack, the fire in the stove was nearly out. Ian raked the coals and added more fuel, but it would take time to burn. A wave of melancholy washed over Laurel. She collapsed on the sofa. Without thinking, she drew the feather from her pocket and brushed it against her cheek. It was like a touch of sunshine. She smiled to herself.

When Ian saw what she had, he started. He went to his knapsack and took out a similar plume.

"I found it," he said softly, "and knew somehow that I had to keep it with me."

Even as he placed the feather to his lips, she saw the change in his features. It was as if a light suddenly shone on his face. The troubled look went out of his eyes. She knew how he felt.

"Laheen must have stopped the Fir-Fia-Caw attacking you, before he saved me." She paused a moment. "He's their king."

"*What?*"

The time had come to tell her story. Ian's eyes widened with astonishment as she spoke of her fall from the precipice and her rescue by the eagle. They grew wider still as she described her vision of the Temple of the Birds and Hy Brasil. But when she told him of the Summer King's war on Clan Egli and the murder of their queen, he swore under his breath.

"That changes everything."

"It changes nothing," she retorted, "except how I feel about it."

He couldn't hide his surprise.

"What will you do?"

"I've got to free him. What choice do I have?"

Laurel got up from the couch to pace the floor. Restless and uneasy, she needed something to do. The room was still cold; the stove slow to heat up. She could feel the damp creeping into her bones, like despair. She decided to light a fire in the hearth. As she stuffed old newspapers and twigs into the grate, she argued her case as much to herself as to him.

"This is bigger than all of us. Laheen himself has agreed to it. He's even suggested an ally—the 'Sea Queen of the West.'"

She struck match after match to light the kindling, but with little effect. A thin trail of smoke spiraled into the room.

"Once the Midsummer Fire is lit," she said, "and the Ring of the Sun is up and working, then Faerie can deal with the King. Put him back in prison or whatever. He's their bogeyman, not mine."

Now she added a few sticks and threw lumps of coal on top of them. More smoke straggled into the room, but still no flame. Her frustration was peaking. She fought back the tears.

Ian came to help.

"I'll do it myself!" she snapped.

"You can't do everything yourself!" he snapped back. Then he added quietly, "Believe me, I've tried."

Something in his tone calmed her. She moved aside to let him work.

First he opened the flue. Then he searched through the kindling for the driest sticks and cracked them over his thigh. These he fed into the smoldering fire before adding more coal. Finally, he held a page of newspaper against the mouth of the fireplace to create a draft. The reaction was instant. With a roar, the flames leaped into life. As the paper itself caught fire, he tossed it into the grate.

"An Irish solution to an Irish problem," he said, with a satisfied grin.

By the time the fire was burning brightly, Laurel had made a pot of tea and set out a plate of ginger cookies.

"Biscuit?" she offered, mirroring his grin.

Both were more cheerful now, and they settled on the sofa with their mugs of tea. Laurel tucked her feet under her.

"You're not happy about freeing him," Ian said quietly, after a companionable silence.

"That's partly it." She shrugged, stared into her cup. "But to be brutally honest, right or wrong, I'd do it anyway."

"For your sister?"

She shook her head. Her time in the eagle's nest had changed everything.

"For *me*. I can't lie to myself anymore. This whole thing is about me. I need to do this for *my* sake. Everyone keeps telling me I can't blame myself for her death, but that doesn't change how I feel. If I had been there, things *would* have been different. I wouldn't have let her go out on that ledge. I would have gone myself if she insisted. Either way, if I had been there, she wouldn't have died."

Ian's tone was ironic.

"I thought I had self-torment down to an art. How can you be responsible for someone's life or death?"

"I was always the strongest. It was my job to protect her."

"Your sister was quiet, that doesn't mean she was weak." He let out a snort. "Remember when we were kids, I pulled her hair and you thrashed me?"

She managed a smile.

"I was only getting her back. She kept pinching me all morning when no one was looking."

Laurel was stunned for a minute.

"You're joking!"

"I was so glad when Nannaflor took the two of you home. The twins from hell."

She laughed along with him, and somewhere in that laughter felt lighter at heart. She laid her hand on his arm.

"I'm sorry for how I acted ... the day she died. For the things I said."

He put his hand over hers.

"You don't need to apologize for anything that day."

They gazed at each other. Regardless of their experiences on the mountain, they were none the worse for wear. Both glowed with health from the sun and wind, and their eyes were shining. The injuries they had sustained were superficial, already healing.

She touched the scar above his eye.

"So, was it the bird on Bray Head or did I give you this? When I pushed you off the bike?"

His grin was wicked.

"Nah. You knocked me on my ass, not my face. I just let you think that, to guilt you out."

"Brat."

There was a moment when she was sure he would kiss her, but he seemed to change his mind. She was both relieved and disappointed. Were his feelings as mixed as hers? Here was another complication in a day as complex as a Celtic knot.

"I'm going to bed," she said, standing up quickly.

He looked surprised, but she was already hurrying to the door of her room. Then she paused, and turned around.

"I just want you to know. I'm really glad you're here."

She saw the flush of pleasure before she left him.

That night, Laurel had a dream. She was standing on the dunes overlooking the sea. The water lay as still as glass, reflecting the dark sky and the silver stars. A faint music came out of the East and trailed over the shadows of Minaun mountain. The sweet sounds made her heart ache. They echoed the sorrow of an exiled spirit, calling up vague longings for a Home faraway.

Lights flickered over the cliffs, moving down to the pale strand and across Trawmore. As they drew closer, she saw the cavalcade of lords and ladies, tall and shining and blindingly beautiful. Some rode on palfreys of white and gray. Others walked with such grace their feet barely touched the ground. Flags and gonfalons fluttered above them. Lanterns glittered with moonlight. Their names were whispered on the wind and over the sea. *The Still Folk. The Noble Ones. The People of the Ever-Living Land. Na Daoine Maithe. Na Daoine Sídhe.* Music surrounded them as they went, and they sang together.

Níl sé 'na lá, níl a ghrá,
Níl sé 'na lá, na baol ar maidin,
Níl sé 'na lá, nil a ghrá,
Solas ard atá sa ghealaigh.

It is not yet day, it is not, my love,
It is not yet day, nor yet the morning,
It is not yet day, it is not, my love,
For the moon is shining brightly.

As she looked upon them, Laurel's eyes welled with tears. Here was a race that would never know the weight of human existence. They seemed so slight and insubstantial, so fragile and precious. A dream at the end of life's heartbreaking journey. She felt a great yearning pierce her; a desire to protect them, to keep them safe.

At the head of the column rode a tall shining man with a star on his forehead. He was dressed in black like the night, and a silver mantle swirled around him. His red-gold hair fell to his shoulders. His eyes were solemn and wise.

Laurel knew he was Midir, High King of Faerie. She

bowed her head. When she looked up again, the cavalcade was gone and a young man stood before her in dark
jeans and a black T-shirt. His hair was tied back in a
ponytail. His smile was friendly. Only the star on his
forehead told of his kingship.

She thought of bowing again but changed her mind.
It seemed ridiculous as he looked her own age. But then
he surprised her by bowing himself.

"I want to thank thee for what you are doing for my
country and my beloved."

"Your beloved," she repeated softly, with a pang.

She knew immediately whom he meant. She was surprised but not surprised. Hadn't Honor suspected that he
was in love with her?

"I wished to undertake the mission myself," he said,
"but I cannot abdicate my duties. The death of the First
King was a shock to the Realm. There are tears and cracks
throughout the Kingdom. And the harm may go deeper
than I can know, for I have yet to come into full knowledge
of myself as Sovereign. I am further weakened without a
Tánaiste, for no one has risen to be second-in-command;
nor is there a Queen in Faerie to be my helpmeet. If you
succeed in forging the *Fáinne na Gréine*, you will have
saved our cause. By the power of the circle, I will be made
whole and the land will be healed. All will be well."

"I'll do it," she promised, "for Honor *and* Faerie." Her
voice rang with determination. Then her throat tightened
and she couldn't stop herself from asking, "Do you know
where she is? Would it be possible . . . to see her?"

Midir waved his hand over the ground between them. A pool of blue light brimmed up like water. And there in the depths she lay, fast asleep. *Honor*. She was like a pale flower, shining and innocent, a newborn soul.

"Oh," said Laurel.

She stared at Midir with mute appeal, and saw her own pain and longing mirrored in his eyes.

"Your sister has fallen through one of the fissures that rends our land. When the Ring of the Sun heals Faerie, she will awaken. Then you and I will be reunited with her."

His declaration was clear and confident, his features serene. Laurel found herself wishing for the same conviction.

"How can you be so sure?"

The blue eyes glittered like stars. His smile was dazzling.

"I believe in you," he said, as he began to fade.

And even as Laurel surfaced from the depths of sleep, his last words were dispelled like foam on the waves.

"I have always believed in humans."

Fifteen

Laurel woke to a bright morning. A cool sea breeze blew through the window. The faint trails of a lovely dream drifted through her mind. Then it struck her. *Two more days to Midsummer's Eve.* She jumped out of bed. She had things to do.

As she pulled on her jeans and a T-shirt, she shivered from the chill in the room. Did the stove go out again? She could never live in Ireland. Automatic central heating was what you needed if you lived by the ocean! She was about to reach for one of Honor's sweaters when she changed her mind. Instead she put on the one Ian bought her. The deep blue showed off her blond hair and the tan she had got on the mountain. As she brushed out her hair in front of the mirror, she wished she had some mascara and eye shadow, but she was happy with how she looked.

As usual, Ian was up before her. He noted the sweater with an admiring glance but didn't comment. He was looking well himself. The white shirt he wore with his jeans accented the dark hair and the newly bronzed skin. He was whistling to himself as he served up their breakfast—grilled tomatoes on toast with mushrooms on the side, juice from squeezed oranges, and freshly brewed coffee. He had been shopping again.

"I could get used to this," she said, sitting down to eat. "The early bird does all the work."

"That's about right." He grinned good-naturedly. "I've been doing a bit of research into your sea queen." He passed her the guidebook with several chapters earmarked. "I knew who she was the minute you mentioned her. She's famous in Ireland, especially in these parts. You'll see her name around the place on shops, hotels, ads, and things. Granuaile. A pirate queen of the sixteenth century."

"A woman pirate! For real? Fantastic!"

She flipped through the pages, hoping to find a picture, but no luck. As she perused the book, Ian filled her in on what he knew.

Granuaile was a daughter of the Chief of the O'Malley Clan whose territory covered most of the western seaboard, including Achill and the islands of Clew Bay. "A most feminine sea captain," she commanded a fleet of galleys and a force of fighting men. Her stronghold was Clare Island from which she monitored the sea. Merchant ships were piloted or pirated, whichever proved most lucrative. She married twice and had four children, the last born aboard ship when she was forty-five.

The dauntless Granuaile ruled as queen in fair Mayo.

Her most hated enemy was the English governor, Sir

Richard Bingham, who called her "nurse of all the rebellions in the province for forty years." She suffered imprisonments in Limerick and Dublin, but ransomed her way out. When she was captured again, during a rebellion in Connaught, only a last-minute reprieve saved her from the gallows.

The last records of the sea queen showed she commanded galleys into her seventies, a pirate till the day she died. She had been born and raised in an Ireland that was free and Gaelic, but lived to see the defeat of her people and the beginning of the long conquest by England.

"Laheen says her spirit is still around," Laurel said. "So I guess we're ghost-hunting."

The words were no sooner out of her mouth than she shook her head. She had come a long way from someone who believed in nothing. First fairies and now ghosts!

Ian didn't bat an eyelid.

"The best place to start would be Clare Island," he suggested. "It's the one you can see beyond the Cliffs of Minaun. Her castle is still standing."

They needed a boat to get there. The old man in the post office was very helpful.

"Sure, Gracie will take ye over. She's moored at the pier in Kildavnet. She won't charge ye an arm and a leg, as she crosses twice a day herself. A great sea woman, has caught many a specimen. She fishes for Ireland, ye know, in the angling competitions."

Back at the cottage, there was a tense moment when Ian wheeled out his motorcycle and handed Laurel the helmet.

"We can pick up a spare in Achill Sound. We'll go there first, then down to Kildavnet."

"I thought we'd take the car," she said, stalling.

He was already seated. His look was impatient.

"We took the old crock yesterday," he said shortly. Then his lip curled. "If you don't want to hold onto me, just grip the bloody saddle."

Annoyed that he had guessed the reason for her reluctance, she pulled the helmet over her head. Climbing up behind him, she put her arms around his waist and pressed against his back.

"Right, let's go," he said, mollified.

It didn't take long to reach Achill Sound where they bought another helmet. When Laurel removed Ian's to give it back to him, she was flushed and exhilarated. They had sped down the narrow roads that spidered across the island's vast blanket bogs. He drove at death-defying speeds, leaning into curves till they were almost flat on the road. She couldn't wait to go again.

Before she got back on the bike, she glanced at the Irish writing scrolled on the tank.

Póg mo thóin.

"What does it mean?" she asked him.

"You don't want to know," he said, and laughed.

Kildavnet was a small village at the southeastern tip of Achill. It overlooked the narrow sea channel known as the Sound. The high stone pier was strewn with nets, lobster pots, creels, and other fishing paraphernalia. Only one vessel was tied up alongside.

The Lady of Doona was a thirty-foot inshore fishing boat, fueled by diesel. The wooden hull was painted dark-green with an occasional white stripe curved like a wave. A small cabin with windows sheltered the helm where the skipper stood to steer the boat. Lifebuoys hung on either side of the wheelhouse, and an inflatable raft was stowed on the roof. Astern of the cabin, a wide flat locker covered most of the deck. The lid was open to air its contents—fishing gear and bait, oilskins, wet-weather clothing, and orange life jackets. Benches for passengers lined the sides.

Basking on a deck chair was the boat's captain, with a copy of *The Irish Skipper* over her face. A corner of the newspaper lifted as they approached, but she didn't bother to move. A cursory glance swept over them.

"Tourists? Want a free shot of the local color? Work away. She's a pretty thing, and I mean the boat, not her skipper."

"Are you Gracie?" Laurel asked.

"Any chance of a lift to Clare Island?" Ian added.

She sat up immediately. In her mid-thirties, she was a stocky woman with curly brown hair and a ruddy complexion from working outdoors. Her strong features had a no-nonsense look and the eyes were sharp, but she had plenty of laugh lines as well.

"'Yes' to the first question and 'maybe' to the second," she said. "It's fresh today."

"You mean the air?" asked Laurel, puzzled.

"I mean the sea," said Gracie, with a snort. She rolled

her newspaper into a tube and fired it with stunning accuracy onto a ledge inside the wheelhouse. "It's fine in the harbor, but once we're out in the open . . ." She shrugged.

Ian looked uneasy, but Laurel persisted.

"Are you saying it's not safe?"

"I wouldn't go out if it weren't. I'm not into drowning foreigners, or putting the fear of God into them."

"We're not afraid," Laurel said quickly, though Ian didn't agree.

Gracie got out of her deck chair, folded it up, and flung it into the locker. Slamming the lid shut, she waved them aboard. As they introduced themselves, she crushed their fingers in an iron handshake. Laurel managed to keep from wincing and watched with amusement as Ian did the same. When the skipper turned away, they both made faces and wrung out their hands.

The smell of fish and diesel oiled the air. The boat was small and needed a coat of paint, but everything was neat and tidy. Gracie got them underway with the speed of an old salt.

"I hate going on the water," Ian hissed to Laurel. "I can't swim."

"Now you tell me! I promise to save you if the boat goes down."

"My hero," he muttered.

He went straight to the locker to get a life jacket.

"Use the wet gear as well," Gracie advised from the wheelhouse.

"It's so warm!" Laurel protested.

Leaning over the side, she dabbled her hand in the cold water. Above, the sky shone a hot blue.

"Suit yourself," the skipper shrugged. "But it's bound to get rough."

Ian didn't look happy at this remark and pulled on the yellow oilskins. Over these went the orange life jacket. Laurel tried not to laugh as he settled on the bench close to a life buoy. Here was someone who drove his motorcycle at breakneck speeds!

The Lady of Doona had just left the pier when Laurel signaled to Ian and pointed toward the village. Several black birds circled the air, as if searching for something. The two of them hunched down.

Gracie had also spotted the birds. She called out to her passengers.

To see one raven is ill luck, 'tis true
But it's certain misfortune to set eyes upon two
And meeting with more—that's a terror!

"What?" said Laurel, recognizing the words.

"Just an old saying," Gracie said, with a shrug. But she didn't look happy. "Sailors are superstitious, you know."

As they sailed south through the Sound, Laurel and Ian kept an eye on the birds, but none appeared to follow. The channel was sheltered by hills on both sides, but once they left the snug embrace of the Sound, they were flung out into the choppy waters of Clew Bay.

The winds blew in from the Atlantic with an icy bite. The waves slapped noisily against the hull. Farther out again, the swell began to heave. The boat seemed tiny on the great rolling sea, a walnut shell bobbing. At times the waves seemed to tower over them, threatening to comb and swamp the boat. Down they would go, into deep troughs without a breath of wind, then up again on top of the rollers.

Ian looked green.

Laurel found her sea legs and stood at the front of the boat, like a surfer enjoying the thrill. When a cascade of water struck the bow, she was soaked.

Ian made no attempt to hide his delight.

"Serves you right for showing off!"

"I warned you!" Gracie called from the wheelhouse.

"It's fantastic!" Laurel shouted back.

At last they spotted the cliffs of Clare Island. The waters grew calm again as the boat sailed into a broad harbor with a high-walled pier. To their right was a half-moon of beach bordered with sand dunes. Beyond it was a scattering of houses and a small hotel. To their left, not far from the pier, was the reason they had come.

Granuaile's castle. Standing sentinel on a rocky cliff, it was a square block tower with slits for windows. From its position it had a full view of the mainland and the entrance to Clew Bay. But even from the boat, they could see it was empty, a broken tooth of stone.

Gracie left them at the pier.

"I've to go back for a party of Germans. I'm takin' them round the bay for 'beeg feesh.' I'll pick you up around one or two, can't say exactly, but if you feel peckish, there's the Granuaile Hotel beyond the dunes. Good food and the drink's not too pricey."

As she stepped back behind the helm, she gave them a wink.

"Hope you find what you're lookin' for."

Laurel was glad of the warm winds that bathed the island; her clothes were almost dry by the time they reached the castle.

The tower was broad and solid, with turreted chambers projecting from the walls. A crenellated parapet lined the roof. The inside was less impressive. Only a hollow ruin was left of the original three stories, and the ground floor was tamped earth. Tufts of grass sprouted from cracks in the stone walls. They could see the remains of a passageway and a few shattered steps that once spiraled upward. A square of blue sky had replaced the roof. Black birds scuttled noisily in the corners.

Laurel looked at the birds anxiously, but Ian shook his head.

"Rooks, not ravens."

They stood at the heart of the broken fortress. The air was dank with the smell of stone and earth. There was no sense of a presence. No trails of the past. No hint of a ghost.

"She's not here."

Laurel's voice rang with dismay.

"This was her home," Ian said, mystified.

"Her home," Laurel repeated. Then she shook her head. "Was it really? She was a pirate, not a housewife. Her home was—"

"—the sea!"

They raced out of the castle. Too late! Gracie's boat had already disappeared around the headland. Laurel let out a groan. How else could they search the bay?

"She'll be back by midday," Ian said, with a shrug. "That still gives us plenty of time. We'll just have to wait for her."

Laurel sighed in agreement. They had no other choice.

"What will we do till then? Too bad we didn't bring swimsuits."

She looked over at the beach. The white sand curved around a sheet of green water. No crowds. No noise. A holiday dream.

Pulling off her shoes and socks, she let out a cry.

"Last one in's an eejit!"

As she raced for the sea, she could hear him running behind her but he hadn't a hope of catching up. She was too fast. Splashing into the water, she let out a whoop. It was so shockingly cold, it cut off her breath. She plunged in regardless. Her brain froze. Her skin burned. Screeching and spluttering, she surfaced in an explosion of spray. Only then did she see that he had stopped at the shore.

His grin was triumphant.

"It's the Atlantic for godsakes. *You're* the eejit."

Her lips were purple, and she was shivering uncontrollably as she waded out of the water.

He started to strip off his T-shirt to offer it as a towel, when he caught the look on her face.

"No way!" he said, and turned and ran.

With the head start, he managed to reach the top of the dunes before she closed in on him. Then she made a flying tackle. In a flurry of arms and legs and sand, they went rolling down the hill. When they hit the bottom, Laurel was winded, and Ian was on top.

He didn't move.

"Get off me!"

"Nope." He pinned her arms and leaned over her, grinning. "I will not be thrashed by a girl again. I'll let you up when you calm down."

"I am calm!" she said, glaring at him.

He snorted.

"Get off me!" she repeated, but less furiously now as the startling eyes watched her like a hawk. A blue-eyed hawk.

"In a minute," he said, and he laughed.

Her own laughter rose up. She could feel the warm sand against her back, and the warmth of his body pressing against hers.

"Come on, get off me," she said, one more time, but her tone was mild and all the insistence had gone.

They both stopped laughing and stared at each other. What was this moment? Who could name it? It was so easy to put their arms around each other. So easy to kiss. Two who had suffered alone for so long, caught off guard by inevitable happiness.

Sixteen

They crossed the beach in their bare feet, carrying their shoes. The clarity of the light was almost blinding. The scene was a blur of white sand, green sea, blue sky. Ian stopped to turn his face to the sun.

"I don't remember ever feeling this good," he murmured.

He let out a low laugh, and regarded her quizzically.

She looked away. Her feelings were scattered. She didn't really know what to say or think.

He offered his hand.

After a pause, she took it.

"I'm hungry," she said.

"Me too. Let's eat."

Beyond the beach, a little road led up to the buildings they had seen from the boat. There was a cluster of houses and a small hotel. The Granuaile House glared white in the sunlight, but it was cool and dim inside. A spacious lounge overlooked the bay.

After ordering her food, Laurel looked around for the restrooms. Her clothes had dried out for the second time, but they were stiff with salt from the sea. She frowned at the two doors on the far side of the room. One said *Mná*, the other *Fir*.

When she asked Ian for help, his face flickered with mischief.

"Right," he said. "You've a fifty-fifty chance. Let's see how the average tourist does. Which would you go for?"

She studied the sign that said *Mná*.

"Well, that looks like 'man.' Sort of. And the other starts with 'f' like 'female'."

As she headed toward the door marked *Fir*, she heard him chuckle behind her even as a man came out. Without slowing her stride, she veered to the left and entered *Mná*.

When she returned, Ian was already eating his toasted cheese sandwich with fries, while a big bowl of steamed mussels waited for her.

"Yum. Squidgy," she said, as she made her way through them. "It's like eating bits of the sea."

"Once *living* bits," he said pointedly.

"Don't start." But then she reconsidered and answered seriously. "Everything on this planet eats something else, not just humans. That's the way it is here. The worms will get me one day."

"Yeah, but first you'll live out your life span."

"Maybe," she said softly.

He blanched as he realized what he had said and began to apologize.

"Don't. It's okay."

They finished their lunch without speaking. Laurel

could see he was upset, and searched for something to
ease the awkwardness.

"Laheen was right about one thing. Granuaile haunts
this place. Her name is everywhere. Like this hotel. And
Gracie's boat. Didn't the guidebook say 'the Dark Lady
of Doona' was one of her titles?"

Ian looked startled, then groaned.

"God, how did I miss it?"

"What?" said Laurel. "What did we miss?"

"Not *we*. Me. You couldn't have known. You have no
Irish. But I . . . Jesus, I'm as thick as two bricks!"

She nearly lost her temper.

"Tell me! What did you miss?"

"Our skipper," he swore. "That's her name in
English. Granuaile translates to *Grace O'Malley*."

Laurel frowned. "So it's a coincidence, or she's a
descendant, but Gracie's a real person, not a ghost. The
man in the post office knows her. She 'fishes for Ireland,'
whatever that means. And she's very solid. Remember
that handshake?"

"Maybe she's a reincarnation," he suggested. "It's too
big a coincidence, the boat and her name."

"Laheen says she's a spirit," Laurel continued to
argue. "How can she be both at the same time?"

"We're looking for a ghost and you want logic?"

In the end they agreed there was only one way to
know for sure: confront the skipper. They were no longer
willing to wait for her return. Gracie or Granuaile, they
were going after her.

Their efforts to hire another boat soon proved futile. The summer season had all on the island employed. Just as Laurel was getting frantic, an old toothless fisherman took pity on them.

"Ye can take your sweetheart out in my *curach*," he told Ian, with a gummy grin. "Mind ye don't upset her."

"The boat or my sweetheart?" said Ian, grinning back.

The old man cackled. Laurel ignored them both.

The old fisherman's currach lay with several others upturned on the sand like great black beetles. The boat was made of wood covered with tarred canvas, ideal for inshore fishing as well as travel between the islands. The stern was square while the bow pointed upwards. It had no keel, and the narrow oars were fixed to the gunwales.

Laurel stared dubiously at the antiquated craft. It was unlike any canoe or kayak she had ever handled. Ian drew her aside.

"This feels right," he said. "Currachs have been used for thousands of years. They belong here. Like Grace."

"You'd get in one of these?" she said, surprised.

He shrugged. "I'm not thrilled about it, but do we have a choice?"

That settled the matter. With the old man cackling and chortling behind them, they hoisted the boat over their shoulders and took it to the water. It was unexpectedly light, far more so than a canoe. But what made it easy to carry, made it hard to control. Once they pushed off, the currach rocked wildly, responding to the waves like a living thing. When they grasped the oars and started to row, they spun round in circles.

Onshore, the fisherman continued to screech directions, between fits of coughing and laughing. When they finally gained control of the boat, he waved them off and they set out for Clew Bay. Their plan was simple. They would row in the direction they last saw *The Lady of Doona*.

Ian grimaced as the waves rose higher and the cold spray splashed over the bow. They were moving at a terrific speed. The currach rode the rollers like a show horse taking its jumps. But where was Gracie? Had they any chance of finding her?

The pier of Clare Island had fallen far behind when it happened. A fist of wind struck the boat and made it pitch like a rocking horse. Then they saw something moving toward them over the waves. It appeared to be a squall on the ocean. Before they could move, they were engulfed in fog.

The mist was a thick milky gray. They could hardly see each other, let alone beyond the currach. The silence was ominous. There was only the slap of the water against the hull. They both stopped rowing. Laurel bit her lip. Though she didn't say it out loud, she realized they had charged off recklessly. Without life jackets or provisions, they were in serious danger if they got lost at sea.

Muffled sounds reached them. A ship's bell clanging. The shouts of men.

"Is it her?" whispered Laurel.

"Let's hope so," muttered Ian.

A huge dark shape suddenly emerged from the fog, as if bearing down on them. Now the haze dispersed as swiftly as it had come, and they saw the ship.

Graceful in line, similar to a Spanish galleon but not as cumbersome, it rested on the waves with its sails furled.

"I think . . ." Laurel began.

She was stunned by the size of the vessel. Their own was like an eggshell beside it.

Some of the crew leaned over the sides to peer down at them. There wasn't a friendly face to be seen. Rough and weathered, each man seemed to be missing some part of his body, an eye, an ear, a hand, or an arm. Several wore eye patches. These were no ordinary sailors or fishermen. There was no question about it: they were pirates.

A rope ladder came flying through the air and landed in the currach with a thump. Laurel and Ian were already scrambling upward before the threats began. What else could they do? When they reached the top, they were hauled onboard.

The crew were a dirty and disheveled lot, long-haired and unshaven, in baggy trousers with leather vests. Most were barefoot. But it wasn't at the men that Laurel stared, but the one woman in their midst. Though she wore leggings and boots, with a saffron-colored shirt, she was as wild-looking as the rest, perhaps even wilder. Her features were hard, her eyes piercing. A large knife was tucked into her belt. Yet despite her appearance, she was recognizable. She had the same brown curls framing her face, the same high coloring from wind and sun. She was the image of Gracie, the skipper of *The Lady of Doona*.

Yet she stared at them as if they were strangers.

At a slight nod of her head, one of the men grabbed Ian and put a dagger to his throat.

"An Sasanaigh sibh?" she demanded.

"Ní hea," he answered, with a strangled noise.

"Leave him alone!" Laurel cried.

A grimy hand was clapped over her mouth.

"We are not English," Ian repeated for Laurel's sake, then explained hurriedly to the captain, who could be no other than Grace O'Malley. "We are not your enemy. This girl can't speak Irish. She comes from a land in the west. On the far side of the ocean."

"I've heard of the new world across our sea," the pirate queen said, nodding curtly. A greedy look crossed her face. She shouted to her men. "More countries, more trade, more ships to plunder!"

They responded with a raucous cheer. There were at least a hundred aboard, all sworn to serve her with their lives. Most came from the two clans the O'Malley's ruled. Grace would go down in history for having said, *Go mbhfearr léi lán loinge de Chloinn Conroi agus de Chloinn Mic an Allaidh ná lán loinge d'ór.* "I would rather have a shipful of Conroys and McAnallys, than a shipful of gold."

The dagger was lowered from Ian's throat and the hand from Laurel's mouth, but they weren't safe yet.

The pirate queen strode toward Laurel and tugged at her jeans.

"What are you doing here? The sea is no place for a girl."

Laurel returned her stare. She knew a test when she faced one. She kept her voice firm.

"You didn't listen when they said that to you. Why should I?"

A heavy silence fell, as everyone waited for the captain's reaction. Grace's eyebrow arched. Then she slapped Laurel's face with the back of her hand.

Ian let out a yell, but was seized before he could move.

Laurel staggered back, her cheek smarting. Recovering quickly, she glared at the sea queen.

"Ní cladhaire í," said Grace, with approval. "No milksop."

They locked eyes. Laurel did her best, but there was no contest. Grace's gaze was overpowering. In that stare was the formidable will that made her chief and pirate in a savage time. Laurel looked away.

The sea queen grunted her triumph.

"Tell me why you are here," she commanded.

The warning in her tone was unmistakable. She wanted the truth, and would know if she got it.

"We came to find you," Laurel answered simply.

Grace nodded.

"Fair enough. And now that you have, you will rue it."

She signaled to her men.

"Throw them in the hold. If no one offers a ransom, you can string them up for entertainment."

Laurel and Ian were about to protest, when a cry erupted from the lookout above. An enemy ship was sighted.

"My glass!" roared Grace.

A young boy raced to bring her the telescope. Peering through it, she chuckled loudly.

"One of Her Majesty's finest. Broad and fat like a goose ready to be plucked. Lost, I'll warrant, took a wrong turn on his way out of Galway. Doesn't know port from starboard, English git."

Her men laughed. But Grace frowned suddenly and raised the glass again. Women's intuition. She shouted to the lookout.

"Further south! T'wards Inishturk! What do you see?"

When the answer came back that a flock of gulls circled the island, she swore blue murder.

"One or more ships in the lee of the harbor. The gulls wait to feed. It's a trap. FULL ABOUT!"

The crew sprang to action as she roared a quick succession of orders. Over the rigging they scrambled, like agile cats. Sails were unfurled. The great sheets billowed. Cannon were loaded. Weapons distributed. Up the main mast ran the flag of the O'Malley's—stallion, helmet, wild boar, three bows affixed with arrows; and at the bottom, the true sign of their strength, a single galley to represent a fleet. *Terra Marique Potens.* Powerful on land and sea.

The minute Grace's ship turned about, the vessel acting as bait knew the game was up. A shot was fired to signal the others. The second and third ships hove into view.

Granuaile let out a great laugh. The lust for battle glittered in her eyes.

"We'll outrun the laggards and take the bait."

The sea chase commenced. The ships that had hidden in ambush were caravels, lighter and faster than the lumbering merchantman in the lead. The latter had a high forecastle and double-tiered deck. But though it was slower, it was better armed and closer. More likely to do damage.

"We haven't a hope if they catch us," Ian whispered to Laurel.

The two had been pushed aside when the alarm went up. Scrambling for cover, they found a hiding place behind the rum kegs lashed to the deck. From there they had a good view. Laurel shivered with excitement as well as fear. It was like an old swashbuckling movie! She kept her eye on Grace, who strode the deck, shouting, commanding, encouraging, laughing. Like everyone else onboard, she took courage from the captain's confidence.

The galley flew over the waves, sails soaring on the wind like wings. The wooden rigging screeched with the strain. The bow rose up in a burst of spray. She was light as a skiff, a proud fast queen.

Taking the helm herself, Grace steered the ship into the maze of islands, reefs, and narrow channels of Clew Bay. This was her domain. Born and bred on these waters which charts had yet to map, she could navigate blind. The threat of running aground forced the pursuing caravels to slow down. But though the others fell behind, the lead ship closed in and fired a broadside at Grace's hull.

A cannonball crashed through the deck. Wood splintered. Men roared. Now the O'Malley ship returned fire. A volley struck the enemy's mast. The vessels almost collided. As grappling hooks swung through the air, the English clambered onboard. All over the ship, the two crews clashed in hand-to-hand combat.

Crouched in the shadows, watching with a mix of fascination and horror, Laurel wondered how anyone knew friend from foe. Except when they cursed in their separate languages, the men were alike—hairy, burly, unkempt and unwashed. After observing them a while, however, she grew aware of the differences. The Irish had shaggy moustaches, and their long hair fell over their faces. The English favored beards and shorter hair. Where the Irish wore trousers and jerkins, the English were dressed in breeches and doublets. At the same time, all of them obviously lived in their clothes, universally tattered and matted with dirt. Swords and daggers were the main weapons used, though some of the English had firearms as well.

As the fighting raged back and forth over the two ships and even up into the rigging, it was impossible to tell who was winning the battle.

"What will we do if the Irish lose?" Laurel hissed to Ian.

"Speak English."

"We need their help. We should join them."

"Are you out of your mind? We don't—"

Before he could finish, Laurel had run from their hiding place and grabbed a fallen sword.

"What are you doing?" he shouted.

"Taking sides!" she called back.

Fired with adrenaline, she ran to join a band of Grace's men where they battled in the stern. She had taken a class in fencing once, but this was nothing like it. There was no room for stance or footwork, no chance to thrust and parry. This was a terrifying scrap involving sharp blades. Slashing wildly with her sword, she yelled, ducked, and even kicked. The absurdity of the situation fueled her courage, as did the sense of unreality. With a little skill and a lot of blind luck, she managed to hold her own for a time.

Then Laurel found herself pressed into a corner beside the anchor winch. She had no room to maneuver, no way of escaping. A heavier sword beat down on hers and knocked it out of her hand. She cried out with alarm, backing up against the bulwark. Now she looked for the first time into the face of her enemy, and nearly fainted. The rage of battle had obliterated all signs of humanity. The contorted features were a livid red. As he lunged toward her, a last thought fled through her mind. *Not here, not now.*

When the plank crashed down on her assailant's head, it was almost comical. His mouth opened wide and

his eyes bulged before he crumpled to the ground.
Behind him stood Ian, looking pleased with himself.

"My hero," gasped Laurel.

"Your shite in knighting armor," he said, with a mock
bow.

Laurel retrieved her sword. Her hands were shaking,
like the rest of her body.

The fighting had moved further up ship, and they
were alone. Together they disarmed her attacker who was
still unconscious.

"He's very scruffy," she said, trying to calm down. "I
thought the English would be in uniforms. And tidier or
something."

Ian tested the weight of the man's sword.

"The British navy came later. At this time they were
much the same as the Irish, raiding Spanish and
Portuguese ships. Sir Francis Drake was a pirate,
remember."

"It slipped my mind," she said dryly. "How do you
know these things?"

"Books. You should try reading sometime. You might
learn something."

"Like fencing?"

"Touché."

When they returned to the fray, they were happy to
find the battle over. With no reinforcements, the English
had decided to retreat. The Irish let them go, cutting the
lines that held the vessels together. There was no time for
plunder. The other ships might arrive at any moment.

Wisdom was the better part of valor. Grace ordered her men home.

As they got underway, the crew tended to their wounded and threw the enemy dead into the sea. When Laurel's attacker staggered up from where he lay, he was taken prisoner.

"Throw him overboard with the rest," Grace ordered.

Laurel objected, horrified.

"You can't do that! He's hurt! And the other ship's too far away. He'll drown!"

The pirate queen laughed and so did her men, but the Englishman pleaded.

"My family have money! They will ransom me!"

"Well, that's a different kettle of fish," Grace remarked. "Take him below. And see to his wounds. There's no payment for a corpse."

The captain regarded Laurel coolly.

"You fought with us. Foolhardy, but brave. I welcome you. For now. But make no mistake, my foreign girleen, you are my guest *and* my prisoner."

Laurel bowed her head. She understood. She had yet to earn Granuaile's trust, but she had done enough. For now.

Seventeen

As Grace's galley sailed for Clare Island, it was joined by the rest of her fleet. Together the ships flew over the waves, bows rising, wood creaking, sails filling with wind. Laurel was thrilled with the speed and beauty of the vessels. So different from the noise and smell of oil and engine! They didn't slow till they approached the island, where they anchored in its natural harbor. Small boats were lowered to take the crews ashore.

The O'Malley fortress stood strong in its heyday. The tower shone iron-gray in the sunlight. The window slits were like narrowed eyes. Flags battered the air above the parapets. Armed guards kept watch along the battlements. A stream of people poured through the front gates; hunters and fishermen with the day's catch, traders hawking their wares, women carrying firewood. In the shade of the walls were stone cabins thatched with mud and hay. Beyond the settlement, the beach was striped with black currachs upturned on the sand. Nets lay drying in the sun. The clan lived as much from fishing, hunting, and husbandry as it did from plunder.

Inside the castle, Grace's wealth was evident. Rich fabrics and fittings told of her trade with the capitals of Europe, while the abundance of gold spoke of her spoils. The main hall was furnished with polished oak, tables draped with damask, magnificent rugs, and tall candelabra. Tapestries warmed the stone walls alongside racks of antlers, war trophies, weapons, and mediaeval maps and charts. A cavernous hearth burned whole logs.

Grace brought Laurel to her own bower to change into fresh clothing. Each donned a floor-length gown of white linen, with long narrow sleeves. Over this was worn an apron-like smock of heavier material. Laurel chose a red brocade with a bodice of pearls; Grace, a dark-yellow wool trimmed with fur. The sea queen clipped a jeweled dagger onto her belt. Around her shoulders hung the chieftain's *brat*, the broad green mantle that marked her status.

As Laurel pinned up her hair with a golden comb, she kept an eye on Grace in the mirror. It was nerve-wracking to be alone with her.

The pirate queen strode around the room, kicking at her skirt.

"When I was a child, I begged to be taken on my father's ship bound for France. They told me the sea was not for girls. I hacked off my hair with a knife to look like a boy."

"Did he take you?"

"Need I say? But enough preening! Let us join the feast."

The banquet was well under way by the time they arrived in the great hall. Mounds of food weighed down the long tables. There were steaming platters of roast beef, venison, braised mutton and pork, along with jugged hares and braces of pheasant. Grilled salmon lay on silver plates alongside heaps of scallops and mussels. Hills of oatcakes were served with butter, curds, and cheeses. The sweets were presented at the same time as the savories; sugared seedcakes, wild berry pies, and a honeyed paste of forest fruits cut in slabs and swimming in cream. The drink was plentiful. As well as home-brewed whiskey, ale, and mead, there were dark ports from Spain, and French wines and brandies.

A riotous revelry attended the feast. The din was deafening. Men and women shouted, laughed, sang, and even wrestled while children raced around the hall. Wolfhound dogs, big as ponies, rolled under the tables in search of scraps. On a dais, a musician strummed his golden harp. The young man's sun-bleached hair fell over his face, but Laurel recognized him instantly. Fionn from the hippie bus! She waved to him, delighted, but he didn't respond. Only when he turned his head did she see, with a shock, the pale blind eyes.

It only added to her unease about the banquet. The revels reminded her of the sea fairies in the Amethyst Cave. She studied the company with a cold eye, but they seemed very human. She also regarded the food with suspicion and had yet to touch it. Beside her, Ian's plate was full. He had foraged successfully, returning with a salad of kale and beetroot, a big slice of artichoke pie, baked mushrooms and leeks, and various cheeses.

He was about to take his first bite when she stopped him.

"Is this fairy food?" she said. "You're not supposed to eat it."

He frowned at his plate.

"Bit stodgy for Faerie, isn't it?"

She knew what he meant. It didn't have the shimmery look of the food in the cave. And there were none of her favorite dishes to tempt her.

Ian swallowed his first mouthful.

"They can't be *Sídhe*-Folk," he said, munching away. "Not pretty enough. Look at your man with the bandy legs, and the one with a face like the back of a bus. They're ghosts."

"Don't Irish ghosts belong to Faerie?" she said, growing more confused.

He shrugged, but kept eating.

"This isn't Faerie. It's Ireland's past. Stop worrying about it. Didn't Laheen tell you to join Grace? She's no fairy."

"And I thought our world was complicated," Laurel muttered.

He laughed.

"Here, try this."

Spearing a clump of wet greenery onto a knife, he popped it into her mouth. It was soft and buttery, with a salty taste.

She made a face.

"Dilisk," he told her. "Edible seaweed."

He scooped a load of it onto his plate.

"You're really at home here, aren't you?" she said.

It was true. She had seen it earlier, when she and Grace first entered the hall. The change was startling. He wore a voluminous long-sleeved shirt of yellow that fell to his knees like a tunic. Over this went an orange jacket, richly embroidered, and over that again, a broad rust-colored mantle. He had chosen to go bare-legged and barefooted as did most of Grace's men. Like them also, he had combed his hair over his face so that his moody features had the same wild look.

Grace herself had commented.

"That's a fine-looking Irishman you've got for yourself, my foreign girleen."

When he came to meet them, he had caught Laurel's admiring look and twirled her around.

"*Go hálainn!*" he said. "You're only gorgeous, *a stór!*"

He had already made friends among the men. Irish was the chief language used and he translated for Laurel, but then she discovered she could speak with those who knew English and French. Spanish also rang out in the hall, along with German and Latin, signs of Grace's trade and military alliances, as well as her religion.

Laurel and Ian were seated together, not at the high table with the pirate queen, but near enough where Grace could see them. From time to time she looked their way with a keen stare. *Who are you and what are you doing here?*

"So, did you ask for her help?" Ian quizzed Laurel, as he started on another helping.

She shook her head. The meat on her plate smelled too strong and gamy. She pushed it aside and reached for a roast duck.

"Why not?" he pressed her. "I thought you'd do it when you went off together. Slip it in with the girly talk."

"She is *not* a girl," Laurel said furiously. "And that kind of attitude could get us killed. Can't you see how dangerous she is? All the nice stuff is just an act. She's sizing us up. And believe me, Ian, if we don't make the grade we are deader than this duck I'm eating."

She tore into the wing and chewed in angry silence. But she was more annoyed at herself, for not tackling Grace. She didn't want to admit that she had no idea how to handle the woman. She had never met anyone like her before. A diva with a murderous streak. As irrational as a storm at sea, the pirate queen was all charm and affection one minute; the next, likely to cut your throat.

Ian gobbled down a mushroom the size of a pancake, slathered with butter. As the juices dribbled over his chin, he wiped his mouth with his sleeve.

"You're disgusting," she said.

"I'm not the one eating a dead animal," he rejoined. "Anyway, look around you."

Knives being the only cutlery, everyone in the hall was eating with their hands. Table manners were rough.

"We're here to get Grace to join us," he persisted. "Let's do what we came to do."

"We can't rush things," she argued. "This is too important. She's our only hope of an ally. Call it women's intuition or whatever, but I'm waiting for the right moment. We have to win her over. Impress her somehow."

"Fine," said Ian. "If that's what you want."

He drained his mug of ale and rose to his feet. With a dramatic sweep of his mantle, he raised his hand toward the high table and shouted at Grace.

"I'd like to sing a song for you, oh captain, my captain!"

Laurel nearly choked. Was he drunk? But it was too late to stop him. The pirate queen banged her metal cup on the table for silence in the hall. She appeared to smile at his request, but her eyes narrowed. The message was plain. If he made a fool of himself—and her—he would pay.

Laurel's heart pounded. There was no chance of escape. All of Grace's men were armed.

Ian's voice rang out, deep and melodic.

Laurel's first reaction was sheer relief. He could carry a tune. Then she realized several things in succession. He was singing a sea shanty, in the Irish language, and while she didn't understand it the others did. What's more, it had a chorus that everyone quickly picked up and sang with raucous glee. Finally and most amazingly, it was all about Grace. He couldn't have done better.

Óró! sé do bheatha 'bhaile!
Óró! sé do bheatha 'bhaile!

Óró! sé do bheatha 'bhaile!
Tá Gránuaile ag teacht thar sáile.

As he finished to uproarious applause, Ian bowed to the sea queen.

Grace raised her cup to drink to his health. Her face glowed.

"Aren't you full of surprises," said Laurel, still clapping, as Ian sat down.

He grinned.

"It's an old ballad. Someone will write it for her in about three hundred years, but I guess this means I sang it first!"

A servant came over to fill his cup. He chugged the drink down.

"I don't mean the song," she said. "You were great! I love your voice!"

His face flushed with pleasure and the sudden rush of whiskey. Mischief flashed in his eyes.

"You speak of love to me?"

Laurel went into a fluster and before she could recover, he caught hold of her for a kiss.

"Stop it! Not here!"

"Look around you," he said again.

Sure enough, as the feast progressed and wine flowed like the river, there were many couples embracing each other, heedless of the company.

Laurel laughed and let him kiss her, then pushed him away.

"Wild Irishman," she murmured.

When the banquet was over and everyone had eaten more than their fill, the night's revels took a new turn. The food was cleared away, the tables moved, and in a short space of time the great hall was transformed into a mediaeval casino. Dice, knuckles, cards, hoops, cups, and board games started up on all sides. Men and women shouted their wagers, money was exchanged, scuffles broke out. The sounds of laughter and argument mingled with the jangle of coins. Vats of black beer were carried into the hall, along with countless jugs of whiskey and mead.

The pirate queen came over to Laurel and linked her arm for a stroll.

"I have many nicknames but *Gráinne na gCearrbhach* is the one I favor. Grace of the Gamblers."

Despite the friendly tone, Laurel shuddered. She tried not to think of herself as a lamb being led to the slaughter.

They stopped near a group tossing hoops.

"Let us pit our skill against each other," Grace suggested.

"Okay," agreed Laurel, warily.

She had seen that look on Grace's face before. During the battle at sea. Sword-eyes.

"What will you wager?" the pirate queen wondered.

She rattled the purse of coins that hung from her belt.

"I have nothing—" Laurel began.

With a noise of disdain, Grace took a handful of coins and flung them on the ground.

"I give you a loan."

Laurel's face reddened. She didn't move. And nor would she. The tension was mounting when Ian arrived. He had a drink in his hand and was looking merry. Immediately grasping the situation, he stooped to pick up the money.

"Women," he muttered.

Laurel was furious with Grace and determined to beat her. She studied the game. The hoops were tossed onto hooks on the wall, positioned high overhead. When she played center on her basketball team, she rarely missed a shot. She grimaced to herself. This was more than sport.

"I'll bet all of it," she said, indicating the coins in Ian's hand. "If I lose I'll be doubly in your debt and take the consequences. If I win, it's mine."

The sea queen was delighted. She shouted for drink. A tray arrived with tall silver cups brimming with liquor. Handing one each to Laurel and Ian, she clashed her goblet against theirs.

"*Uisce beatha!*" she shouted, and quaffed it down in one swallow.

Laurel peered at the golden liquid.

"Mead?" she asked Ian.

"The water of life," he translated, before swigging his draught. "Pure whiskey."

"Firewater," she choked, when she took a sip.

She put the cup down.

"You won't drink?" Grace demanded.

"I like to keep a cool head when competing," she countered.

The pirate queen considered this remark.

"A cool head," she echoed.

Then she flung her own cup across the room with such force that several people ducked before it clanged against the wall.

Laurel's eyes widened but she didn't react. Grace was even more fearsome at home than at sea. Restless and irritable like a wild thing caged, she kept tugging at her female attire. The characteristics that made her a leader among men and a queen of pirates made her almost unbearable at close quarters. One of her enemies would say of her, "No warlike chief or Viking has a bolder heart than she." Knowing some of her history, Laurel could reflect on the hardships she suffered; a murdered lover and a murdered son, long spells in prison, a close shave at the gallows. Yet, despite a lifetime of rebellion and piracy, she would live to old age still in command of her fleet. An amazing woman.

"Let the challenger begin," Grace declared.

Laurel was thinking fast, her survival instincts alert.

"I'd rather you went first," she said, adding quickly before Grace could erupt, "I'd like to see how it's done and I bet you're the best player here?"

Her hunch was right. Flattery was good. Grace nodded, pleased, and took her position to throw.

As each hoop went sailing through the air to land on its hook, the spectators cheered. Twelve throws made a game. The pirate queen tossed with a steady hand and stunning accuracy. Laurel and Ian exchanged uneasy glances. Then a ring fell short of its mark. Grace cursed vociferously. And moments later, another one. But the rest reached their target till her turn was done.

Laurel stepped up to the line. She tried to relax and calm her breathing, while young boys clambered up the walls to retrieve the hoops. Her stomach was in a knot, her palms sweaty. When she was handed the rings, she tested their weight. They were light, and jangled like bracelets.

A crowd had gathered to watch, placing bets among themselves.

Laurel threw the first ring.

It curved a high arc in the air.

Then went wide of its mark, hit the wall, and ricocheted over her head.

A titter of laughter rose up. Laurel bit her lip. Her hands were shaking.

Before she could toss the second ring, Ian came up behind her. Slipping his arm around her waist, he drew her to him. His lips caressed her ear.

"Breathe," he said softly, his own breath warm on her neck. "This is not about you. It's for Honor."

She steadied immediately. He was right. This was not a contest of egos between Grace and her. This was Laurel alone, pitted against the odds, against death itself, for her sister's sake. She imagined Honor in the crowd giving her the thumbs up, the way her twin used to do when she attended Laurel's events. The memory brought with it a steely confidence.

The next ring landed on its hook.

And the next.

And the next.

As each hoop sailed into place, the spectators grew quieter. Coins were already changing hands, though surreptitiously as no one wanted to be seen betting against the chief. The tension in the hall was growing. People slipped away, back to their own amusements, unwilling to be witnesses to the sea queen's defeat.

Grace was thin-lipped with rage. She was not a good loser. As the twelfth hoop landed on its hook, she roared for more drink.

"You have won the loan," she spat.

Laurel kept her features blank, not daring to look victorious. Ian gave her a furtive wink. They wouldn't celebrate . . . yet.

"We play cards!" Grace cried.

They took seats at the end of the high table, just the three of them. Grace used her personal cards. The backs were illustrated with the O'Malley coat of arms. Though larger than a modern deck and artfully hand-painted, they had the same suits of hearts, diamonds, spades, and clubs.

"They were made in France," she said airily, as she shuffled with the mastery of a professional. "Cards are war in the disguise of a game, is that not so?"

Laurel didn't answer. Her mouth was dry. Card

games were not her forte. Across from her, Ian sat stiff and silent. His jaw was clenched. They both knew the pirate queen was playing with them in more ways than one. Cat-and-mouse. Grace herself was a study in concentrated poise. But though her face was stony, her eyes burned.

Don't be intimidated, Laurel told herself. Focus on the game.

Grace explained the rules as she cut the cards. It sounded something like poker, but without flushes or straights. The only values were in two or three or four of a kind, with face cards high and aces highest. There was also a lone wild card called the Fool. It showed a court jester in red, holding a staff of silver bells.

"Like the Joker," Laurel murmured.

The first round was simple. The best five out of a seven-card deal, one draw, no raises, maximum discard of three. A short sharp war.

Grace dealt.

Laurel picked up her hand. Not too bad. A pair of nines, a jack, and a queen. But the other three were useless. These she would discard to draw three new ones in the hope of making a second pair or perhaps three of a kind or, if luck was with her, maybe four. She was happy with her place at the table, as she would play last. Having split her coins with Ian, she waited for Grace to call the bet. At least without raises, the round would be quick and fairly painless.

The pirate queen had yet to look at her cards, but a

faint smile twitched at the edges of her mouth. She drew her dagger from her belt and slapped it on the table. A beautiful piece of finely worked metal with a jeweled hilt, it was undoubtedly worth a small fortune and more than the total of Ian and Laurel's coins.

"That is my wager," she declared, to their dismay.

Alarm bells rang in Laurel's mind. This was a trap. She watched as Ian placed his money on the table and wasn't surprised when Grace pushed it back.

"Something of equal value," said the sea queen, evenly. Then a crocodile smile. "Or something agreeable to me."

Ian was about to protest, but Laurel shook her head. They had no choice but to play Grace's games.

"What do you want us to bet?" Laurel asked.

The pirate queen filled a goblet with whiskey and set it before Laurel.

"If you lose, you drink it down in one gulp."

"Fine," said Laurel, with a trace of impatience.

Really, Grace was as petty as a playground bully.

"Same for me?" said Ian, wryly, lifting his cup.

"I think not," said the sea queen with a little laugh. "That would be no hardship for an Irishman." She called to a serving girl and whispered in her ear, then turned back to Ian. "You did not take meat at the feast, I believe."

Ian already looked sick before the girl returned with the cooked heart of a deer.

"If you lose, you eat it," Grace confirmed.

She laughed out loud at his glare of hatred. When he

stood up to leave, her men pushed him down again and crowded him menacingly with their weapons drawn.

Laurel gave him a look of sympathy but there was nothing she could do.

Dazed like a man caught in his worst nightmare, Ian checked his hand. Blinked. Checked it again.

Grace lifted her cards and studied them impassively.

It was up to Ian to begin the round. Discarding a single card, he spoke coldly to the sea queen.

"One."

Laurel was relieved. He had a good hand. But just to be certain, she would play to lose. She couldn't risk adding to her pair of nines or her face cards. She would not be the reason he broke his taboo.

"Pass," she said quietly.

A satisfied look crossed the pirate queen's face. Laurel saw it and wondered.

"I'll take two," said Grace.

The moment of truth had come. Ian lifted his cards to his lips before laying them down. Three queens, two sevens. With a little smile, Laurel showed her pair of nines.

It was the pirate queen's turn. Snorting with disgust, she revealed her hand. Three tens, two aces.

Close.

Both Ian and Laurel let out their breath.

"I believe this is mine," said Ian, taking the dagger.

He did not hide his triumph. With exaggerated glee,

he admired the gems on the handle and made a show of tucking the knife into his belt.

Grace's eyes flashed angrily at his antics, but she was nowhere near as furious as Laurel expected her to be.

"Come, my foreign girleen, time to drink up!" she commanded.

There it was again. That smug look.

Laurel chugged the drink down. As the fiery liquor coursed through her bloodstream and exploded in her brain, she suddenly understood. In one fell swoop, her enemy had ambushed and disarmed her. It was on Laurel's loss that Grace had wagered, not Ian's win. She had no doubt bargained on Laurel playing to lose for Ian's sake.

A deadly gambler indeed.

Laurel slammed the empty cup onto the table.

"What do you want?" she hissed at Grace.

The sea queen's eyes darkened till they were almost black.

"Have you not heard of the Devil's card game? We are playing for your soul."

Laurel shuddered. Her head was buzzing. The room seemed to blur. The faces around her looked distorted. She tried to sit up, but her body kept slumping. The whiskey was burning through her veins. Her face felt hot. And though she fought to keep her mind clear, she was already thinking fuzzily. How silly it all was. What a funny old world. She started to giggle. Then she hiccuped.

Ian looked concerned.

Grace looked pleased. "Next round!" she announced.

It was Ian's turn as dealer. He chose to keep things simple and called the same game; the best five out of seven cards, one draw, no raises, maximum discard of three. But before he could deal, Grace called to one of her men to sit down at the table.

An affable young ruffian, he had a mane of fair hair and a handsome face.

"This is Cormac, my First Mate," she introduced him. "A most able seaman in every way."

Her lascivious wink made Laurel laugh out loud, resulting in more hiccups.

"Is he joining the game?" Ian asked, suspiciously.

"No," said Grace. "He is my wager."

Ian's eyes widened.

Laurel was struggling to grasp what she meant.

"And you will be Laurel's. This round is between the girleen and me."

Ian's face went livid. Again he rose to leave and again he was stopped.

"'Sh no prob," Laurel assured him, waving her arm limply. "I'm perfeckly fine. 'T's good game."

Cormac eyed her with approval.

She grinned tipsily back.

Ian glared at the two of them. Then, surveying the hall quickly, he spied what was needed and signaled to his friends to bring it over.

When the basin of water arrived at the table, he pushed it in front of Laurel with a meaningful look.

She blinked at him blearily.

He sighed and muttered, "Sorry about this," and reached over to grab her. With one swift move, he plunged her head into the water.

It was like a cold slap in the face. Laurel jerked back and jumped up, chair falling behind her, wet hair flung in the air, and comb flying loose. With a roar of fury, she picked up the basin and hurled it at him.

Ian and the men near him were soaked. Grace was splashed, too, but she didn't appear to mind. She was howling with laughter.

By the time everyone had calmed down, and linen was brought to dry off the players, the game resumed.

Ian dealt the cards, though he was no longer included.

Laurel had sobered a little and was trying to concentrate. She had two pair, queens and nines. She discarded the rest, hoping to gain three or four of a kind. Another queen! But nothing else. Still, it wasn't a bad hand. Three of a kind, even low, was good enough to win most pots, and these three were high. Her heart beat rapidly. She waited for Grace.

The sea queen's face was composed, but there was a gleam in her eye.

"One card."

Both Laurel and Ian flinched. Not a good sign.

Time to show the hands.

With cautious optimism, Laurel displayed her three queens and two nines.

Grace let out a whoop.

And threw down four tens.

Ian's face went red, then white, then resumed its own color. He looked around the hall. His friends among the men raised their cups and cheered. Maybe it wouldn't be so bad.

Cormac shrugged at Laurel and left the table.

Laurel pressed her lips together.

"It's my turn to deal," she snapped.

"Fair enough," said Grace, with a casual shrug.

The pirate queen leaned toward Ian and placed her cup to his mouth. He glared at her helplessly and took a sip. Her grin was wicked, her meaning clear. He was hers.

Laurel shuffled the deck violently. Over her dead body. She dealt the round. When she lifted her cards and saw what she had, she couldn't stop her reaction.

Grace heard the gasp and snorted.

"You think such ploys convince me you hold a winning hand?"

Laurel fought to keep her face straight, but she could hardly breathe. She checked her cards again. Yes, there it was. The reading she had got on the hippie bus! Face cards all: Queen of Hearts, Ace of Hearts, Ace of Spades, King of Spades, King of Clubs, Ace of Clubs, King of Hearts. *A bright thing may lie hidden inside the dark.* Well, here was the silver lining inside the cloud. Fingers trembling, she rearranged her cards to choose the best five.

Three aces, two kings. An excellent hand. The kind of luck you could bet your life on. But Laurel knew in her heart this was more than chance. It was a sign, and she was ready to put her faith in it.

Her tone was quiet as she challenged the sea queen.

"Let's up the stakes. I want more than Ian."

Grace raised an eyebrow. Ian looked startled.

The hall was now deathly quiet. All other games had ceased. Everyone was crammed in that one corner. Some had even climbed into the rafters above. Jugs of whiskey were passed around. Another whole log was thrown on the fire. The air grew thick and smoky.

The pirate queen studied her cards. Her face was blank.

"Name your terms," she said in the same quiet tone as Laurel.

Laurel took a deep breath. The moment had come. The cards had told her. It was now or never.

"If I win, you will place yourself, your fleet, and your men at my disposal."

The words were no sooner out of her mouth than Grace's men reached for their weapons with angry shouts. It was an outrage.

The pirate queen remained still. Only the slightest flutter of her eyelashes indicated she had been taken by surprise. A slow smile twitched at the edges of her mouth, but the eyes were cold. Sword-eyes.

"I like you."

She signed to her men to stand down, barely glancing at her hand a second time.

"And if you lose?"

Laurel paused, but she knew the words had to be uttered.

"You win my soul. Forever."

"Are you crazy?" Ian burst out.

Grace's eyes flashed. Her gaze was locked on Laurel.

"I like you," she repeated. "I could get used to your company. Your dark-haired Irishman surpasses my bard, but methinks he would not like to stay here alone. He will sing only mournful songs of lost love and have us all weeping in our cups."

Her men guffawed until she raised her hand.

"The two of you together are most entertaining. You would keep me amused throughout the long winter. I accept the wager."

It was time to draw and discard.

"Pass," said Grace.

The crowd cheered. Ian clenched his fists.

A tremor passed through Laurel, but she steadied herself.

"I pass too."

A collective gasp sounded. Ian looked stunned. Grace's eyebrow arched.

It was time to show their hands. With a grand flourish, Grace stood up and spread her cards across the table.

Four jacks, plus the Ace of Diamonds.

An unbeatable hand.

No wonder she had accepted the terms. The chance

this hand could be trumped involved such astronomical odds, no gambler would have reckoned them into her calculations.

And Grace was right not to do so.

Darkness descended over Laurel. It came with a whirring sound, like wings beating at the back of her head. Her stomach twisted, as if a knife were gutting her. How could she have been so wrong? How could she have been so stupid? In one move, one reckless gamble, she had lost everything! The mission. Her chance to save Honor. Her own life and Ian's.

A sob escaped her lips. Ian shuddered as he registered her response. Grace threw back her head and crowed.

But the cry choked in the sea queen's throat when Laurel flung down all her cards.

Three kings, three aces . . . and the red Fool.

Laurel barely managed to stop her own cry of surprise.

The Fool now stood in the lost queen's place, granting Laurel four aces. Only the wild card could have won her this round. The random element of magic in the universe.

Laurel scanned the hall quickly. There by the hearth stood a small figure in red. But he was gone in a second, leaving only the flames roaring up the chimney.

Grace staggered back from the table. Silence filled the hall.

"You were playing with me? You let me think I had won?"

The flash of rage was as bright and murderous as lightning. She reached for the dagger in her belt, but it wasn't there. Instinctively Ian gripped it himself. An eternity seemed to pass as the pirate queen stood speechless, face working with emotion. Her fists closed and opened and closed again.

A thought snaked through Laurel's mind. *How many people has this woman killed with her bare hands?*

Grace's shoulders began to shake, then her entire body, as she roared . . . with laughter.

They let her laugh alone for a while till they were certain, then her men joined in. Laurel and Ian managed brief smiles.

The pirate queen leaned on the table. Her features were clear. Her voice firm.

"A game well played, my foreign girleen, a gamble well risked. I knew the moment I clapped eyes on you that you meant to ask a boon. And I tell you now that regardless of your cause, I would not have granted it. In a world where allegiances change by the day, I keep my power by fighting no battles but my own."

"There won't be a battle—" Laurel began.

Grace struck the table with her fist.

"There is always a battle."

Eighteen

L aurel woke the next morning to the sound of birds scrabbling on the castle walls. Her eyes shot open. And she groaned. The pain was excruciating. It splintered through her brain, threatening to crack her skull, and throbbed like an engine behind her eyes. Disoriented, she didn't move as several insights struck at the same time. The pain was a blinding hangover. The ground was damp beneath her. She was snuggled against another body snoring loudly. Ian, with his arms around her. She held herself rigid, determined not to wake him. First she needed to remember what happened. Images from the previous night were slowly seeping into her mind.

Grace clasping her hand with an iron grip and an iron-clad promise.

"I'll be there when you need me."

A call to celebrate. Cups of *uisce beatha*.

Many cups.

That explained the bursting head and the queasy stomach. Ian had stopped snoring, but didn't stir. Was he asleep or pretending? She wasn't ready to deal with him yet. She raked her memory. Where did she go to bed? Ah yes, in a chamber high up in Grace's stronghold. Soft blankets on sweet-scented rushes. A crockery night-jar filled with hot water to keep her warm. Moonlight streaming through the slit of a window in the massive stone wall. The sound of the sea on the rocks below. And from above, the clank of sword against stone and the murmur of male voices on the night watch.

But how did she get there?

Oh no.

An image of Ian helping her up the stairs. Carrying her, in fact. She was laughing loudly and singing out of key and making a lot of noise as she insisted that he join her. *You sing like a bird, like the birds you love.* Cringe. Those startling blue eyes, filled with laughter. He had drunk a lot too, but held it better. Much better. An earlier memory. The two of them dancing in the hall to wild reels and jigs played on pipes, drums, and bones. They spun across the floor, like figures on a music box. The golden comb went flying again. Her hair and skirts swirled. Clasping her waist, he had lifted her up and swung her around before he kissed her.

A different image now. A massive cringe. When he finally got her up the stairs and flopped her on the bed, she had insisted he stay. The blue eyes sparkled with amusement.

It's not on, darlin', you'd only kill me tomorrow.

Now Laurel bolted upright, pushing his arm away.

Ian didn't move.

"I know you're awake," she accused him.

"Is it safe?" he said, as he opened his eyes, grinning.

They both scrambled to their feet.

She let out a moan as lights exploded in her brain.

"All right?" he asked, concerned.

"Not a word!" she warned.

Suppressing a laugh, he raised his hands in surrender.

"I'm sayin' nothin' and repeatin' it."

They stood in the empty shell of Granuaile's tower. It was early morning. Through the ruins of the doorway they could see *The Lady of Doona* moored at the pier.

When they reached the boat, they found Gracie sitting out on deck, reading her paper and sipping a mug of coffee. She squinted at them as they climbed onboard.

"Well, if it isn't my missing persons. When you didn't show yesterday I made inquiries. Wasn't I told the old currach you hired had come ashore without sight or sound of you? I almost put out an alert for an air-and-sea rescue." Despite her words, she didn't appear in the slightest bothered. "I couldn't wait around, I had a party of Japanese booked. Howandever, you don't look any the worse for wear."

She winked at the two of them. They didn't know what to say or think. Despite the hints to the contrary, she acted as if she knew nothing of her other self. Indeed, she ignored them on the journey back to Achill, though she did offer Laurel two aspirin when she saw her looking a little green and leaning over the side. And yet, when Gracie left them on the pier at Kildavnet, where she had first picked them up, she seemed to add weight to her parting words as she shook their hands with her iron grip.

"Keep in mind, now, I'll be here when you need me."

Laurel had revived by the time they returned to the cottage, but her feelings of shame and guilt still lingered. She had let herself go in Grace's castle, dancing and flirting like someone who hadn't a care in the world. Like someone whose twin hadn't died.

There was also a smaller matter that niggled her conscience.

"We didn't win fairly," she said to Ian. "The cluricaun's help was cheating. Grace might've been a bully, but she played an honest game."

"Cop on," he said, with a snort. "Did you see that last hand she got? What are the odds? She stacked the deck. You beat her at her own game. All's fair in love and war."

"And that kind of attitude can only lead to good things."

"Winning is all that matters," he argued. "That's how both worlds work. We've only got two days left. Grace is with us. Let's free the king."

Ian's plan was simple. Strike immediately. Gather Grace's army and storm Slievemore, the mountain where Laheen said the Summer King was imprisoned. They needed to act fast and take the enemy by surprise. A short sharp war.

Laurel disagreed. An attack was exactly what the Fir-Fia-Caw expected. They would be ready to fight, and any kind of a siege would be disastrous. The king's jailers had only to hold out past Midsummer's Eve and all would be lost. Yes, surprise was the answer, but it had to be something that would truly catch them off guard. Something small and furtive. Guerilla tactics. If she and Ian went alone into the mountain, they could free the king themselves. Grace and her men would be the backup, a last resort. No matter what the pirate queen said, Laurel wanted to avoid a battle.

"Aren't you overlooking something? What if we get caught? There's no one to lead Plan B!"

"If we're captured, Grace will come for us," she insisted. "Don't you see? She's our trump card. We don't play her unless we have to, but we can take risks knowing she's there."

"You're the gambler," he remarked wryly. Then he grinned. "You know the saying about that?"

She didn't.

"Lucky at cards, unlucky at love."

That ended the discussion.

They were sitting together at the living room table. Ian had made them some tea and toast, as there was nothing else to eat in the house. Now he slipped his arm around her and leaned forward for a kiss.

She drew back.

"Don't," she said. "We've got work to do and so little time. We need to figure out how to free the king."

A flicker of annoyance crossed his face, then he relented.

"Right, no messing. It's your turn to hit the books.

Find out everything there is to know about Slievemore. I'll go buy some food and cook us a meal. I could eat a farmer's arse through a thornbush."

"What?"

Laurel shook her head. Irish expressions were bizarre.

After he left, she spread the map of Achill over the table and riffled through her grandparents' guidebooks. There was plenty about Slievemore, "the Great Mountain." In her mind, she thanked Honor for all the nights of enforced study. Who would have thought it could prove useful? She was already sifting through wads of information, jotting down bullet points, and earmarking pages with slips of paper.

"And you call yourself the dumb twin?" was Ian's comment, when he returned.

He had stopped to look over her shoulder before heading for the kitchen. Soon the cottage was filled with the savory smells of onions, tomatoes, and peppers simmering in the pan with olive oil and basil. He whipped up a pancake batter and grated some cheese.

"You're an amazing cook," she said, looking up from her work.

He stood at the stove, his back toward her, stirring the pan.

"I learned young. I didn't want to eat meat, and both my parents do. My mother tried her best, but she's a traditional cook—meat, spuds, and two boiled veg. In the end, it was easier if I looked after myself."

She saw his shoulders slump.

"That must have been lonely," she said quietly. "It's hard when you feel it in your own family."

Though she was referring as much to herself as to him, he looked angry when he turned to face her. She steeled herself for a cutting remark even as it occurred to her that this was how he shielded himself. Then his features changed and he smiled briefly.

"We shouldn't fight so much."

"Yeah," she agreed, smiling back.

Lunch was vegetable crepes sprinkled with parmesan, and a green salad on the side. Neither spoke as they ate, they were both so hungry. When they were finished, Laurel presented her research on Slievemore.

"From what I've read, it's like a sacred mountain. There are ruins scattered all over it, not only abandoned villages but megaliths and portal tombs. I looked for any legends about it. I remember reading in one of my Granda's books that folklore is a kind of ancient memory.

"The guidebooks say there's a web of tunnels inside the mountain which no one has found for centuries. There's even mention of 'the King's Cave,' but nothing about where it might be.

"I started to think about why the Fir-Fia-Caw imprisoned him in the mountain and not somewhere else. They were the Temple guard. In the vision of Hy Brasil, I saw swarms of them. They must have had a barracks or stronghold or something."

"Of course!" Ian swore. "What better place to keep him than in their own fortress?"

Both were silent a moment as they acknowledged what that meant.

Ian looked grim.

"Any idea how many there are of them?"

She bit her lip.

"I think most were massacred, and when Laheen mentioned survivors he didn't give a number. We know there are at least seven from the night they attacked us, but after that . . ."

"Right, it's seven or seventy. Hopefully not seven hundred. Stealth mode all the way. You got a plan?"

She did.

"My guess is the King's Cave is at the heart of the mountain and most likely high up. It wouldn't make sense to keep him on the lower levels or the outer fringes. That would only help a rescue or escape attempt. So this is our mission: go deep inside headquarters, find him and get him out, while avoiding the guards."

There was another moment's silence.

"You found a way in?" he asked, in a quieter voice.

She showed him the map and the places she had circled.

"I looked for anything about entrances or secret door-ways and came up with two. One's somewhere near the Deserted Village, the big ruins at the southern base of the mountain. The entrance has an Irish name."

He checked what she had written.

"*Teach Faoi Thalamh,*" he read out loud, and then translated for her, "The Underground House."

"The second entrance doesn't have a name but it's on the northwest slope of the mountain, above Blacksod Bay. It's just outside a place called Dirk, one of those booley villages, like the one we found on Croaghaun."

He nodded. "But what are the entrances like? Are they caves? Potholes?"

"That's the bad news. No descriptions or details. And they could be blocked up, destroyed, whatever. We won't know till we find them." She sighed. "We don't know 'what' but at least we know 'where.' Once we get there, we use our eyes."

He studied the map again.

"We should go for the Underground House first. It's the easiest to reach. If we don't find it or can't get in, then we head up to Dirk." He stopped a moment and frowned. "But maybe we should check out Dirk as well? I mean, before we go inside? Confirm two exits? That'll give us a second escape route."

"There isn't time. We've got to get moving. Keep it simple. Whichever way we go in, we go out."

"You're the boss," he conceded, and though he looked worried, he said no more.

But she had caught his look. She, too, was beginning to dread what lay ahead. Who knew what waited for them inside the mountain?

They packed their knapsacks with flashlights, compasses, ropes, candles, matches, and bottles of water. The eagle feathers were tucked in their back pockets where they could reach them easily. When Laurel offered Ian charms against the Fir-Fia-Caw—packets of salt, a bag of white stones, several daisy chains—he didn't refuse this time. He also packed his switchblade and the dagger he had won from Grace.

"You got to keep it!" she said, surprised.

"You kept what you won."

She heard the intimation and chose to ignore it. He changed the subject.

"Once we free the king are we bringing him back here?"

She shook her head.

"He could be hostile, according to Laheen. Even with the feathers to bind him, I'd be nervous about trying to control someone so powerful. Best to take him to Grace. She can lock him up in her castle. Then we'll have her ships to get us to Hy Brasil when the island appears."

"You've covered all the angles," he said, admiringly. "Brains to burn."

He reached out for her.

She backed away.

It was the last straw. He had only so much patience.

"What is it with the hot and cold game? Are you messing with me?"

"I can't do this," she pleaded. "Not now. Not when I'm so close to saving her. I've got to stay focused."

He opened his mouth to argue when he suddenly froze. His eyes widened.

"*Saving* her?" His voice was incredulous.

Laurel started to tremble. She hadn't meant to tell him. It was a slip of the tongue. Not something to be uttered.

He gripped her arms before she could flee.

"What did they promise you?" he demanded.

She refused to answer. She could see the fear in his eyes. The fear for her. But she didn't want to see. He spoke urgently, firmly, as if to a child. But she didn't want to hear.

"The fairies are tricksters, Laurel. They can't be trusted. No matter what they've told you, you can't save her from death. It isn't possible. Honor died. You can't change that."

"What do you know about it?" she cried, breaking away from him. "It's my mission, not yours!"

Both were already tense, it didn't take much to push them over the edge. Grief and guilt bled into her emotions, bad temper fueled his.

"I should never have got involved with you," she said. "You're distracting me. You could ruin everything!"

"Are you talking about last night? It's my fault again, is it? Because you let yourself be happy for a few bloody hours? You managed to forget her?"

She wanted to hit him but instead, to her horror, she started to cry.

Her tears shocked him out of his anger. He was dismayed by his outburst.

"I'm sorry, I shouldn't have said that. But, look, we've got to talk about this. Her death—"

"Get out of here!" she screamed.

"Laurel—"

"Get out!"

White-faced, he grabbed his knapsack and left the cottage.

She heard the motorcycle start up, heard it howl away into the distance.

And then the pain hit. That was the nature of grief. It waxed and waned, pulling on the emotions like the moon on the tides. It could be low and quiet, a dark understream of hurt and loss. Then it would surge with sudden violence, set off by any twist of feeling: a rogue wave breaking against the rocks. She uttered a strangled cry and clutched her stomach, then dropped to her knees, torn apart by sobs.

When the wave withdrew, Laurel staggered up. She was alone again. It had to be that way. Anything else was a diversion. She was here for one reason and one reason only: to save Honor. Though her eyesight blurred with the last of her tears and she felt so weak she could barely move, she finished her packing and left the cottage.

She drove the Triumph Herald through Keel and turned left for Slievemore. The mountain loomed up immediately, at the end of a long, narrow road. The great whale-backed ridge glowered down at her, a colossus standing guard. The peak was lost in a veil of mist. The landscape all around was flat and bleak, sparsely inhabited. It was raining and everything was shrouded.

She parked the car at the foot of the mountain, near the graveyard beside the Deserted Village. The ruins of the old settlement stretched across the southern slope. More than a hundred families once thrived here; men and women working the potato beds, children playing between the cottages, cows tethered to rings on the outside walls. Now nettles sprouted in the empty doorways and a cold wind blew through the eyeless windows. All that remained were stone skeletons, picked clean by time. It was a desolate place, echoing loss and defeat. Laurel could feel the despair seep into her bones.

"Where are you?" she whispered, her face wet with rain and tears. "Where have you gone?"

According to her research, the Underground House was somewhere outside the village, on the slope above it. Yet she didn't move to look for it. She had come to a standstill, plagued by doubt. What was she doing here? Could she really save Honor? Was Ian right? Was it impossible? Her sister's death seemed more real in this place, the promise of her resurrection a cruel delusion.

Laurel didn't see the danger. The trap she had fallen into.

They were pushing their way up through leaf mold and soil, thick viscid toadstools skulking in the grasses, their bloodred caps pocked with white warts. They made a ring around her. *Amanita muscaria*. Fly agaric. Fairy mushrooms.

Believing her eyesight to be dimmed by tears, Laurel didn't realize that she had gone blind. Immobilized by grief, she couldn't sense the paralysis that crept through her limbs. Had she thought to cry out, she wouldn't have been able, for she was already struck dumb. And because of the deafness that blocked her ears, she didn't hear the sound of the motorcycle in the distance . . .

Heading her way.

Nineteen

He was there, outside the ring, prowling around it like a panther; trying to find a weak spot, an opening. He kept calling her name. His voice was frantic. She didn't respond. She couldn't hear him. Couldn't speak. Her body stood stationary in the rain.

"They've caught you. Can you see them?"

He was urging her to fight.

"Where are your charms?"

Her knapsack was on her back.

Now he stood directly opposite her, fixing his gaze on hers. Rain trickled down his hair and over his face. His eyes glittered with intensity. She sensed him near her, but couldn't react.

"Give me your hand. Try."

He mouthed the words carefully, but still she didn't move. In desperation, he reached over the toadstools. His body jerked back from the shock. Fury flooded his features. He kicked at the mushroom in front of him. Another jolt hit him, stronger this time, but it only made him angrier. He started stomping on them all, roaring with rage and pain. The ring was being smashed to smithereens.

Laurel felt its hold loosen.

Then Ian pulled her from the circle and into his arms.

She leaned against him, like a bird seeking solace in the lee of a cliff.

"I'm sorry," she said.

He held her tightly.

"Me too."

He kept his arm around her as they made their way up the mountainside. Her body tingled with pins and needles as the last of the paralysis withdrew.

"Thanks for coming back," she said.

He gave her shoulder a squeeze.

"At least we know we're on the right track," he pointed out. "That was like a perimeter defense back there. We need to watch out for traps."

He kept his voice neutral but she heard the undertone. Something else to worry about. He was already scanning the sky for ravens. His concern was contagious. Was her plan too risky? Should they have gone with his instead?

The ground was boggy, covered with heather and grass. Though the slope appeared smooth from the base of the mountain, it rose in a series of ridges that led to the final summit over to their right. The lack of trees or bushes left them exposed and vulnerable, but it also allowed them to search more easily.

Laurel's research had convinced her that the Underground House was just beyond the Deserted Village, and they both assumed they were looking for a cave or something similar. The first thing they checked were visible outcrops of rock, but none had openings. Next they investigated any patch of ground that looked different, either hillock or hollow. Ian used his switchblade and Laurel, the dagger, to stab at the grass. If they struck stone, they would clear away the turf to see what lay underneath. More than an hour passed as they hunched over their task, wet and cold from the incessant drizzle, but neither mentioned giving up. And all the time they kept watch for ravens.

"Maybe you're right," said Ian, scanning the empty sky. "They're waiting for an army."

"Let's hope that's what it means," she answered.

Then at last they were rewarded.

It was Ian who found it and called her over to work alongside him. Cutting away furiously, they uncovered a stone slab overhanging a little cave. The opening was small and dark, like a badger's hole, but there was enough room to squeeze through.

"This must be it," she said, afraid and excited. "The Underground House."

Still smarting from her defeat by the fairy ring, Laurel insisted on going first. With flashlight in one hand and a fistful of salt in the other, she crawled into the hole on her elbows and knees. The wet ground soaked into her jeans. It was hard to move in such a tight space and the bulky knapsack didn't help. A sudden flashback to the Amethyst Cave brought a panic attack. Her heart beat rapidly. She couldn't breathe. The sea fairies had

been bad enough, but the Fir-Fia-Caw were far more terrifying. And she was entering their lair! She gripped the
salt in her palm.

"All right?" came Ian's voice behind her.

It was muffled. He was still outside.

She forced herself to calm down.

"Yeah," she called back. "It gets wider. Follow me in."

She could see where the burrow opened ahead. Was it
some kind of air vent? It seemed too narrow for an
entranceway. Then she crawled out into a chamber that
allowed her to stand up.

Round in shape, like a megalithic tomb, the room was
built of stone blocks with a corbeled roof. Only five or
six people could fit inside it. Her flashlight picked out
niches carved in the walls. For weapons, she guessed,
judging by the scattered remains on the ground—a piece
of bronze sword, a pile of sling stones, some chipped
metal discs. Moving closer, she was able to make out
inscriptions in the stone. The same feathery hieroglyph-
ics as the archway in the gorge. The place felt long abandoned, but that wasn't what upset her.

When Ian arrived he, too, looked around with dismay.

It was a dead end. There was no other opening
besides the one they had come through.

"We'll have to head up to Dirk."

"No wait," she said, thinking. "It doesn't make sense.
If this is a military stronghold, why would they have a
room like this? What's it used for?"

"Good point." Ian kicked at the broken sword. "The Underground House," he muttered. "Guardhouse, maybe? First defense post?"

The same thought struck them both, and they ran to the walls to push against the stone.

Nothing happened.

"Try the parts where there's writing," Laurel suggested.

Now as she pressed a certain spot, a deep rumble sounded. One of the blocks began to move. They had found the way in.

The passage was dark and breathed cold air onto their faces. Pointing her flashlight ahead, Laurel stepped cautiously into it. She felt as if she were being swallowed by the mountain. Cracks fissured the stone walls. The elegant inscriptions were covered with black mold. Where the stone had broken away in places, the earth was bared like a flesh wound. Something crunched underfoot. *Bones?* She aimed the flashlight down. Brittle bits of stone. The dankness clawed at her throat. She heard Ian cough behind her. Judging by the state of decay, the tunnel had been unused for centuries. The cobwebs were the worst part. From time to time, she had to fight her way through sticky curtains of them. Only pride stopped her from asking Ian to lead.

Then something dropped on her head.

She smothered a shriek and signaled urgently to him. *Get it off me! Get it off me!* He ducked as something landed on him too. They both kept whipping around, trying to see with the flashlights, flailing their arms as more things rained down on them. In a fit of wild panic, they ran down the tunnel, heedless of the dangers that might lie ahead.

When they finally came to a halt, out of breath, they trained their flashlights on each other. Both were peppered with black mold which they had obviously disturbed when they brushed away the webs.

Overcome with hysterical laughter, they stuffed their fists into their mouths to muffle the noise. Tears pricked their eyes as they fought for control.

"What are we like," said Ian, catching his breath at last.

"Eejits," she agreed.

Moving deeper into the mountain, they discovered a vast network of passageways. New tunnels continually branched out on either side of them. With the help of a compass, they kept heading north and, when faced with choices, always took the way where the ground appeared to rise. Their strategy was simple. Further in and further up. Though the incline was subtle, they knew they were climbing; their legs felt the strain, and so too their lungs. As the air grew icier, their breath streamed like mist.

The silence weighed down on them, like the mountain itself. They were alert at all times for the slightest sound. The rasp of their own breathing began to unnerve them and they covered their mouths to keep quiet.

Sometimes they came to a cul de sac and had to retrace their steps. Both were beginning to suspect they were going in circles, despite the compass. It was Ian's idea to mark the entrance when they next entered a new tunnel. They scratched their initials in the stone above the opening. Sure enough, it wasn't long before they found themselves staring at their own graffiti.

Their hearts sank.

"It's like one of those labyrinth puzzles," Laurel said. "You know, the ones where you have to draw a line to the center? But this seems to be in spirals rather than squares. That's what's throwing us off."

"Another line of defense," he agreed. "We could be here forever trying to guess the pattern."

"We need to change the way we're moving," she suggested. "Put away the flashlights and compass. Go on instinct."

Neither liked the idea, but they agreed to try it for awhile.

"Safer too," Ian pointed out. "They might see the light before we see them."

The pitch-blackness was a shock. It engulfed them like dark water. Disoriented, unnerved, they proceeded slowly, groping their way along the walls. The open mouth of a new passage was always a nightmare. One minute they were handling stone, the next, nothing, and a blast of cold air would strike them.

Laurel could feel her heart pounding against her ribs. How long could she keep this up? The suspense alone was harrowing.

They had waded through the darkness for quite a

while before the sound they most dreaded reached their ears.

Whoosh whoosh.

The whirr of great wings!

They pressed against the wall, holding their breath. The sound was ahead of them. In the same tunnel or one of the offshoots? Minutes stretched like hours. Their hands met in the dark and gripped tightly. They strained to hear. Was it drawing nearer or fading away? One bird or more? Good thing they weren't using their flashlights! Now they let go of each other to slowly, quietly, reach for their weapons. Ian slipped a knife into each hand. Laurel retrieved the salt she had stored in her pockets. Was the sound receding? The beat was steady and rhythmic. No sense of urgency. A routine patrol. As the whirr faded into the distance, they breathed more easily.

Neither spoke as they resumed their slow progress through the darkness. Meeting the guard was confirmation that they had finally breached the inner defenses. Laurel was attacked by doubts once more. How many patrols would they have to avoid? What if they couldn't find the King's Cave? And if they did, would they be able to overcome the guards and escape? It was a daring plan, but it was beginning to look foolhardy.

They hadn't gone far when a raven came screeching from the mouth of a new passage. There was a flurry of wings, sharp talons, and beak. Ian struck out blindly with his knives. Laurel threw the salt, then pulled off her knapsack to get at her flashlight. By the time she aimed it at the huge bird, it was flying away.

"We've got to stop it!" Ian cried. "Before it warns the others!"

But they hadn't a hope of catching it. With a *whoosh whoosh* of wings, it disappeared down the tunnel.

They had to think fast. Continue with the plan or flee? Could they hide out in the tunnels? Do battle for the king? But the Fir-Fia-Caw had the advantage of numbers as well as home ground.

"We've lost the element of surprise," Ian said quickly. "It's too dangerous now. Time for Plan B. Grace and her army."

Laurel wasn't happy, but she had to agree. They had little chance of reaching the king now. The guard around him would be doubled, even trebled. All hope of a covert operation was gone.

Sounds broke out in the tunnels beyond, confirming their decision. A clamor of shrill squawks. The alarm had been raised. Worse still, the closest cries came from the direction of their escape route. They couldn't go back to the Underground House.

Laurel pulled out her compass.

"Dirk is to the northwest. On one of the lower slopes. We can go that way, moving downward. But there's no guarantee it's open!"

"We'll have to take the chance," said Ian, gripping his knives. "You lead. I'll cover our backs. Let's go!"

Fear spurred them on as they raced through the

tunnels. Behind them, they could hear a whisper that grew, like a wave rushing toward them. The swift beat of wings.

They were being hunted by a terror of ravens.

Laurel clutched her side. Her breathing was ragged, and she had a stitch. It was more annoying than painful, but it was slowing her down. She could hear the birds gaining. Wings were faster than feet.

"We could do with the bike right now," Ian swore.

Every time they came to a fork, it was Laurel's decision which way to run. Always northwest. Always downward. But now they were traveling through ruinous passageways. Many had collapsed, with great blocks of stone barring their way. They had to clamber over the rubble. It was awkward with flashlights. Sometimes they had to remove their knapsacks to cram them through the narrow spaces, then scrape through themselves. Haste made them reckless. The jagged stone cut and bruised them. The disrepair of the tunnels only increased their worry about the state of the exit. And all the time they were hounded by the harsh sounds of pursuit.

Kra-a-a-w. Kra-a-a-w.

Then they stumbled into a wide open space. Pointing their flashlights around, they gasped with surprise. They were in an immense hall of impossible proportions. The roof disappeared beyond their sight. The floor was a vast chessboard of splintered stone. The walls bristled with weapons of every kind and more were stacked in heaps around the chamber—swords, spears, disks, javelins, strongbows, and axes. Even in the dimness Laurel could see the faint image embossed on the shields: a great golden eagle. But all the weapons were rusted and broken. This was the arsenal of an elite legion, long dead and gone.

There was no time to dwell on the past. Their pursuers were closing in on them.

They trained their flashlights across the room, but couldn't see to the far side. They had no idea if there were other ways in or out of the hall.

"Salt!" Laurel cried.

She pulled the packets out of her knapsack and started to pour the salt across the mouth of the tunnel. Ian did the same. Hands shaking with adrenaline, they drew a straight line. They should have brought more! It took all they had to bar the way.

They were running across the broken floor when the ravens arrived. The shrieks were deafening. Laurel couldn't stop herself from looking back. All she could see in the dark were the white eyes, flashing like lightning.

The barrier held. The birds couldn't cross it.

On the far side of the hall at last, the two were relieved to find another exit. But they weren't in the clear yet. The ravens had left the salted passage. They would know other ways to catch up to the intruders.

Laurel and Ian ran on.

"Should be near," Laurel gasped out, keeping an eye on her compass.

She was picturing Dirk on the map in her mind and assessing how far they had traveled inside the mountain.

"Please let it be this way," she prayed.

Then they came to a dead end.

Ian swore wildly. Laurel was almost sick. Until it struck her.

The stone that blocked their way was covered with writing.

"This is it! It's like the other one!"

Frantically she pushed against the wall, pressing the inscriptions.

The rumble was more like a screech this time and the door only partially opened. As soon as they squeezed through, they saw why. This guardhouse was in ruins. Most of the walls and half of the roof had collapsed. It was filled with rubble. *Where was the way out?* They shoved their flashlights into a niche on the wall to give them some light, then searched frenziedly through the debris at the edges.

Harsh cries broke out in the tunnel. The *whoosh whoosh* bore down on them. They ran to block the gap with rocks. But did they want to brick themselves into a space with no exit?

Ian stopped suddenly, his chest heaving. He ran to turn off the flashlights. Yes! In the dark they could see it: a speck of light. They hurried to the spot to fling aside the rubble that covered the opening.

"Go! Go!" he shouted.

The Fir-Fia-Caw had arrived at the gap. They were shrieking and pecking at the stones with their beaks.

Now a more horrifying sound. Hands pushing the rocks aside. At least one of the ravens had changed to humanoid form.

Laurel and Ian scurried through the burrow like rats in a run.

And scrambled out on the other side.

A quick look around and they knew where they were. Immediately to their left was the booley village of Dirk. The cluster of stone huts stood on a slope overlooking the bay. Directly below was a rocky cove. All around rolled the broad back of Slievemore, open and boggy and swirling with mist. They needed to get back to the Deserted Village, where their vehicles were parked. It was over the ridge behind them and down the southern slope.

There was no time to block off the exit against the ravens, and they had no more salt. All they could do was run.

As they hurried away from Dirk, Laurel spied it on her left, leading up to the summit: a craggy promontory, like a stony gray face. The King's Cave? So close, but unreachable! The cries were already rising behind them. Soon the ravens would be in the air. There was nowhere to hide. No trees, no cover. They were out in the open, stumbling across a sodden bog.

Ahead was a lake bordered with rushes. Laurel frowned, disoriented. This wasn't on the map. There was only Lough Aigher on the eastern side of the mountain. Could they have gone the wrong way? Taken a wrong turn? At the center of the tarn was a small *crannóg*, a manmade island overgrown with brambles. A little stone cottage peeked out from the greenery, with smoke curling from the chimney. The door opened and Grace stood on the threshold, waving to her.

"She's come!" cried Laurel, overjoyed. "We can go back for the king!"

She ran toward the lake, too excited to hear Ian's protests.

"Wait! There's something wrong. Grace belongs at sea not—"

He rushed to catch up with her, but she was too fast.

And as Laurel reached the water's edge, the image of the pirate queen dissolved. There stood a tall figure cloaked in black, with a wide-brimmed hat. The leader of the Fir-Fia-Caw. Now he took to the air in his raven form, emitting a shrill cry.

Laurel had no time to react. As the island disappeared in a wisp of smoke so too did the ground under her. She was not at the lakeside, but deep in the mere and sinking fast.

Struggling out of her knapsack, she kicked her legs to surface, spitting out the brackish water.

"Stay back!" she screamed at Ian, remembering he couldn't swim.

He stopped, just in time, on the true bank of the bog pool, but almost lost his balance.

Laurel began to swim toward him when something caught her foot. Glancing over her shoulder, she saw a green tendril twist around her ankle. Was she caught in some pond weed? She turned on her side to kick it away. The leafy grip tightened.

And pulled her under.

She was submerged for a few seconds, then fought her way up again. Now that she knew she was under attack, her resistance was fiercer.

Ian was rushing from place to place on the bank, trying to find the spot that was closest to her. He had the rope from his knapsack. It hit the water with a splash. Just beyond her reach. He swore with frustration. Cast it out again. In his haste, he almost fell in.

"Be careful!" she shouted.

The bog pool was deep. Deep enough to drown him.

The thing that clutched Laurel's ankle felt like a hand. Thrashing wildly, she tried to swim away from it. She had to get nearer to Ian.

He tied a knot in the end of the rope and threw it again.

She lunged with all her might.

Her hands closed on the knot. It burned her palms, but she didn't let go.

"Yes!" he cried.

Now he twisted his end of the rope around his hand and leaned back for more leverage. With him pulling and her kicking, it looked as if they would win the tug-of-war. But their triumph was short-lived.

Kra-a-aw. Kra-a-aw.

The raven swooped down on Ian. He struck at the

bird with one hand, clinging to the rope with the other. The beak stabbed his arm. He roared with pain.

Laurel was shouting too. The tug on her foot was relentless. She couldn't keep her grip on the rope. With an anguished cry she let it go, only to be dragged farther away from the shore. Now the thing wrenched her underwater again and she caught a glimpse of her adversary. Something green and wizened, with long flowing hair. *Greenteeth.* She kicked out against it with her one free foot and surfaced again, gasping for breath.

The rope abandoned, Ian was slashing at the raven with his knife and dagger. The bird managed to stay out of reach, but kept flying behind him. As the great black wings battered his head, he backed away to avoid them.

With horror, Laurel saw that the raven was driving him into the water.

Now he cried out as he fell into the bog pool, flailing and splashing.

"Hold on!" screamed Laurel, "I'm coming!"

She had only begun to renew her struggle, when her ankle was released.

And a green streak arrowed through the water, straight for Ian.

It was like a shark attack. One violent pull and under he went. There was a gurgling sound and bubbles. But he didn't surface again.

Then the bubbles dispersed and there was only silence.

For one interminable moment, Laurel tread water in that bog pool high on the mountain, knowing there was no one around to help. Then she wailed with despair.

"*No, Ian! No!*"

He was gone.

Twenty

There was no sign of Ian. She had to dive and find him before he drowned; but she didn't get the chance. A great bird swooped down at her.

"*No!*" she cried, as the talons gripped her shoulders.

She was pulled from the water with brutal force. Choking with despair, she struggled against her captor, then stopped when she realized it was Laheen.

He carried her into the sky, soaring over the mountain. The bog pool receded below to the size of a puddle and the ravens buzzing over it, to black specks like flies. Now a rush of cold wind and a blur of sea-washed cliffs as they flew westward toward the precipice of Croaghaun.

The moment he dropped her into his nest, she begged him to return to Slievemore.

"Please save my friend!"

His golden voice echoed with sympathy.

"There is nothing I can do for your companion."

She felt herself going numb.

"No . . . this can't be happening."

Instinctively she joined her hands together as she pleaded with him.

"Then take me back! Please! Before he drowns! Before it's too late!"

"Your friend is no longer in the water. He was captured by the Fir-Fia-Caw."

Laurel received this news with a mixture of relief and fear.

"He's alive then? Will they hurt him?"

"I do not know his fate."

"You're the Lord of Clan Egli. Can't you stop them? Tell them to let him go?"

The dark eyes regarded her with an old sorrow.

"Long has it been since the Fir-Fia-Caw obeyed my command. They follow only their kinsman, Ruarc, who is blind and deaf to all but vengeance."

"And you won't fight this evil?"

Her accusation was bitter.

The sadness in his eyes deepened.

"Your kind are quick to call 'evil' what they do not know or understand. Ruarc was my Queen's champion and the Captain of her guard. He has gone mad with grief and guilt, because he still lives when she does not."

Not for the first time, Laheen's words cut the ground out from under her. Laurel didn't know what to think. She yearned for the simple division of good and evil instead of this tangle of right and wrong. For she understood her enemy. Knew exactly how he felt. The grief of the one who didn't die. The guilt of the survivor. In that moment, she was able to pity him.

"With his brothers and sisters, the last of the Fir-Fia-

Caw, Ruarc guards the Summer King inside the mountain. Only his noble nature has stayed him from slaying in cold blood the one whom he hates. But he would die rather than see the king freed and he will kill any who attempt such a deed."

Laurel felt sick. She couldn't bear to think that Ian might be dead. She clung, instead, to the hope of her mission. If by saving Faerie she could save Honor, didn't that mean she could save him as well?

Laheen spoke again, and his voice took on a timbre that seemed to echo through the mountain.

"When you come to the edge of all that you know, you must believe one of two things: either there will be ground to stand on, or you will be given wings to fly."

As he spoke, he spread out his own wings in a grand gesture of gold plumage. Warmth and light shed from his feathers to fall around her. The tightness in her heart eased. Courage surged in her veins.

His golden voice resounded once more.

"Death is not the enemy. Light the fire!"

With the eagle's words ringing in her mind, Laurel was set down at the foot of Croaghaun beyond Keem Bay. She looked like someone who had been lost on the mountain for days. Her clothes were wet and dirty, she was covered in cuts and scrapes. Trudging down the road to Keel, she could only hope that a passing car might give her a ride.

All her thoughts were of Ian. Was he okay? Was she abandoning him? Was she doing the right thing? It was all her fault. If they had gone with his plan, not hers. If only . . . *if only* . . . She stopped short when she realized what she was doing. Tormenting herself, as he would say. And it did her no good, only made her weaker. She needed to be strong, for his sake as well as Honor's. Laurel closed her fists so tightly her nails dug into her palms. She would not wallow in self-pity or blame. She would join up with Grace, raise an army, and return to the mountain to free the Summer King and Ian too. Then tomorrow they would set sail for Hy Brasil to light the Midsummer Fire and wake Honor from her sleep.

"And we'll all live happily ever after," she said, through clenched teeth.

Laurel was not long on the road when she heard a clopping noise behind her. She stepped into the verge as an old-fashioned jaunting car pulled up beside her. It had two wooden benches in the back, facing outward on each side, and a high seat in front for the driver. The donkey that pulled it was gray and round like a barrel. The driver was a big teddy bear of a man, almost too big for his old tweed suit. His face was covered with whiskers the same gray color as the donkey. His baggy trousers were tied with rope instead of a belt, and his jacket was closed with safety pins. A battered Walkman sat on his lap, while a pair of enormous headphones covered his ears. Lively music spilled out. His whole body twitched.

"Would ye like a lift?" he roared over the Walkman. "Take the weight off your feet!"

It was the Walkman that somehow reassured Laurel. She climbed up beside the stranger.

"Janey Mack, would ye look at the state of ye," he said. "You're like the wreck of the Hesperus."

He reached back into his cart and hauled out a plaid blanket. As he tucked it around her, he passed her the headphones.

"*Éist nóiméad*," he said. "Have a listen to Altan. They're only powerful, a fright to God and the world!"

The wild-paced Donegal music clamored in her ears. Fiddles, pipes, flutes, and bodhráns played in a frenzy. Instinctively her feet began to tap.

"Now list to this. It'd make the stones weep."

He fast-forwarded the tape. A sad tune keened in her ear with such yearning and loss that her eyes filled with tears. She thought of Honor and Ian.

"The three great gifts of music," he told her. "Songs that bring the comfort of sleep, songs that make ye dance, and songs that make ye weep."

He took up the reins and told the donkey to "gee-up."

When she told him she was heading for the Deserted Village to pick up her car, he let out a great laugh.

"Amn't I goin' that way meself?" he said. "What a grand coincidence!"

The donkey trotted along at a leisurely pace, but Laurel was happy enough not to walk the long road. She was happier still when he handed her a little straw basket. Under the clean cloth were buttered slices of soda bread and a small round apple cake, along with a flask of hot sweet tea.

"Thank you so much," she said, between bites. "I didn't realize how hungry I was!"

Her spirits were reviving.

"Think nothing of it, *girseach,* don't we owe you that much in the heel of the hunt?"

Laurel turned to him, aghast. It was the cluricaun, and she had eaten his food! She was about to fling away the last of the cake, when he caught her arm.

"Don't be at that! 'Tis not from Faerie. I bought it in a shop. And, begob, the price of it! Cost me a bloomin' fortune! That oul Celtic Tiger would devour your wallet, so it would."

"How can I believe you?" she demanded, trying not to panic.

Her mind raced. What did fairy food do a person? It could trap you in Fairyland forever. But she was still on Achill. What else could it do? Put you under their control!

"I can prove it," the cluricaun assured her. "Look, I'll give ye an order, and if ye don't follie it, ye'll know you're not under me sway."

She waited for his command. He rolled his eyes skyward, thinking hard. Her fear dissipated as she grew impatient.

"Well, do it," she prodded him.

"Don't be rushin' me. It's not every day I get to be makin' suggestions to a fine girl like yourself."

"You're being creepy."

"Right then. Touch the tip of your nose with your tongue."

"What?"

"Go'wan. Let me see ye do it."

"That's ridiculous."

"Well, the fact you're arguin' proves me point. The food's the real Ally Daly."

Satisfied, Laurel finished off the cake, but now there were more serious matters to discuss.

"You've been lying to me from the start," she accused him. "You told me the Summer King was lost and it was my mission to find him. That's a long way from the fact he's in prison and for very good reasons. And what about the Fir-Fia-Caw who guard him? Who will kill anyone who tries to free him? You didn't think I needed a heads-up on that? Oh, and let's not forget that the Summer King is the bad guy and doesn't deserve to be set free! Or was that just another 'slight oversight' on your part?"

Her voice grew louder and higher as she warmed to her tirade. Here was a fitting scapegoat for all her worry about Ian.

"It's been lies, deceit, and betrayal from the very beginning. And why? Because Faerie wants me to do something none of you would dream of doing your-selves!"

He hung his head as she berated him and didn't once interrupt or make excuses. By the time she was finished, he was no longer the burly jarvey who had driven up to her, but was now his own diminutive size. His legs swung over the seat and he was barely able to manage the reins.

"Are you shrinking again?!"

"Forgive me quick!" he urged her. "Or I might dis-appear altogether!"

Her eyes narrowed. She didn't believe a word he said, but at the same time she didn't want him to go just yet.

"I forgive you," she said.

His features collapsed with relief.

Then she added immediately, "If you promise me something."

He looked alarmed again.

"Not my store of *poitín*!"

"Of course not," she said impatiently. "I don't even know what that is. I'll forgive you if you promise to tell me the truth."

"I'll do me best," he swore fulsomely. "Swelpmegod."

"Do you know anything about Ian?" was her first question.

"Who?"

His eyes squinted in a shifty manner.

"My . . . my friend who's been with me on the mission. Dark-haired guy, motorbike. Do you know what's happened to him?"

The cluricaun smacked his lips.

"Can't say that I do," he declared, "and that's the truth of the matter."

It sounded true. But whether it was or not, there was nothing she could do about it.

They were approaching the village of Dooagh. Though they passed cars and a few pedestrians, no one seemed to find the cluricaun or his cart out of the ordinary. Whenever he nodded hello, they always greeted him back.

"As for me not tellin' ye the whole shebang," he said, "Ye hardly believed in us at'all at'all. How was I supposed to be recitatin' the Doom of Clan Egli, one of the Twelve Tragic Tales of Faerie? Sure 'twould take days to tell it, and that's only the fairy half. The human tale is another story, but none of us knows it or what happened to that gobshite of a king once he got his comeuppance, the curse of Cromwell upon him."

He spat into the ditch beyond the jaunting car.

"His fate was kept on the QT. All hush hush. A matter of national insecurity, as your kind do be callin' it. The only one who knew the ending was the First King, for wasn't he the headbuckcat and Boss of the business? But that knowledge was lost along with himself." The cluricaun heaved a huge sigh. "So much was lost. I've a terrible drooth just thinkin' about it."

Gripping the reins with one hand, he reached under the seat to grab a big earthenware jug. Unstoppering the cork with his teeth, he took a long swig.

When he offered the jug to Laurel she declined, but she was less angry now. Though she hated to admit it, she was beginning to see his side of the story.

"But how could you expect me to carry out the mission with the wrong information?"

"All the better," he said. "It made you an innocent. Humans can boldly go where fairies can't, and innocent humans can go even further. Doors unlock. Hearts open. And those who have stayed silent may find their tongue."

"Laheen," she murmured.

She saw him start.

"Ah," he said, and he sounded pleased. "I was thinkin' of the *boctogaí* meself, but that's even better. They say he has not come out of his eyrie since the day she died. We dared not hope. Has he told ye where the king is, then?"

"Yes."

The cluricaun waited for her to say more, but she didn't.

They had left Keel behind and were on the straight and narrow road that led to Slievemore. Though they appeared to be sauntering along, the donkey was covering the distance with incredible speed.

Laurel tried to look nonchalant as they approached the Great Mountain. The cluricaun was watching her closely out of the corner of his eye.

"The car's up here, is it?" he said, slyly. "And were ye doin' at the Deserted Village, I'm wondrin'?"

"Picking mushrooms," she snapped.

"Now, *girseach*, we've got to pull and pull together. Amn't I here to help and not to hinder ye?"

Laurel frowned. Did she trust the cluricaun? Not for a minute. There were only two people she was prepared to put her faith in—herself and Grace O'Malley. Between them they would get the job done.

"I don't need your help," she said. "I know what I'm doing."

The cluricaun was so surprised he nearly fell off the cart. He took another slug from the jug, a rather long guzzle, till his face grew red as a beetroot.

"I'll ask ye only one thing," he said, when he finally put the jug down. "Do ye mean to do battle?"

She didn't want to say, but felt somehow she should.

"Yes," she said quietly.

His red face darkened.

"Then ye've agreed to the extinction of the Fir-Fia-Caw?"

"What?"

Her stomach churned.

"Ye know the truth of it. They'll fight to the bitter end and won't yield up the king till every last one of them is dead."

His words stabbed at her heart. The one great flaw in her plan. She would have to kill an enemy who were not evil, who were simply doing their duty, and for the right reasons at that. She didn't reply to his charge. How could she?

"Well if it has to be, it has to be," the little man said with a fatalistic nod. He reached again for the jug. "The end justifies the means, I suppose."

"It does not!" she retorted miserably. "It cannot! But what choice do I have?"

"Ye can let me help."

By the time they drew up at the Deserted Village, Laurel had let the cluricaun into her confidence and changed her plans to include him. She felt that trusting him was the lesser of two evils.

There was a moment before she got into her car, when she wavered. Her glance settled on Ian's motorcycle.

Tears pricked her eyes. She looked upward to the dark summit of Slievemore. Was he imprisoned there? Was she wrong to leave him? Then she forced herself into the Triumph and drove off.

The sun had already set when she arrived at the cottage. The house was dark and cold. The stove had gone out. She didn't try to light it. There were groceries on the kitchen counter, things Ian had bought. She put them away. She wouldn't eat that night. The place was dreary without him. Her thoughts began to circle again. Was he still alive? Shouldn't she go back and find him? Was she doing the right thing?

She grabbed her cell phone and ran outside. The reception was bad, but she persisted. The moment her father came on the line, she gulped back her tears. Assured him she was fine. "I just wanted to hear your voice," she said. Then her mother was there. It was the first time since Honor's death that she had reached out to them.

"I love you," she said softly. "I love you."

"We love you," they kept saying back.

Then she phoned her grandparents.

"Thank God, pet. Your Granda and I . . . every minute . . . all right? . . . home soon?"

Nannaflor's voice was as good as a hug.

Then Granda came on the line. His anxiety was palpable.

"Any trouble there? You're not in danger, are you?"

"Of course not," she said, keeping her voice neutral. "How could I be? Everything's fine."

Back inside the house, she didn't intend to go through his things but they were strewn over the couch. A leather bag contained his shaving gear. She inhaled the familiar scent. There were several shirts and T-shirts. She folded them neatly. Then she picked up his books one by one. *The Selected Poetry of Rainer Maria Rilke.* Emily Brontë's *Wuthering Heights.* An odd blue-covered volume with an even odder title. *The Time Falling Bodies Take to Light.* She shook her head. He was such a strange boy, so different from any she had ever met.

She got a jolt when she found it, the strip of photographs. They were from the previous year, in Dublin. The two them horsing around in a photo booth. As she looked at the pictures, she saw it so clearly. The first flush. How happy they were, laughing, sticking out their tongues, giving each other rabbit's ears. There was even one of them kissing.

In her bedroom, Laurel undressed and crawled under the quilt. She slipped the photo strip under her pillow, beside the picture of Honor. She felt as if she were drowning, falling through the darkness of a bottomless sea. Tomorrow was the last day. Her one and only chance to save Honor, Ian, and the land of Faerie. She folded her arms across her chest, holding herself tightly, and she fell asleep whispering.

I believe.

Twenty-One

The next morning, Laurel woke with an overwhelming sense that something wonderful had happened. Birds were singing outside her window. She felt like singing herself. The air in her room seemed crisp and magical. Like a child waking to Christmas Day, she knew in her heart the world had changed.

She threw on her clothes and ran out of the cottage. There it was. Out on the water, beyond Keel Strand, like a shining creature that had surfaced in the night. The enchanted isle of *Hy Brasil*.

Though it seemed faraway, like a cloudbank on the ocean, all its features were visible. White cliffs rose above a silver strand. Hills and valleys were cloaked with green woods. Bright rivers splashed into fountains and waterfalls. Above elegant dwellings rose a palace of amethyst, its spires jutting upward like living crystals. And rising again, above the palace, the crown of the island. The radiant peak of Purple Mountain.

The beauty of Hy Brasil was astonishing to see, yet Laurel's view was shadowed. It was hard to believe such a glorious place belonged to someone like the Summer

King. A thought whispered through her mind, though she couldn't remember where it came from: *a bright thing can nurse a dark heart, even as light may lie hidden inside a dark creature.*

Too nervous and excited to eat, she put a few things together before setting out. She pulled on the sweater that Ian bought her, as a kind of armor, then stuffed what charms she could in the pockets of her anorak, mainly white stones and the last of the salt. She had lost her knapsack and everything in it in the bog pool on Slievemore, but she still had the golden feather. She borrowed a brass compass and an old-fashioned flashlight from the dresser drawer. She was traveling light. Courage was the best shield for what lay ahead. Her time had come. *For Honor. For Ian. For Faerie.*

Driving down the road to Keel, her anxiety increased when she saw the flocks of birds everywhere. Many were crowded onto telephone wires, walls, and the roofs of houses. Many more crossed the sky in squadrons. There were those she could name such as swans, mallards, hawks, crows, swifts, swallows, seagulls, ravens—a huge number of ravens—and others she couldn't. It was as if all the birds of Ireland were descending on Achill. The more she saw, the more worried she grew. She wanted to believe they had come with Hy Brasil, but she knew that couldn't be. No bird would sing in the realm of the king who killed their queen. They were obviously there for a more ominous reason: to swell the ranks of the Fir-Fia-Caw. Clan Egli was preparing for battle.

She stopped at the shop in Keel to buy more salt. In the checkout line, she was surprised to hear an old man and a little girl chatting about the island.

"It's so pretty, Granddad. I wish we could go there for a visit! "

"The time will come when we will, my pet. Did ye see the wee house up on the hill to the right? The one with daisies growing in the thatch and a *súgán* chair outside the door?"

The child nodded eagerly. She was five or six years old, and clasped her grandfather's hand as she gazed up at him.

"Now listen to me, *a leanbh*. There'll come a day when I am gone and they'll tell ye I won't be comin' back. Well, that's where I'll be. Ye just look over when the island comes and I'll wave to ye. Have ye got that now?"

"Yes, Granddad."

The others in the queue laughed. The woman at the cash register chided him gently.

"You and your stories, Michael Keane. Filling the child's head with fancies."

The little girl looked surprised, then puzzled.

"Can't they see?" she asked her grandfather.

"Not a bit of it," he said, with a sigh. "They've gone all mod'rn."

When Laurel left the shop, she almost bumped into a blind woman who stood stock-still on the sidewalk, gripping her cane.

Aware of Laurel, the woman spoke aloud. Her voice trembled.

"It's there, isn't it? The blessed isle. 'Tis the seventh year. I can't see her, but I can smell her. Sweet woodsmoke and the perfume of flowers beyond compare."

"Yes," Laurel said softly. "It's there."

Across the road, a silver Mercedes pulled up and a businessman jumped out of his car. He had binoculars in his hand and he trained them over the water. Now he let out a whoop and started waving at the island.

Nearby, a housewife came out to her yard to hang up the washing. She looked tired and worn out. When she shaded her eyes to look out at sea, her face lit up. Then she resumed her work, humming an old tune.

I have been to Hy Brasil,
And the Land of Youth have seen,
Much laughter have I heard there,
And birds among the green.

Laurel drove the Triumph to Kildavnet. There were more birds on the pier, strutting along the stone walls and circling the fishing boats. Tension crackled in the air, like that before a thunderstorm. She touched the feather in her pocket.

With relief, she spotted *The Lady of Doona* making its way into harbor. When the boat docked, Gracie jumped ashore and greeted her with a clap on the back. Exuding health and high spirits, the skipper wore faded jeans and an old shirt rolled up at the sleeves. A baseball cap was clamped down on her curls.

"I've earned enough this morning to take the week off!" she declared, looking pleased with herself. "Am I right in thinkin' you need me today?"

"I do," said Laurel, bemused.

It was hard to know whom she was talking to, the present-day skipper or the infamous sea queen.

"Where's the boyfriend?" asked Gracie, looking over at the car.

"He's . . . I . . . I think he's inside Slievemore."

Her distress was evident in her voice.

"Fret not, my foreign girleen," said Grace, with a glint in her eye. "We'll do this together, you and I."

The indomitable will of the sea queen rang in her voice. For the first time that day, Laurel believed the plan might work.

"I want you to take the boat to the cove below Dirk," she explained to Grace. "I'll meet you there with Ian and another passenger. I don't know how long it will take, but you've got to get us before sunset to . . ." she hesitated a moment, "the isle of Hy Brasil."

Gracie didn't even blink.

"Fair enough. But let me add, my friend, if you don't arrive well before twilight, I'll come looking for you, under hill and under mountain."

Laurel felt the weight on her shoulders ease.

"Till we meet at Dirk."

As Laurel drove to Slievemore, her hands shook at the wheel. The Great Mountain loomed ahead of her. Though the rest of Achill was bathed in sunshine, a dark mist hovered over the ridge. Drawing nearer, she spied what the fog helped to hide. Clouds of birds spiraled above the summit. As if from a jagged tear on the peak, they fanned out in a steady stream. Her heart sank. Their number was countless.

She parked the car near the Deserted Village where she had agreed to meet the cluricaun. When she passed Ian's bike standing alone in the drizzle, she looked away. There was no sign of the little man. As she wandered through the ruins, all her doubts about him returned. Had he talked her out of her original plan in order to betray her? Was he a Judas goat leading her to the slaughter? In a situation where good and evil weren't clearly defined, how could she know who was friend or foe?

Then she saw something scurrying down the mountainside, jumping over the heather with flying leaps. A little red mouse. When it arrived at the village, it stopped before her and unraveled its shape. There stood the cluricaun in his old red suit. His clothes were damp from the rain and a little muddied. With a wink and a nod, he sat down on a wet stone to catch his breath. As his glance took in the birds above them, she saw him wince.

"Have we a hope?"

"A fool's hope," he answered, "as is the way with these things." Then he turned to her with a twinkle in his eye. "Still an' all, the Fool's been known to beat the odds."

They set off up the slope together.

"Did you see any sign of my friend Ian?" was her next

question. "He's been taken prisoner too. At least I hope he has," she added quietly. For she couldn't—wouldn't—believe he was dead.

The cluricaun coughed.

Laurel saw his uneasiness and her throat tightened.

"I didn't see him," came the reply, "and that's the truth of it. But listen to me now, *girseach*. Ye must stick to the job at hand and not be worryin' about anything else. You've only the day that's in it and none other. If ye fail us now, all is lost."

She knew he was right, but her heart ached. Was she the only one who cared about Ian?

"I've done me part as promised," he continued. "A bit of transmogrification helped me at it; a wee mouse is not a thing them big birds could be bothered with. I scouted the premises as best I could. Your hunch was right. The gray crag beyant Dirk, on your way to the peak, is the King's Cave."

"Did you find a way into it?"

"I did. A class of a front door, ye might say, long shut and locked. But today we'll knock and it will open, for Midsummer's Eve magic is stronger than most, and in the seventh year is stronger agin. The only snag—once you're in, the door'll close and I can't get it open for another seven years."

Laurel shuddered.

"*Éist* to me now. That's your way in, but there's another way out. The Captain's Quarters is right benext to the King's Cave, as he likes to keep an eye on his prisoner. That's how ye'll get out. Through his private entrance."

Laurel swallowed. An image of Ruarc flashed through her mind. The terrifying features, the eyes burning with madness. She felt a little sick. The cluricaun had done exactly what she asked; discovered the fastest way in and out of the King's Cave. But could she do it? Snatch the king right out from under his deadliest enemy?

Sensing her fear, the little man's voice was kind.

"Be of good courage. I've done more than ye axed me. I got up to a little mischief and mayhem this mornin'. Each troop thinks the other is mindin' the king and they're all out and about, chasin' shadows. Once they meet up, they'll discover me trickery, but that gives ye a smidgeen of time."

Laurel felt a rush of gratitude and began to thank him, but he waved her words away.

"Just remember that next time you're ready to eat the head off me and, to be sure, we both know that'll come agin."

She would have laughed if she wasn't so nervous.

They were halfway up the mountain and in sight of the gray crag, the King's Cave, when they came upon a massive quartz boulder she remembered from the guidebooks. *An Réilt*, the islanders called it, the Star. Pure white, though veined with amber lichen, it was five feet tall and just as wide.

The cluricaun stopped in front of the stone and groped for the bottle inside his jacket. With a doleful look, he unstoppered the cork and emptied the *poitín* onto the ground.

"A little libation," he said, mournfully.

The words were no sooner out of his mouth than the clouds above them parted and a shaft of sunlight struck the Star. There was a burst of light, then a low rumble like thunder, and the great stone rolled away. A black hole gaped before them.

Laurel switched on her flashlight and peered inside. A stone tunnel, like the others, but not in ruins. It ran straight ahead and disappeared into darkness.

"It'll take ye further in and further up," said the cluricaun. "But don't dilly dally on the way. They won't be fooled for long. May the White Lady shed light across your path."

"You're not coming with me?"

She already knew the answer. The mission was hers and hers alone. She turned to thank him again, but he was already away, a little red mouse scampering down the hillside.

Laurel took a deep breath. Alarm bells were ringing in her mind. It was madness to go in alone. What if she was attacked? She slipped a packet of salt out of her pocket, tore it open, and clutched the grains in her palm. Then, aiming her flashlight like a gun before her, she stepped into the passageway.

She hadn't gone far when a thunderous noise sounded behind her as the great boulder rolled back into place. Except for the beam of her flashlight, she was plunged into darkness. The finality of the moment made her blood run cold. She was sealed in a tomb.

If the tunnel had continued to lead her into the dark, she might have lost her nerve. But after a time, she came to a great stairway that climbed upward. It was very different from what she had previously seen in the mountain. Torches burned in metal brackets to light the way. There was no sign of cobwebs or mold, and the air was dry and clean. The steps were carved of white quartz, smooth and polished and faintly gleaming. On either side of her, the walls were a glassy black stone with no cracks or breaks. They were covered with the familiar inscriptions which she now realized were Fir-Fia-Caw art as well as writing. These were inlaid with silver and elaborately adorned.

The stairs rose steeply, tracing the slope of the mountain. The roof arched overhead. She doused her flashlight. The torches went all the way up. As she climbed, she peered into corridors and other stairwells that branched off in all directions. Despite the cluricaun's warnings, she couldn't forget that Ian might be here, and she clung to her hope of finding him as well as the king.

The glimpses she caught of dim rooms and hallways surprised her. One area even appeared to be some kind of playground, though long deserted. She passed an arch that opened into a great chamber and stood transfixed for a moment. It was a library. The countless shelves that reached the vaulted ceilings held not books but rolls of parchment and papyri. There were long reading tables and high-backed chairs. The more she saw, the more she understood. While she and Ian had discovered the military side of the fortress, this was where the Fir-Fia-Caw lived. This was their home. The insight brought a lingering sadness, for the halls were lonely and echoed with loss.

As she neared the end of the staircase, she instinctively slowed down. Her breathing came quicker. Her legs felt weak. An orange-red light glowed ahead of her, reflecting off the walls. The flames of a hearth? She reached the top. The landing ran a short distance and forked at the end. Two entranceways faced her. She knew immediately what they led to. The King's Cave and the Captain's Quarters.

With the golden feather in one hand, her only defense against the king, and a fistful of salt in the other, her only defense against Ruarc, she moved forward. The firelight was shining through the arch on the left. She would go there first.

Hurrying to outrun her fear, Laurel crossed the threshold and gasped with shock.

Too many impressions assaulted her at the same time. It was the King's Cave, but not the dungeon she expected. The spacious room was furnished with every kind of luxury. A roaring fire cast its bright shadows over elegant furniture, a canopied bed, and a table laden with a feast. A jeweled chessboard stood on a carved bench, and a white hound with red ears sprawled on a rug by the hearth.

Yet it wasn't the prison's bounty that made her cry out, but the prisoner himself. He wore rich garments trimmed with fur and a circlet of blue stones on his brow. As he sat by the fire, absently scratching the dog's head, he looked into the flames with a weary sadness. His ankle was bound with an iron chain that trailed across the floor. This was not the cruel king she had come to free.

"Ian!"

Twenty-Two

He jumped to his feet at the sound of her cry. To find him there, so suddenly and unexpectedly, was overwhelming.

Laurel ran to Ian and threw her arms around him.

"You're alive!" she cried, weeping with relief.

He held her tightly for the briefest moment, then pushed her away.

"Get out of here, Laurel! Before he comes back!"

She was so happy she could hardly think. Pulling at the chain that bound him, she inspected the lock on the anklet.

"We've got to break this."

She looked around for something heavy.

Ian backed away.

"You don't understand!" he implored her. "It's worse than we thought. Get out of here! Right now! You must go away!"

Something in his voice made her stop. She stared into his face and was shocked by what she saw. He looked tortured.

"What have they done to you?" she whispered.

There was no time to talk. The sounds of an uproar broke in the distance. The cluricaun's ruse had been discovered. The Fir-Fia-Caw were on their way.

"We've got to go!"

Laurel was frantic. She followed the chain to where it was attached to the wall and struck at the metal ring with her flashlight. Sparks flew, but to no avail. She hurried back to Ian and tried to pick the lock.

"Do you know where the king is? I've got an escape route."

His face darkened with impatience.

"Use the key!" he snapped.

"What do you mean?" she snapped back. "What key?"

"The golden feather!"

"Why didn't you say so?" It was back in her pocket along with the salt. "Let's not all panic at the same time."

She had no sooner touched the feather to the anklet than the chain fell away.

"At last!" he cried.

"You're welcome," she said, dryly. "Now where's the king?"

He hesitated. His eyes narrowed.

"They moved him to Croaghaun. Left me as a decoy. Once we get out of here, we can go and get him. Did you bring weapons?"

She handed him some packets of salt.

He threw them on the ground with a noise of disgust.

"These are useless against a full guard!"

She scrabbled to pick them up.

"Stop being a jerk! I know it's been hard, but—"

"We must go!" he cut her off.

Drawing the switchblade and dagger from the folds of his clothes, he stormed out of the cave.

Laurel hurried after him. The screeches of the Fir-Fia-Caw were growing louder, drawing nearer. Ian was already at the stairs when she called him back and pulled him into Ruarc's quarters.

The room took her by surprise. It was spartan, with weapons on the wall, as to be expected of a soldier's quarters, but there was more. The furniture was elegantly crafted. The shelves of rolled parchment were reminiscent of the library, and there was a desk with brushes, quills, pots of ink, and paper. A soldier poet? As well as the swords and shields, there were musical instruments like lutes and lyres. But it was the shimmering cloth laid so carefully on a frame that made her heart tighten. She recognized it from her vision of the Temple of the Birds: the golden cloak of the Queen of Clan Egli.

Laurel's quick scan of the room showed no other doorway, but she wasn't deterred. Checking her compass, she ran to the north wall and began pressing against the writing carved in the stone.

"What are you doing?" demanded Ian.

"What do you think?" she said, impatiently. "Give me a hand!"

But it wasn't necessary. The familiar rumbling had already sounded as the stone began to move. A dark passage was revealed.

"If we are where I think we are, it's a short run," she told him.

The tunnel twisted and turned around several corners, but it was when they neared the end that Laurel's anxiety peaked. A circle of light shone ahead. Why was the entrance open? Then the light blinked, like an eyelid closing. Or did she imagine it? She readied the salt in her hand and hissed a warning to Ian.

Knives drawn, he pushed ahead of her.

The mouth of the tunnel was wide, but once they crossed the threshold their way was barred.

There stood Ruarc, Captain of the Fir-Fia-Caw, garbed in black battle-dress with weapons drawn. Each hand gripped a curved sword. The dark corvine features were twisted with fury.

Aaawwrrrccckkk.

Ian didn't wait for Ruarc to attack but charged him, roaring.

Despite her horror, Laurel was glad to see that Ian's street-fighting skills were a match for his opponent. The two fought with such force it was hard for her to know what was happening. Neither had shields, but both wielded double weapons: Ian, two knives; and Ruarc, two swords. Yet it seemed as if each had six or even eight blades, they moved so swiftly. Ian's face was pale and determined. Ruarc's dark eyes burned. At times they were locked together in a murderous embrace, bashing against the rocky crags of the cave. Except for the harsh grunts and the clash of metal, their struggle was silent and terrible to watch.

Laurel didn't know what to do. She picked up a rock in the hopes of disabling Ruarc, but she had to be careful. She couldn't risk doing more harm than good.

First blood was drawn by the Fir-Fia-Caw captain. His sword slashed Ian's hand. There was a streak of red. Ian jumped back with a cry, clutching the gash.

Heart pounding, Laurel ran behind Ruarc and smashed the rock against his head. Caught off guard, he fell forward and dropped one of his swords. Ian leaped to grab the fallen blade and charged at the captain. But Ruarc was back on his feet in time to parry the blow. The two swords rang as they met in the air.

New terror gorged in Laurel's throat. There were noises in the tunnel. Reinforcements were on the way!

"They're coming!" she screamed to Ian.

Tearing packets of salt, she ran to line the passageway; but she didn't have enough for so wide a space. She let out another yell, one of pure frustration.

Now Ian hurled his full weight against his foe. They both crashed to the ground, with Ian on top. His sword arm blocked Ruarc's throat, pinning him down, while the dagger hand rose to strike.

With a sudden twist, Ruarc shifted his body, lifting his arm to block the blow. But he let out a screech as the knife tore through flesh and tendon. A red wound gaped from shoulder to wrist. He began to shape-shift into raven form.

But Ian was faster. He jumped up and brought his foot down with a violent stomp onto the injured arm that was now a wing.

Laurel heard the bones cracking, saw the blood seep through long black feathers, heard Ruarc's cry of agony. Half-man, half-raven, he lay dazed on the ground, unable to move.

With a yell of triumph, Ian lifted his arm. The jewels on the dagger glinted.

Laurel saw that he meant to kill.

"No!" she cried.

With a flying tackle, she knocked Ian over. His aim went wide, his dagger slashing the air as he fell. Laurel landed near Ruarc. There was a moment when their eyes met, and she registered his surprise and acknowledgment. Then she scrambled upright

Ian was also on his feet, cursing her.

"There's no time for this!" she said, furiously.

Grabbing him by the arm, she dragged him away, running toward the western side of Slievemore.

"Keep down!" she hissed, indicating the sky behind them.

The flocks of birds wheeled over the peak like a swarm of bees. Laurel and Ian were on a lower slope, out of sight of the summit, but once the alarm went up, they could easily be spotted. They had to get off the mountain.

Keeping low as they ran, they traveled downward over rough ground. To their right spread the blue sheet of Blacksod Bay. Ahead, in the distance rose the ridge of Croaghaun. All around rolled the broad boggy flanks of Slievemore.

Laurel led the way, keeping the stone huts of Dirk in sight, her marker for the cove where she had agreed to meet Grace.

"Where are the others?" Ian demanded, as they ran. "Surely you are not alone?"

She didn't answer him. Her mind was racing, adjusting her plan. Overjoyed as she was to have freed Ian, she needed to find the king. Thankfully Croaghaun was not too far away and, better still, accessible by boat. They would get there all the faster.

When they reached the slope below Dirk that led down to the cove, she nearly wept with relief. There on the water, anchored like a gull on the waves, was *The Lady of Doona*. And there on the shore, beside an inflatable raft, stood Grace herself, in a red anorak as bright as a beacon. The sea woman leaned on her oars as if they were spears. She waved up at Laurel.

A steep cliff path plunged to the cove through patches of rock and briar.

"Is this all you've brought?" said Ian, incredulously. "Where is our army?"

She stopped herself from yelling at him. She could see he had suffered at the hands of the Fir-Fia-Caw. And was he angry that she had taken so long to find him? With a pang of guilt, she conceded that if things had been reversed, he would have come for her sooner.

She spoke firmly but patiently, as if to a child.

"We don't need an army. It would only attract attention. Look, the birds haven't even noticed us yet. This is not what they're looking for. A few people on a beach. A lone fishing boat. They're expecting a big attack. If Ruarc didn't see which way we went, we just might get to Croaghaun without a fight. We've got to free the king and head for Hy Brasil, but Grace will help us do that. And maybe Laheen."

His grunt showed that he saw her point.

"There won't be a battle?"

"Not if I can help it," she said. "No birds will die today."

They hurried down the cliff path, dislodging stones as they went, and then raced across the beach toward the skipper.

Grace had pushed the raft into the water by the time they reached her. The sea woman's face was creased with concern as she eyed the birds in the sky.

"The king is at Croaghaun!" Laurel said, catching her breath. "We need to move fast. Our best bet is Laheen. He must know where they've hidden him."

Grace was already glaring at Ian when he planted himself in front of her.

"We go to Hy Brasil!" he commanded. "Now!"

Her face flushed angrily.

"I give the orders. I don't take them!"

One of the oars was in the raft, but she still held the other. She raised it like a weapon.

Ian was faster. He grabbed hold of Laurel and put his dagger to her throat.

"Do as I say or her blood is on your hands."

Laurel was dazed with shock. What was going on? The world had suddenly turned upside down. Ian's grip was hard, deliberately hurting her, and his tone so cold it sent a chill up her spine.

Grace lowered the oar, and nodded curtly.

Ian climbed into the raft, holding Laurel in front of him as a shield.

Laurel exchanged looks with Grace. A mere flicker of the eyelids. An almost imperceptible nod. The skipper looked fit to kill.

"You row," Ian ordered Grace.

He settled astern, pulling Laurel down with him. She sprawled helplessly as the knife pricked her skin.

White-faced, Grace got into the raft. Her movements were awkward and she fumbled with the oars. As she struggled with their weight, she dropped one in the water.

"You'll have to help," she said to Ian. "I can't do it alone."

"Useless woman!" he swore. "Ever weak!"

Laurel saw Grace's look. Sword-eyes. He would regret those words when chance allowed.

And that chance came the moment he reached for the oar.

Laurel moved first, jabbing him with her elbow and ducking out of the way. Grace was already lifting the other oar high and brought it down on his head with a mighty whack. He keeled over, stunned. She hit him again for good measure.

Laurel winced at the sound of the crack on his skull, but reflected grimly that he deserved it.

"I don't know what they did to him!" she said to Grace, "but he's been acting crazy since I found him."

Sliding the oars into the water, Grace rowed the raft toward *The Lady of Doona.*

Laurel moved Ian's limbs to make him more comfortable, and gazed with worry into his unconscious features.

"I should've rescued him sooner."

The sea woman let out a sigh. The look she gave Laurel was one of pity.

"You won't see, girleen, what you don't want to see, though it is right in front of you."

Laurel stared at her, bewildered. Then it struck her. The dark truth she had denied since she found him in the King's Cave. Her voice echoed her dismay.

"Ian's under the Summer King's spell!"

Grace sighed again and shook her head.

"Ian *is* the Summer King."

Twenty-Three

"That's crazy! Ian's a human being!"
Laurel was still arguing her point as the raft drew up alongside *The Lady of Doona*. She was a little surprised to see Cormac, the pirate queen's first mate, on the modern fishing boat. In jeans and a T-shirt, he was leaning on the gunwales and winked over at her. Then he moved to haul the unconscious Ian aboard and, on Grace's orders, bound him hand and foot. Laurel opened her mouth to protest, but thought better of it. The skipper's rage was unappeasable. Pale with fury, she pulled open the deck locker, pitched out its contents, and signed to Cormac to heave Ian inside. Then she slammed the lid shut and locked the hatch.

"Weak woman, is it?" she said, with a satisfied snort.

When they were underway, Laurel tried again.

"The Summer King is fairy. Ian is human. My grandmother's a doctor, she delivered him. And I saw the king in a vision. Ian doesn't look anything like him!"

"Of course not," Grace said, shortly. "Ian looks like

his human parents. But that does not change the fact he is the Summer King. Have you learned nothing from your quest?"

She stood at the helm, feet planted apart, hands gripping the wheel. The smell of diesel greased the air. The engines growled. They had left the shelter of Dirk's cove and were skimming over choppy waters on their way to Saddle Head. They had to sail around the tip of Achill to turn south for Hy Brasil.

"Am I Gracie of your time or Granuaile? Is the island to which we sail real or imaginary? Is Ian of Faerie or of the Earthworld?"

She trained her fearless gaze on Laurel.

"Far more importantly, my foreign girleen, the question you have struggled with since your sister's death. *Are we mortal or immortal?*"

In the immensity of that setting of mountain and cliff, endless sky and water, Grace's words carried inexorable weight.

Laurel choked back the tears.

"I want to believe."

As the sea woman guided her small boat over the waves, her voice grew calm.

"Perhaps it is not a question of belief, nor even one of hope. Perhaps it is something you already know. Let the soul rise over the intellect, as the sun rises over the sea."

But Laurel felt lost and confused. Though she understood what Grace was saying, she couldn't accept that Ian was the king. There had to be another explanation for his behavior.

When they rounded the tip of Achill Head, the isle of Hy Brasil appeared in the distance. Despite her worries, Laurel's heart lifted. Over the waves came scented breezes and the faint strains of a sweet song. *Gile na gile.* Brightness of brightness. Shining cliffs rose above blue bays and zawns. Hills and glens bristled with woods. *Agus fasann úlla agus géaga cumhra ar an chrann is ísle bláth.* And apples and fragrant blossoms grow on the low bough. *Ceol as binne de gach ceol.* Music sweeter than all music wafted on the air. Laurel found herself longing for something only dimly remembered. *An grá a théid fán chroí, cha scaoiltear as é go brách.* When the heart finds what it loves, it will never lose it.

"It's so beautiful," she murmured, with tears in her eyes. "Like heaven on earth."

They were crossing the borders of the Perilous Realm, where the world dissolved into myth. No longer sailing in Gracie's small boat, they now stood on the deck of Granuaile's galley. The crew scrambled over the rigging. Cormac, in the lookout, trained his telescope on Hy Brasil. The air resounded with the creak of wood and the whip-crack of the sails that snapped overhead. The ship raced over the rollers like a horse on the plain.

Standing at the prow, cloak swirling around her was Grace O'Malley, the pirate queen.

"Like heaven on earth," she repeated to Laurel, but

her eyes darkened as she surveyed the island. "Yet every garden has a serpent. Even heaven had its war."

Ian's muffled protests could be heard from a hold below. Loud thumps erupted as he kicked against the hatch.

Grace grinned with wicked glee and ordered her men to bring him before her. Though he was still bound, strong arms gripped him and a sword was held to his throat.

"Did you have a fair crossing, my liege?" she asked him.

Dirty and disheveled, he shook with rage.

Laurel searched for signs of the Ian she knew, the Ian she cared for. The familiar features were almost exploding with rage. The same blue eyes glittered beneath the dark hair. The same mouth twisted in a snarl. She recognized that snarl. It only added to her confusion.

"Your mission has failed." He spat the words at her. The same voice, edged with venom. "I will never light the Midsummer Fire. Let Faerie fall, I care not. A fitting punishment for all who left me imprisoned. Hy Brasil will survive below the sea. And if humanity fades because it loses its dreams, all the better. I will celebrate its passing. The Earthworld would be a paradise without your race."

Though she flinched to hear his voice so filled with hatred, Laurel remained calm. She drew the golden feather out of her pocket.

"I can make you light the fire," she said quietly.

His face went white, but with fury, not fear, and his laugh was so cold it made her shudder.

"You may try to bind me to your will, but even if you

succeed—and I doubt you could—it will do you no good. Once we set foot on Hy Brasil, my people will fight to free me."

Stunned, Laurel turned to Grace.

"Is this true? Or a lie?"

The pirate queen looked grim.

"The truth, I'm afraid."

Laurel was speechless. No matter what she did, she was blocked at every turn.

The sea queen drew her aside.

"All is not as it seems. You hold sway over the king, though he tries to hide it. And so, too, does Ian. The king is caught in the human body, for it is heavier than his own, and though he appears to have the upper hand for now, that does not mean he can keep it. Appeal to the one whom you hold dear. He is there also."

Though the situation was bizarre, Laurel was beginning to understand. For one, it explained many things about Ian. She approached him warily. Two burly seamen guarded him with a sword at his throat, but she found herself wondering—which was stronger, ghost or fairy? She laid her hand over Ian's heart. He trembled visibly but she couldn't tell if it was with disgust or distress.

"Ian, are you there?"

Her voice was low, concerned. She felt as if she was fighting for his life.

The king's voice was cold.

"I know what you are doing, but it will not work. He is only a part of me, and the weakest at that. I chose to enter a mortal child who would come one day to free me from the mountain. He has been mine since he was born, and I have resisted all human efforts to reform him. My nature will always triumph."

"That's not true," she said, with sudden confidence. "Ian has always struggled against you, I can see that now. He's a good person. And he hates what you did to Clan Egli and the Queen. He *loves* birds."

"You lie!" the king screamed.

But she had struck home. She knew immediately that Ian was there, by the light in the blue eyes and the familiar torment in his features. It all made so much sense now.

"I'm sorry, Laurel. I can't fight him. He's stronger than me."

"He isn't! Keep trying! You're so much better than him!"

She was about to embrace him, when a harsh laugh cut her short.

"Come near me and I'll tear you apart," he swore.

"Enough!" Grace signaled to her men. "Throw him overboard!"

Before Laurel could object, the men dragged Ian to the side of the ship and heaved him over.

Hands and feet still bound, he hit the water headfirst.

"He'll drown!" Laurel cried.

Grace was already spinning the wheel and shouting orders at her crew. They scrambled to obey her. The ship came around and was flying from Hy Brasil.

Laurel ran to the side to look. There he was, swimming toward the island, slicing through the water like a shark. It was that little detail that convinced her at last—the fact he could swim—and something broke inside her as the truth struck home. Ian was the enemy.

She strode over to Grace and demanded angrily, "Why did you let him go? We need him to light the Midsummer Fire!"

The sea queen raised an eyebrow at her tone, but answered evenly.

"He was playing with us. Even I was distracted. Meanwhile, his people were gathering to attack. Had we taken him with us, they would have pursued. We are outnumbered. I only fight when I can win."

Laurel glanced back at Hy Brasil. Though it was fast fading behind them, she could see the flashing lights on the shore. Weapons glinting in the afternoon sun.

Grace finished implacably: "We must gather an army. I know you hoped to avoid it, girleen, but as your friend and advisor I tell you now—for the sake of the mission, battle must be joined."

Twenty-Four

Laurel stood alone on the ramparts of Grace's castle, overlooking Clew Bay. Waves crashed on the rocks below her. Beyond lay a multitude of islands. From the tower's position she could see across to the mainland, but her gaze kept returning to the beach below. She was observing the arrival of the pirate queen's army. Countless ships had dropped anchor around Clare Island. Currachs were rowing back and forth to bring the captains and commanders ashore. The men were handsome and broad-shouldered, with shaggy manes of hair and long flowing cloaks. Armed to the teeth, they greeted each other with loud guffaws and friendly blows. Some were accompanied by pipers skirling tribal marches. The air crackled with excitement. The Queen of the Sea had called a *gairm slógaidh*. A hosting of war.

Laurel regarded the proceedings with a cold eye. She did not think battle was thrilling or glorious, and it was not what she had set out on her quest to achieve. Yet she had to acknowledge the truth of the matter: with Faerie you always got more than you bargained for.

Her thoughts kept returning to Ian. She could hardly

believe he was the Summer King. Of course it explained his erratic behavior, but were they two different people in one body? Or two sides of the same person? Did she really know him at all? She could see the dunes where they had lain together. Was that the Summer King too? The more she brooded on the matter, the more lost she felt. If only Honor were there. Her twin had always helped her sort out complications, whether with friends, boyfriends, parents, or teachers.

She's not here, Laurel reminded herself bitterly, and that was the core of the matter. Regardless of anything else, she had to save Honor, and if that meant going to war against Ian, then so be it.

She was about to leave when Laheen dropped out of the sky and alighted on the parapet.

"You are troubled."

His voice was kind and soothing.

"Things are getting worse, not better," she said.

He was like a great golden statue. He had yet to furl his wings, and they stretched out on either side of him, radiating light.

She felt her spirits lift.

"I bring you good news," he said, folding his wings. "The Fir-Fia-Caw will fight by your side."

As always, his words caught her by surprise.

"Even though I freed the king? I thought—" Then she stopped. Of course. "They want to capture him again," she said, nodding.

"That is not the whole story," Laheen said, quietly.

"Something greater has happened. Long has Captain Ruarc been lost in madness, knowing nothing but vengeance. Though it meant the fall of Faerie, he would not free the one who murdered his queen, nor would he let the fire burn that destroyed his people.

"Now a light has shone to ease the darkness wherein he dwells. Just a short while ago, after years of silence and exile, he came to me with a mystery he could not fathom.

"On a certain night when he led his troop against you, he discovered the existence of your friend, Ian. It was a shock. For he sensed this man was of the king and yet not the king. From that time on, he endeavored to capture him and finally did so yesterday on Slievemore.

"Determined to understand the riddle, he brought his new prisoner to the King's Cave. The moment the Summer King saw Ian, he became enraged.

"'You fool!' he shrieked. 'You let them catch you! You are no use to me now!'

"Your friend staggered back, looking pale and distressed, and said, 'I . . . know . . . you.'

"'Of course you know me, idiot,' the King said. '*I am you.*'

"It was a strange exchange, all the stranger because Ruarc felt the link between the two, yet could also perceive the difference. His new captive vehemently denied the charge and begged to be taken away. Alas, too late, for the Summer King reached out for your friend and subsumed him."

Laurel's face drained of blood. She felt faint.

"He killed Ian?" she choked.

"No. He claimed him. For Ian carried a part of the king sent into your world to set himself free. Reunited, they exist as one. While this must cause you pain, good may come of it. Your friend's nature impressed Ruarc. He believes that Ian can conquer his kingly self and tame the fiery nature that has done so much wrong. He will help him do this."

Laurel struggled to understand what Laheen was saying. She recalled the battle between Ruarc and Ian outside the King's Cave. No wonder it was so vicious. She had witnessed mortal combat between two ancient enemies. It made the eagle's words all the more poignant and, just for a second, she forgot about the Midsummer Fire and Faerie, forgot even about Honor.

"Are you saying Ruarc wants to save his enemy?"

Laheen's eyes shimmered with tears.

"Before he fell into madness, Ruarc was the most noble of my children. He believes in redemption, for is it not his hope also?"

"And mine too," she said softly.

After Laheen left, Laurel went to the main hall to deliver his news. A Council of War was in progress. Grace stood at the head table, looking over a map of the western seaboard that showed the islands of Achill, Clare, and Hy Brasil. With her commanders around her, she was issuing orders and debating strategy. They spoke in Irish together, but when Laurel arrived, they switched to English. She had just told them about their new allies, when the Fir-Fia-Caw arrived.

In three troops of seven moving as one, they fanned out across the hall like birds in flight formation. Jet-black eyes rimmed with gold scanned the room with the fierce stare of the predator. Both male and female were garbed in dark battle-dress of leather jerkins, tight trews, and knee-high boots. Their long feathered mantles had a violet sheen. In place of the wide hats, glossy dreadlocks fell to their waists. And though they bore almost human form, dark-skinned and sharp-featured, their spirit was that of the raven: proud and solitary, cold and dangerous.

As they approached the head table, they let out their battle cry—*kra-a-w kra-a-w*—and the harsh sound shattered the air. Though no one cowered, most did step back. A terror had come among them.

Captain Ruarc strode forward. His right arm lay motionless at his side, bound in a splint, but the opposite hand rested on the hilt of a great sword. In a guttural voice, he called out the names of his kindred, the last of their kind, as they presented themselves to Grace. It was Aróc who commanded the *Mná-Fia-Caw*, the troop of seven sisters. Cádac was chief over the second troop of males, while Ruarc led the first; but the Captain of the Queen's Guard and their eldest brother was also leader over all.

When Ruarc turned to Laurel, his gaze was one of such unflinching ferocity she thought she might faint. Regardless of what Laheen had said, the captain's face was still ravaged.

"*Awrrrcckk.* Not enemies. You and I."

She suppressed a shiver of primal fear. He was truly terrifying. But though her instincts told her to flee, she stepped closer to him. She wanted to say words only he could hear.

"I have also lost someone I loved . . . and failed to protect."

A shudder passed through him. The raw anguish in his eyes was painful to meet; but it was a mirror of her own. Both acknowledged that, and bowed to each other.

Grace invited Ruarc to view the battle plan. Pleased with the reinforcements, she was happier still when he told her that the birds of Clan Egli would also join them. An auspicious addition to the company. Tactics were adjusted and a new plan drawn up.

The Council of War was almost over. Time was growing short. In the few hours left before sunset, they had to invade Hy Brasil, capture the Summer King, and light the Midsummer Fire. Each had a part to play. Grace's army was to fight the king's forces while the birds built the pyre on Purple Mountain. It was the Fir-Fia-Caw's task to take the king prisoner, and Laurel's to bind him and make him light the fire. All knew the gamble. If any one of them failed to do his or her part, the day would be lost.

A final pact was agreed. If they were successful and the Ring of the Sun was forged, the Summer King's fate would be determined by the Fir-Fia-Caw. Exchanging looks with Ruarc, Laurel knew what that meant. It would be up to Ian whether or not he remained a prisoner.

The Council was disbanding when a commotion

broke out at the entrance to the hall. Two guards carried a small bundle between them that hissed and spat like a wild cat. All in red, his cap askew, the little man kicked his legs in the air.

"Put me down, ye big bollockses!" the cluricaun was bellowing. "It's a gross indignification! A thundering disgrace! I'm an Ambassador of Faerie! I should be treated with the respect due me station!"

Grace's men laughed and jeered. Though Laurel recognized the captive, she didn't speak up.

"We do not tolerate spies," the pirate queen warned.

"Roast him till he reveals where he keeps his *poitín!*" someone shouted. "Me throat is parched!"

There were more roars of laughter. The cluricaun paled.

"She knows who I am!" he screeched, looking at Laurel.

Grace raised an eyebrow.

Laurel glared at the little man.

"Did you know Ian was the Summer King?"

The cluricaun went limp between the guards. Legs dangling pathetically, he hung his head.

"I did and I didn't," he confessed at last. "We suspected the blaggard had made a *scáth*—a shadow of himself sent into the Earthworld—but they're not aisy to detect. Not like a changeling. And when the *scáth* mingles with the mortal soul, it becomes its own man, and might not act like a fairy at'all. We could never be sure, and by the time we were, you and him were an item. It seemed best to leave ye's be."

Laurel frowned.

"When I asked you about Ian, you said you knew nothing."

"Did I now?" said the cluricaun quickly. "I'm thinkin' that isn't so, *girseach*. Ye asked me if I knew what happened to him and if I'd seen him. And I didn't and I hadn't and that wasn't a lie. I'm a divil for sins of omission, not commission."

He stumped her there. Lies were never the problem, but rather all the truths he failed to tell her.

"You're hopeless," she said.

The cluricaun managed an apologetic shrug in midair.

Grace signed to her men to let him go and they dropped him on the floor. He picked himself up, straightened his clothes, and bowed to the sea queen.

"Hail, Granuaile. I greet you on behalf of Midir, High King of Faerie. He thanks you for aiding she who furthers our cause. He sends word of warning that all the sea fairies of Ireland will join the *boctogaí* of the West to fight at the side of the Summer King. He is their liege-lord and they must follie him, even to their doom. On the High King's order no other fairy troop will join the fray, either for or against, but all will hold vigil for the Midsummer Fire."

"He's not coming?" Laurel burst out. "Not bringing troops? But this is Faerie's battle! How can he—"

Grace cut her off.

"The High King is wise. Faerie is to be strengthened by the Ring of the Sun, not riven by war. Long have the sea fairies been sundered from their kinfolk by fault of their king and the Doom of Clan Egli. For other fairy troops to join this battle would only widen the breach. Some might fight for them, others against, and strife would be everywhere.

"Take this message to Midir. Granuaile sends greetings. Since our two races first met together, the rescue of Fairyland has been the charge of humanity. Today will be as it has always been."

The cluricaun bowed to her.

"Our thanks, great lady. I do as you bid."

The Council of War had come to a close. The plans were drawn. The time was nigh. Laurel glanced out the narrow window at the westering sun. Soon the Midsummer Fire must be lit. But first, a great battle. She felt the shudder in every part of her. Terrible things would happen before her mission was fulfilled. And how much worse would it be, if she failed!

Twenty-Five

L ate in the day of Midsummer's Eve, a mighty arma-
da set sail for Hy Brasil. Like a flock of white birds,
the galleys and caravels flew over the waves, sheets
swelling in the wind, bows rising through the spray. Each
vessel carried a full complement of men, not only Grace's
sailors and pirates, but troops of warriors loyal to the
O'Malleys. At the prow of the flagship stood the sea
queen herself, cloak billowing behind her. Overhead flew
squadrons of birds, shadowing the fleet like a mass of
storm clouds. The susurrus of wings was like the sea
below, surging with sound. Leading the birds were the
ragged forms of the Fir-Fia-Caw, moving in formation
across the sky. The great black wings beat in unison. The
eyes flashed like lightning. At the head of the vanguard
flew Ruarc, dark and terrifying.

Laurel looked up as he passed by. He flew toward the
last battle with his ancient enemy. Would this day see the
two redeemed?

Like the pirate queen, Laurel was dressed in battle-
clothes of leather and mail, with a green cloak wrapped
around her. She bore a shield emblazoned with a golden

eagle; but where Grace bristled with weapons, Laurel had only a short sword and a dagger at her hip. Her chief weapon was the feather clasped to her belt.

Nervous and edgy, she was surprised to sense the same tension among the men.

"If you're all ghosts," she said to Grace, "doesn't that mean you can't die in this battle?"

The sea queen snorted.

"Would that were so, my foreign girleen. What a glorious game it would be! Alas, the truth is not as pleasant. Being otherworldy all, neither side has immunity from the other. We may harm and be harmed, even unto death."

The truth hit Laurel like a blow.

"What will happen if you die today?"

"Who can plumb that mystery?" The pirate queen shrugged. "I do not fear death. I have faced it already." She grinned broadly. "And it didn't kill me."

The gallows humor was lost on Laurel. She didn't feel like laughing. There was one last question she had to ask.

"Can I die here?"

Grace was not a woman who minced her words.

"You can. And those of Clan Egli, both the Fir-Fia-Caw and the birds. For we have entered the Perilous Realm and not all who do may return."

Laurel could feel her stomach churning. That meant the battle was real, not a fantasy. Many would die today, and so might she. She wished with all her heart it was only a dream. She wanted to wake up.

As the fleet approached the shores of Hy Brasil, they were confronted by a formidable sight. Their enemy ranged along the coastline behind a wall of shields and a forest of spears. Like a shadow cast behind, the ranks in the back were a host of fell creatures. Ever skilled at war, the Summer King had called a hosting, not only of his own people, but also of foul things that dwelled in the nether regions of Faerie. Goblins, demons, red-eyed pookas, bogles, giants, hags, and glashans all swelled his forces. Creeping from the depths of nightmares, they looked the true enemy, grimacing and evil. They were what one expected to fight. But they were only the rearguard.

Laurel's heart ached as she viewed the front lines. In golden mail and glimmering with light stood the *boctogaí*, the sea fairies of Ireland, commanded to fight by their bellicose king. It was like warring with angels. Yet what made them beautiful, also made them terrible. For they were as cold and indifferent as the drowning waves of the ocean, ready to kill without mercy or remorse.

Surveying the vast numbers, Laurel blenched. This was a far bigger army than they were prepared for.

The onset was fierce and sudden. A rain of burning arrows lacerated the air, striking the ships as they anchored. White sails burst into flame. The fleet responded immediately. Cannon lobbed missiles at the shore. Sand and earth exploded. The front lines broke.

The slaughter had begun.

The sea queen and her commanders were shouting orders. From every vessel, small boats dropped like spiders into the water to land the troops. As men splashed ashore, the battle was joined.

Laurel watched, appalled, as the tapestry of war unfolded. Clouds of arrows whistled overhead. Swords flashed. Spears skewered. Axes rose and fell as if hewing trees. The din itself was a shock, an uproar of howls, screams, and battle cries. She tried to tell herself it was only a dream turned briefly to nightmare. But the shrieks of pain were real, and patches of red bloomed everywhere. It was as if the heart of the island had been pierced and its blood was flowing.

Grace signaled to Laurel to follow her. Their boat waited to take them to the battle.

Laurel felt her courage desert her. Every part of her was shaking. She felt sick. She was not like the pirate queen reared to pillage and plunder. Growing up in a quiet neighborhood in a small town, she knew nothing of war. As her legs buckled under her, she gripped the gunwale to hold herself up.

"I can't do this," she whispered. "I want to go home."

Her eyes were already filling with tears when her glance strayed eastward, beyond the fleet. There a shaft of sunlight danced on the waves and a spiral of mist rose up from the foam. Out of the mist rode the White Lady upon her pale horse. Laurel heard the words whispered in the deep of her mind.

Death is not the enemy. Light the fire.

Now it coursed through her, singing in her veins, the truth she had struggled with throughout her mission.

Even if she died today she would live again, she would live forever. She was immortal.

"Are you ready?" Grace roared from the boat.

"I am!" she shouted back.

The moment Laurel set foot on Hy Brasil, she was assailed on all sides. The enemy had been waiting for her. She raised her shield and gripped her sword. *For Honor.* The onslaught was a blur of chaos and noise. Blows thudded on her shield. Shouts rang in her ears. In the press of battle, bodies bashed against her and it was all she could do to keep on her feet. The clash of metal shattered the air. Arrows whined overhead.

Despite her newfound courage, Laurel slipped quickly into shock. She was sluggish and slow to react. Luckily Grace shadowed her, parrying the strokes that would have killed her. The rest she fought off herself as she gained momentum. Soon she, too, was caught up in the madness.

The horror was unrelenting. Her shield arm grew numb from the force of constant blows. Her clothes were soaked in sweat. Her sword dripped blood. She could hear herself grunting as she hacked and slew. The imperative to stay alive had become an imperative to kill.

Even as the battle raged around her, Laurel's glance strayed to the sky above. The sun was sinking in the West. Time was also an enemy they had to fight.

Then the inevitable happened. She was separated from Grace. Tripping over a fallen body, she nearly lost her balance. As she struggled to right herself she lowered her shield, exposing her side. A goblin leaped toward her, screeching, his spear aimed to strike. She raised her arm. Too late.

It all happened in slow motion. Laurel saw the horrible creature rushing at her, saw the deadly point of his spear. Then she watched, with a strange detachment, as another point protruded from his chest. He was skewered on a javelin. And even as the goblin was tossed into the air, she faced the one who had saved her. There stood the Master Riddler in shining mail, laughing out loud. Before she could react, he grabbed her roughly and flung her aside.

Laurel hit the ground with a cry of pain. But when she scrambled to her feet, she saw that he had thrown her out of harm's way.

Like a great wave rushing to shore, his troop surged against the O'Malley lines. Tall, splendid, and lethal, they were masters of *Bruíon Amhra,* the Wonderful Strife, the deadly game of Faerie war. And in voices beautiful and terrible, they sang like the sea as they swept all before them.

The battle had taken a turn for the worse. Everywhere Laurel looked, the sea fairies were wreaking havoc on their foe. Grace's army was being driven back to the sea.

Then the Fir-Fia-Caw dropped out of the sky.

Wings battering, beaks slashing, they drove a wedge between the armies where they could land. Swiftly, silently, each changed into warrior shape to form a phalanx. With two scimitars apiece, they spun their blades like propellors. Now they marched forward, grim-faced and deadly, cutting a great swathe through the enemy ranks. Their captain was the only one to wield a lone weapon, his shattered arm bound to his side; but his aim was unerring and he struck more blows than all of his kin.

Even in the fog of war, Laurel saw how the *boctogaí* reacted to the Fir-Fia-Caw. The joyous charge of the sea fairies wavered and broke. There were looks of shame and guilt. Some fell back, unwilling to engage. Those who had stayed to fight did so without enthusiasm. The clash itself was disorienting to witness. Terrifying creatures fought against bright beings, but it was the dark ones who stood for what was right, while those who looked like angels were defending evil.

Grace's men were heartened by the Fir-Fia-Caw assault. With a clamor of horns and trumpets, their soldiers regrouped. It was time to gain ground, to advance on Purple Mountain. Swelling forward, they fell upon the enemy, broke, reformed, then charged again. Each onslaught cost them dearly; but every time they stopped, they were farther ahead, moving in increments like the incoming tide.

The battle plan was back on course.

From the skies above, the larger raptors swooped down to skirmish with beak and talon. Under cover of these flying columns, the smaller birds set out in twos and threes to accomplish their task. To Purple Mountain they flew, carrying in their beaks the wood that would make the Midsummer Fire. All the trees of Ireland had offered twigs and branches: rowan for protection; birch, which promises a new beginning; alder for prophecy and hawthorn to cleanse; apple for beauty and ivy for self; beech for old knowledge; oak for strength; ash, which stands in both worlds at once; and long-living yew, the tree of rebirth. As each piece fell upon the summit, the sacred pyre grew.

Laurel saw the first birds reach the mountain. So far, so good. She took a deep breath to steel herself. It was her turn to act. Gripping the feather in her shield hand to protect it, she joined her guard. They were warriors sent by Grace, all brandishing broadaxes. Though they looked fearsome, she was disappointed that Ruarc wasn't with them. Strategy had changed to suit the situation. Since the Fir-Fia-Caw were leading the army, it was these men who must help her capture the king.

She had seen him arrive on the battlefield in his dark-blue chariot with fiery wings on the side. As glorious as an archangel, he wore golden armor and a crown of gems. Fluttering above him was the oriflamme, his crimson banner. Whenever Laurel caught sight of him, her heart tightened. He looked so like Ian. But though he fought with kingly strength and courage, his features were cold, his eyes cruel, and he smiled as he slew.

Laurel's sortie had just set out when the king spied the birds over Purple Mountain. He signaled to his bowmen. The archers ran forward, took up position, and let fly their arrows.

A flock of birds fell from the sky.

The Summer King ordered another volley.

More birds fell in a hail of blood and feathers. But even as they died, others flew to take their place, defying the arrows—robins, sparrows, swifts, swallows, linnets, thrushes. Small beings with great courage.

Wild with rage and sorrow, Laurel broke from her guard and ran for the king. Dodging in and out of the press of fighters, she advanced on his chariot. The battle-car was open at the back, with a running board. Hunkering low, she crept up from behind and leaped into the car. Before he could react she had touched him with the feather and uttered Laheen's words. *By that which you kill are you bound.*

The effect was instant. Both she and the king were suddenly elsewhere. A milky void. The silence was more shocking than the change of place. Neither of them was armed, for they had no corporeal form. They were two columns of energy, locked in conflict. And they were not alone. The White Lady rode toward them, accompanied overhead by a beautiful she-eagle. Only then did Laurel realize that the feather wasn't Laheen's, but belonged to his wife and queen. She could feel Ular strengthening her, as did the Lady, while she fought the king's will.

The struggle was horrific. It was like gripping a serpent. He shrank and expanded, twisted and contorted, resisting with venomous rage. He was fiery and explosive like a volcano erupting, but also searingly cold like the depths of the sea. Her grasp began to slip. He was too wily. Too strong. Now she sensed another presence straining to emerge in the void. *Ian!*

But Laurel lost her hold on the king.

They were back in the chariot. The din of battle broke over them like the roar of a wave. The king was too quick. He blocked her arm, knocked the feather from her hand. With a panicked cry she tried to catch it in midair, but it fluttered beyond the battle-car. Before she could see where it landed, he seized her brutally.

His laugh was exultant.

"Your male kin was stronger."

Grabbing a fistful of her hair, he yanked back her head.

"Never send a girl to do a man's job."

Her mind was already shutting down as he swung the sword to cut her throat. She had forgotten to call her guard. Forgotten the dagger in her belt. Forgotten how to fight. His violence overwhelmed her. She had never faced such a savage force, all the worse for being embodied in someone so dear to her.

The sword didn't land. Before it could strike, a great raven smashed into the king and sent him sprawling out of the battle-car. By the time the king was back on his feet, Ruarc had transformed to face his ancient foe.

They did not stop to circle or assess, but charged at each other with murderous roars. Neither bore shields. The king had kept hold of his sword as he fell and also drew his dagger. He moved with a swift, fluid grace, striking with mastery. Ruarc evaded his blows, and wielded his lone scimitar as if it were two. Sparks flew from his blade as he parried the king's thrusts, retaliating with lightning speed and ferocity.

The combat was so vicious, all around them gave way, granting them their own arena.

Crouched in the chariot, Laurel watched with horror. It looked like a duel to the death. Had Ruarc forgotten his pledge to capture the king? To try to save Ian? Then she began to see that he was fighting defensively, and striving to disarm his opponent. A rush of gratitude came over her, followed by a wave of fear. That meant the Fir-Fia-Caw captain had two weak points: the limb that couldn't defend itself, and the intention not to kill. It wouldn't be long before the king took advantage of both.

Laurel was frantic. She had to help Ruarc. Her only hope was to find the feather and bind the king again. Her guards were now surrounding the battle-car, and she scrambled out to search the area. The ground was churned up with sand, blood, and gruesome things she didn't want to see. But no feather. Was it under the chariot? Accustomed to war, the king's horses held their positions despite the press of the throng. She had grabbed the reins to nudge the car forward when a terrible cry pierced the air.

Ruarc reeled backward, clutching his heart. Blood poured from wounds in his shoulder and chest. He had taken a mortal blow. As his death cry rose to the heavens, it was answered by shrieks across the battlefield. The six brothers of his own troop raced toward him. His raven sisters bore down from above. The third troop transformed and took to the air.

Ruarc fell to his knees; but the king had no time to deal a final stroke, nor was he able to enjoy his victory. The seven sisters swooped, screeching vengeance like harpies. Had the king's own captain not died to save him, he would have been slain. As it was, both king and guard were now beleaguered and fighting for their lives.

Laurel ran to Ruarc where he lay amidst the slain. Cradling him in her arms, she tried to stop the bleeding; but it flowed from his heart and there was nothing she could do.

His eyes fluttered open. They were dazed with pain, yet she saw that he knew her.

"I'm sorry," she said, weeping. "I lost the feather."

With a low moan, he tried to pull his arm forward, the one bound to his side. It was drenched with blood.

Though she had no idea what he wanted, she loosened the bindings. It was then she saw the golden feather tucked inside his arm, and she knew this too belonged to Ular. The queen's champion had worn it into battle as his lady's token.

Gently Laurel laid the feather on Ruarc's chest. It shone against his black battle-dress like a blade of light. As his eyes rested upon it, his face changed. Despite the pain, all grief and madness left.

"I go now . . . *aaarrcckk* . . . to seek her . . . forgiveness."

Then he was gone, and Laurel wept over him.

She had forgotten about the battle. Though the fighting swirled around her, she seemed to be in a still quiet place, the eye of the storm. Wiping away her tears, she saw that Ruarc's own troop had replaced her guard, forming a cicrle around her and their fallen chief.

Now Laurel rose up, heartbroken and raging, with the golden feather in her hand. She moved with steady purpose, and as she went, so too went the brothers, clearing a path around her. She came to the place where the Summer King was beseiged by the rest of the Fir-Fia-Caw. All his guard had been slain. Livid and screaming, he still brandished his weapons. The brothers and sisters were taking turns fighting him, slowly wearing him down. Deaf to his curses, grim and unyeilding, they kept him in the circle and all others out.

The moment Laurel arrived, Aróc, captain of the female troop, let out a screech. Falling upon the king with a flurry of blows, she disarmed him in minutes and struck him down. Then she pressed her foot against his throat.

"Do it!" she cawed at Laurel, eyes dark and terrible.

The torment she suffered from not slaying him outright was evident to Laurel; but evident, too, was the discipline of the Fir-Fia-Caw, unbroken through time and all their trials.

Laurel approached the king where he writhed on the ground like a worm caught by a bird. Though he screamed with dismay, she laid the feather across his heart and bound him instantly. There was no contest this time. Not only did she have her own strength and fury bolstered by Ular and the White Lady, but the feather was stained with Ruarc's blood. The spirit of the queen's champion came to her, renewed, and together they defeated their enemy.

"Oh God, Laurel! Are you all right?"

There was no doubt it was Ian. He looked anguished.

Aróc removed her foot from his neck, but it was Laurel who helped him up.

"Quick!" he urged her. "Get me to the bonfire! Before it's too late!"

The sun was sinking into the horizon. Fiery colors seeped through the sky, drenching the clouds red. There was little time left.

They ran for the chariot. Ian flung the king's weapons out on the ground. With his jeweled dagger, he cut a strap from the reins and thrust it at Laurel.

"Tie my hands behind my back!"

She hesitated.

"Do it!" he ordered. "You know how strong he is!"

"How does he keep returning?" she cried with frustration.

Ian grimaced. "He draws life from *me*."

White-faced, Laurel bound his hands. Taking up the reins, she goaded the horses toward Purple Mountain. Though she didn't know how to drive a chariot, the horses knew what to do. Slowly but surely they pushed their way through the press of bodies.

Then someone spotted the bound king. A hue and cry went up. Fairy troops assailed the chariot. The Fir-Fia-Caw beat them back, but more charged forward. The battle-car was like a small boat in a storm, pitched and tossed by waves of violence. It was obvious to Laurel they would soon be overcome.

At the heart of the battlefield, Grace saw their peril. Rallying her own company of cutthroat pirates, she swept toward them.

"O'Malley *abú!*" she cried.

Together the pirates and the Fir-Fia-Caw cleared a path to the foot of the mountain. There was a frenzied edge to the fighting now. Time was running out. The mission hung in the balance. Laurel urged the horses onto the road that led to the peak. Behind her, Grace and the Fir-Fia-Caw closed ranks to block the way. Shields up and weapons poised, they would hold their posts to the death.

Laurel drove the chariot onward, but couldn't stop from looking back. It seemed as if the whole battlefield was rolling in a great wave against the last line of defense. How few in number were Grace and her men, and the tall dark forms of the last of the Fir-Fia-Caw! How slight the barricade!

She saw Grace buckle under a flurry of blows. Then rise up again. But the sea queen was lurching around with her shield lowered. Laurel slackened the reins. She had to go back. To help her.

As the horses slowed down, Ian began to object but then stopped.

It was the pirate queen herself who let out a roar when she saw the chariot halt.

And Laurel drove on, face wet with tears, already mourning her friend whose cry rang out behind her.

Death is not the enemy. Light the fire!

Twenty-Six

L aurel urged the horses up the mountain. There was little time left. The last rays of sunset were fading in the sky. Soon dusk would fall. She knew which way to go. She had only to follow the trail of broken birds.

Ian gazed at them with horror.

"What have I done?"

"It wasn't you," she insisted. "It was the king."

"I am he. I carry his darkness."

"Then we're all guilty," she said grimly. "We all carry darkness."

Despite her words, she couldn't look at him. In her mind burned images of the Summer King killing Ruarc and the birds; trying to kill her. And he looked exactly like Ian. The truth was a stone inside her. She would never feel the same about him again.

The road circled the mountain, winding ever upward. As they neared the summit, the air grew sharper and colder: rare air, almost too pure for human lungs. She felt dizzy and her body tingled as if immersed in icy water.

The higher they went, the more she could see with an enhanced clarity of vision. Below her lay the island of Hy Brasil. Despite the roiling nightmare at its heart, she could see green hills beyond, untouched by war. Across the water she spied Grace's stronghold at the tip of Clare Island. And to the north, secreted in its crevice on the precipice of Croaghaun, Laheen's eyrie stood sentinel over the ocean. Gazing westward into the distance, she even caught sight of the pale shores of her homeland.

At last they reached the top of Purple Mountain. It was a level grassy space, strangely still and quiet. At its center stood a tall mound of wood. The brave songbirds did not die in vain.

Laurel led Ian to the pyre. The sun was sinking below the horizon. The waters encircling Hy Brasil glimmered gold. Beyond lay the living map of Ireland with its sea-washed coasts shadowed with mist. On every peak girding the land were the pyres raised up by Faerie as well as those made by humans who followed the old ways. And there on the sacred Hill of Tara rose the sister-pyre to that of Hy Brasil's.

Laurel looked upon the bonfires waiting to be lit. How fragile was the hope that held all together!

"Untie me," Ian said quietly.

Her eyes narrowed with suspicion. But what choice did she have? She kept the feather ready as she freed his hands.

His rage flared in an instant. The Summer King had

returned. He moved so swiftly, she hadn't time to react. The jeweled dagger, hidden in his clothes, flashed in the air. Cut her hand. With a cry she dropped the feather.

As he dragged her away from it, Laurel looked around wildly. Her weapons were in the chariot. There was no one who could help.

"Ian!" she cried desperately.

He laughed, an ominously carefree laugh. Almost affectionate.

"What sport this has been. And now you have lost your feather. You know I will kill you before I let you near it. But I do not want to kill you." He laughed again. The mildness of his tone was chilling. "I would rather make you wish for death."

Though she struggled with all her might, she couldn't escape. His grip was hard and cruel. There was a pettiness to his malice, to the delight he took in hurting her.

"Ian," she gasped.

The blue eyes were cold.

"That will not work again. Not ever. Do you not know yet? Ian and I are one. Though he resists me, his efforts are futile and will soon cease as I draw him deeper inside me. It is not as difficult as you may think. He shares much of my nature. Though you hate to see it, you know how alike we are."

"He's not like you!" she cried furiously. "He can be good and kind. He suffers for the things you've done."

That led to a laugh which froze Laurel's blood.

"The things *we* have done, you mean. Would you like to see what we have done?"

"I don't need to see it. I know already. You murdered the Queen of Clan Egli. An act of pure evil."

That laugh again. She wanted to cover her ears to block it out.

Ian's voice broke through.

"No! Please don't. I'll stop fighting you! Laurel, get away from him. You must get away!"

When the king's voice returned, it was remorseless.

"Look upon our crimes, dear Laurel. See what we did!"

Still holding her tightly, he fixed his gaze upon her and she could feel his will bearing down like a mallet. She tried to look away, but couldn't. She was drowning in the cold sea of his eyes.

And then she was surfacing, in a strange dreamlike manner, and found herself somewhere else entirely.

It took her a moment to grasp what was happening. She was scaling the precipice of Croaghaun, high above the Atlantic. Waves crashed on the rocks below. The sun was setting in the sky. A fiery red glow lit up the water and the crags around her. Though she had no control of her body, it was moving swiftly and effortlessly up the cliff.

She passed a stone platform jutting out from the rock. With a start, she recognized the ledge from which she fell the time Laheen saved her. But the broken gorge wasn't there, and the finely carved arch opened into a passage that tunneled through the mountain. Now she understood. She was in the past, before the destruction of the Temple of the Birds, reliving a memory of the Summer King.

A sick feeling came over her and with it, dread.

"No," she begged. "I don't want to see this."

Her pleas were in vain. Inexorably, pitilessly, she was drawn up the cliffside. She was powerless against him, unable even to look away. She had reached the second platform that led into the eagle's eyrie. It looked very different, with white pillars and intricate latticework trailing flowers and greenery; a lovely balcony overhanging the sea.

Now she scuttled sideways, over to one of the many niches that scarred the rock face. Here she waited in the shadows.

"No," she moaned.

For there, flying toward the royal bower, was the Queen of Clan Egli. Ular's beauty was breathtaking to behold. The great tawny feathers, so like Laheen's, were tipped with gold. The splendid wingspan was that of an angel's. The golden eyes were wise and joyous. Queen of the Eagles. Mother of the Birds.

Around her flew her raven guard with their silver-white eyes. In front flew Ruarc, her captain and champion. Alighting on the balcony, they shape-shifted to their wingless form. The golden-skinned queen was a tall, slender beauty in shining raiment. The first troop of the Fir-Fia-Caw were garbed in black battle-dress.

Ular spoke to the Captain of her guard, a light

remark, and they laughed together. Laurel couldn't take her eyes off Ruarc. He looked so youthful and passionate, so proud and noble. Her heart ached to see him before his downfall, before the Doom of Clan Egli cursed him with madness and despair.

In the shadows, Laurel felt the Summer King raise the great bow to his shoulders. Felt him nock the arrow. Though she knew it was only a memory, a deed long done and gone, she tried to scream a warning. But the only sound was the whine of the arrow as it shot through the air.

And the cruel laugh of the king as he struck at the heart of his enemy.

Then the cry of the Queen as the arrow pierced her heart, and she toppled from the ledge.

Her death cry was drowned in the wild shrieks of Ruarc as he leaped from the cliff after her, changing form in midair.

And his cry was echoed by Laheen inside the eyrie, who had felt his own heart stop and knew what it meant.

Laurel was devastated by the scene, yet the vision didn't end.

The arrow was loosed so close to the Queen, and with such force and enmity, that it tore through her body and continued onward. Over land and sea it flew, across plains and mountains, penetrating a rend in time and space caused by the weakening of the fabric of Faerie. Now it began to drop, plummeting toward a rocky coast on the eastern seaboard.

Laurel could hardly breathe. She recognized the small mountain that fell into the sea and the ledge skirting the cliff face. The ledge on which stood a young woman with long blond hair, making her way carefully. Carefully and with confidence, for she expected no mishap.

Until the arrow struck her heart.

And she fell backward into the waters below.

A new voice joined the anguished cries of Clan Egli.

"Honor!"

Twenty-Seven

L aurel went limp in the Summer King's arms. She had lost all will to oppose him. The truth was shredding everything she had come to believe in. Everything she was fighting for.

He released her, smiling cruelly as she backed away from him.

"Collateral damage. Isn't that what your people call it? An innocent casualty of a war she knew nothing about. How ironic. If Faerie did not exist, your sister would still be alive." His shrug was casual, pitiless. "Faerie is not the land of your dreams. It is the home of your nightmares."

Laurel stared around her, dazed; at the pyre that stood waiting, heaped with wood, and the bodies of the birds who had died to build it. What was the point? Shattered wings, blood-soaked branches, broken dreams. Everywhere she looked, death wiped out life. Why keep trying? There was nothing at the end but the dark of night.

Ian's voice called to her, as if from far away.

"Forgive me, Laurel. Please forgive me."

She was drowning in despair, gulping for breath

between her sobs. When he tried to reach out to her, she pushed him away, weeping for Honor, for Ular, for Ruarc and Laheen, weeping even for Ian and also for herself; and for a world where nothing was purely right or good, not even the land of hopes and dreams.

The Eve of Midsummer was passing. The last rays of sunset faded in the sky. The last shimmer of light sank beneath the waves. Dusk was falling over the land. The dark was rising.

The Summer King's voice rang with triumph.

"Let us part now. You to your world and me to mine. The time to light the fire has passed."

His voice was low, even charming. He almost sounded like Ian. "Give up your mission. Forget the world of Faerie, the cause of your sorrow."

In all that he had said and done to her, this was his greatest mistake. His undoing.

"I have a mission," she whispered.

The moment of remembering was but a blink of light, a mere flicker of hope, yet it was enough to offset the darkness.

Laurel reached out for the Summer King and pulled him toward her.

By that which you kill are you bound.

And she kissed him on the mouth.

They were back in the nether place, locked together, and her hold was so strong he couldn't move. There in the void the White Lady rode toward them, and Laurel saw that she smiled with Honor's smile. And with the strength of the kin-blood of she who was slain, Laurel vanquished the Summer King and threw him down.

As he lay at her feet she felt hatred surge through her. She wished him dead, but she couldn't kill him; certainly not in cold blood. And what would happen to Ian if the king died?

She sensed Ian beside her. Torment echoed in his voice, and it seemed as if he could read her mind.

"I'd kill him for you, no matter what it did to me, but we need him to light the fire. He's the one who has the spark."

His words filled her with dismay and dread.

"Then *you* must control him, Ian. I've done all I can."

They were back on the summit of Purple Mountain. Ian fell to his knees and buried his face in his hands.

"I killed her. Oh God, I killed your sister."

Laurel dropped beside him, too numb to respond. She couldn't console him. Yet she made a last effort to speak.

"Death is not the enemy," she said hoarsely. "Light the fire."

Though lost in his own nightmare, Ian stretched his hand toward the pyre. She could see the titanic struggle in his features as he fought to command the king. Now a single blue spark flew from his fingers and struck the branches. The wood began to burn, but the flames were slow to rise. Would the other bonfires see the beacon?

The sun had set. The sky was gray with twilight.

"Is it too late?" she whispered.

From above came the beating of wings. A golden shadow fell over the pyre as Laheen descended. He landed on the bonfire, but before the flames could touch him, he rose up like a phoenix, bearing in his beak a burning branch. And as he soared into the sky, light exploded around him.

The signal was seen on every hill and mountain. The Midsummer Fire had been lit.

It was as if fireworks were embroidered on a cloth of gold. Wildfire snaked around the coast of Ireland as one pyre was ignited after the other. When the circle of flame enfolded the land, Midir stepped forward on the Hill of Tara. From the star on his forehead flashed a ray of light that set the heart-fire ablaze. As the last link was made and the chain was forged, a cord of light flared. *The Fáinne na Gréine.* The Ring of the Sun.

And then the Summer King returned.

With a last gasp, he lurched toward the fire and stepped inside it. As he raised his arms, Laurel knew what he meant to do. He would use the fire as a weapon once more, and destroy them all.

Steeling herself against the pain, she reached through the flames. It was the only way to stop him. She almost fainted; not from the scorching heat, but from the surge of power. Storms of light whirled around her. She stood at the heart of the sun. It was only for a dazzling second and then, as she caught him, they were back in the void.

Laurel saw immediately that it was no longer her battle. Two fiery columns writhed together in mortal combat. Within the streaks of light, dim shapes were visible:

the Summer King as she remembered him from her vision, and Ian. Even in that nether place, the Ring of the Sun burned, and both were drawing on its power. For the first time since the king had claimed him, Ian was on equal ground. And while the king had only rage to goad him, Ian fought also from grief, remorse, and love.

When she saw who was winning, Laurel's heart lifted. The Summer King was on his knees. In those final moments, she thought Ian would kill him.

But Ian's stance was not that of a warrior. He opened his arms. There was strange pity in his voice, though he spoke fiercely.

"It ends here. I am no longer your shadow. You are mine."

The Summer King howled, knowing that his doom had come, but there was nothing he could do. As Ian embraced him like a fallen brother who must yet be owned, the king was subsumed.

Out of the void and back in the fire, Laurel expected the worst; but Ian put his arms around her and kept her safe, even as he surrendered the stolen power to Faerie. As part of the circle, she was able to see the end. The *Fáinne na Gréine* inundated the Realm with waves of light and energy, healing all in its path. When it reached Midir where he stood on Tara, it illuminated his person, bringing him into full knowledge of himself and his sovereignty.

Just before Ian took her from the flames, Laurel glimpsed something else: a slender figure ran across the Hill of Tara, into the arms of the High King of Faerie.

Twenty-Eight

Once the Ring of the Sun was forged, the battle of Hy Brasil came to an end. The darker creatures fled the field, returning to the shadows from whence they came. The sea fairies threw down their arms to surrender. Yet instead of wails of defeat, ragged cheers rose up and then rapidly swelled as the word spread like wildfire. Clan Egli had made peace with the Summer King. The strife in the West was over.

The Amethyst Palace was thrown open to fairy revels. A thousand lights glittered from the chandeliers and were reflected in the mullioned windows. Delicate harmonies filled the air. Dancers twirled on floors of purple glass between fluted pillars. A fabulous feast was served on jeweled dishes; wines flowed from fountains. Music and laughter echoed everywhere.

Though they had pardoned the Summer King, the Fir-Fia-Caw did not attend the celebrations. With Aróc as their Captain, the twelve survivors of the battle retrieved the bodies of their slain and carried them back to Slievemore. There they held funereal rites for their fallen leader and comrades. It would be long before they were seen in the two worlds again, but they would return; for not all that is gone is gone forever.

Laurel had also declined to join the festivities. Unlike the fairies, she could not make war one minute and carouse the next. Her experiences on the battlefield and inside the fire had left her solemn and pensive. She was amazed she had survived. And she was mourning the loss of Grace. Though she now trusted that her friend existed elsewhere, she missed her all the same.

Sequestered in a bower high in the castle, she sat in a window seat overlooking the gardens. She wore a gown of green silk with a golden bodice. A crespine of emeralds bound her hair. Outside, sporadic fireworks illumined the night, while burning tapers lit up the spacious lawns. This was Ian's domain, over which he was now lord and sovereign. But though Laheen and the Fir-Fia-Caw had forgiven the Summer King, she had not. From the time he took her from the fire, she wouldn't speak to him, and though he ordered his people to look after her, she refused his company. She had made it clear that she would remain in her chambers till Faerie fulfilled its promise to her.

And yet, as Laurel waited for her sister, she grew nervous and uneasy. Beneath her anticipation, she found herself nursing a vague foreboding.

Her solitude was broken when Grace herself strode into the room, dressed in pirate gear.

"I thought you died!" Laurel cried.

Overjoyed, she jumped up to greet her friend but

stopped short of a hug. Grace was not the type for shows of affection. They clasped hands instead.

"We shall make this brief," said the sea queen, briskly. "There are two things I like to avoid—a lingering death and a lingering good-bye."

Laurel spied the bandages under her clothing.

"Close enough!" Grace agreed, when she caught her look. "But I have an excellent leech, a Parsee I rescued from a corsair slave ship. It takes more than a few hobgoblins to kill an Irishwoman!"

Laurel laughed along with her, but grew serious again.

"I want to thank you—"

"No lingering! 'Twas a great gamble, well-played and most entertaining. Fare thee well, my foreign girleen, till we meet again on the high seas."

To Laurel's surprise, the pirate queen smothered her in a warm embrace concluded with a hearty thump on the back. Then she gripped Laurel's shoulders and stared into her eyes.

"What you face next is hardest of all. Be of good courage."

Laurel caught her breath. She didn't ask what Grace meant. She couldn't.

It was not long after the sea queen departed that Laurel had a second visitor. He sidled into the room, his rust-colored beard twitching nervously. He was dressed as the Fool from the O'Malley deck of cards in a costume patterned with red and silver diamonds, and a peaked cap with a bell. In his hand he carried a slender rod with more bells attached, shaped like silver apples. Yet despite the merry garb, there was a serious air about him and neither of them laughed.

"The king has sent me to escort you to the ball."

"I'm not going near him or his feast!" she said furiously.

The cluricaun took off his cap and started to fidget.

Laurel returned to her window seat, expecting him to leave. Instead, he shuffled over to her, all bells tinkling, and sat down opposite her. Though he waited patiently, she continued to ignore him, gazing down at the garden. Immediately below was a great labyrinth of boxed hedge trimmed in the shapes of birds and animals. Like the lawns and flower beds, it was lighted by torches that flickered in the night breeze.

From where she sat, she could see the solution to the maze.

"There's nothing like a bird's-eye view," she murmured.

Sounds of music and merriment spilled out of the palace windows and onto the terraces. She watched the fairies, bright as fireflies, playing chase and calling to each other with peals of laughter. Some danced barefoot over the grass that glittered with evening dew.

"Will ye not join the hooley?" said the cluricaun. His voice was unusually gentle. "'Twould do ye a power of good. Ye deserve a bit of happiness after all's been said and done."

"I'm not here to have fun. I'm just waiting for what you promised me."

Her voice trembled. She noticed that the cluricaun looked apprehensive himself and she recognized the shifty look in his eyes. He squirmed in his seat, making the bells jitter. It was as if a cold hand suddenly clutched her heart. All the warnings rang in her mind. *They are not like us. You always get more than you bargained for. The fairies are tricksters. They can't be trusted.*

"You said I could save her," she whispered.

As she implored him with mute appeal, she saw something much older and graver look back at her, and there was compassion in that gaze.

"The time has come," he said quietly, "and you must face it. 'Twas not the Summer King who sent me to escort you. He has stayed away, mindful of your feelings. 'Tis the High King himself who awaits your pleasure. With him has come—"

The cluricaun didn't get to finish his sentence. Laurel had already run out of the room. Catching up her long skirts, she raced down the marble staircase that seemed to spiral forever, and into the great hall.

Like Cinderella arriving late at the ball, she was dazzled by the scene before her. Beautiful sea fairies mingled with the Gentry of the High King's court, all dressed in rich raiment and sparkling jewels. As Laurel made her way through them, the throng parted before her, bowing and curtseying as if she was the guest of honor. And as they drew aside, she saw ahead of her two stately figures enthroned on the dais.

It was Midir whom Laurel recognized first. He wore a golden tunic sprayed with stars and a fiery mantle. His red-gold hair shone like the sunset. As he stood up to greet her with a smile of friendship, beside him rose another, her hand resting on his arm.

Laurel could barely take in what she was looking at. It seemed so long since they had last met. An eternity of loss and despair, guilt and mourning.

Tall and fair, Honor was dressed in a silken gown fili-greed with silver. Her long blond hair was wreathed with white blossoms. She looked more elegant and beautiful than Laurel had ever seen her; and though this was the prize, so eagerly sought, it was almost too much to accept.

Almost.

"Honor!"

She ran to her twin and, nearly fainting with happiness, clasped her in her arms. How light she felt! Like an armful of air!

"Is it you? Is it really you?" she said, touching Honor's face, hugging her again.

It was too good, too incredible, too miraculous to be true.

They were both crying and laughing.

"I had a dream," Honor told her. "I fell out of the sky and into the sea, but before I could drown, you fished me out and wrapped me in a shawl of golden feathers."

"Did I?" said Laurel happily.

More laughter. More tears.

"Then I dreamed you needed *me*," Honor continued. "And I rode out on a pale horse to bring you succor."

"Yes, yes, you did," said Laurel, too dazed to really hear. "Oh God, I've missed you so much! I can't believe you're here! I've dreamed and hoped and worked for this. And I'm sorry, I really am. I've so wanted to say that to you. I'm really sorry."

"Sorry?" said her twin, laughing. "For all you have done for me?"

"No, not that. For before . . . I should've . . . I was so selfish. Just thinking of myself."

"And did I think of you?" Her sister's voice was gentle. "Though some might call it selfish, we each must follow our own star. It's not right that you should blame yourself. I chose my destiny, and it is you who have brought me to it."

That was the moment when an icy sliver entered Laurel's heart. And though she could already see the truth emerging, she made a last effort to deny it.

"I was told if the Midsummer Fire was lit, if the Ring of the Sun was forged, that I could save you. That's what they promised me."

"You did save me," her twin said softly. "You woke me from a sleep in which I was lost, and here I am, in Faerie, where I wish to be."

"But . . . but aren't you coming home? To Mom and Dad? To me?"

"Oh, my dear one." Honor touched Laurel's face and took her hands. "I cannot return to the Earthworld. You know that. I died there."

The pain was so strong that Laurel thought it might break her, and yet she wasn't really surprised. Wasn't this what she had dreaded all evening? The true reason for her reluctance to join the feast? Deep inside, she had always known what lay in wait for her. But against it she had clutched a handful of hopes—that Honor would come home, live out her life, change and grow old along with her. Now those hopes withered like fairy gold turned to dried leaves in her hand, crumbling into dust.

She stood pale and trembling.

It was Midir who stepped forward and bowed to her. A hush fell over the hall as he spoke in solemn tones.

"We thank thee for all thou hast done for Faerie. By restoring the *Fáinne na Gréine* you have healed our land from the hurt caused by the death of the First King. And not only have you brought me into my kingship but you have given us our Queen. On this day do I declare thee a Companion of Faerie. As with all so named, thou shalt not suffer the Spell of Forgetting, and thou shalt be called again into the Kingdom. Though you have lost your sister in the Earthworld, you have not lost her in Faerie."

Laurel bowed her head to acknowledge his words, but couldn't yet speak.

Honor clapped her hands so that the music and dancing resumed in the hall.

"All's well that ends well," she said with a little laugh. "I am in Faerie and, rumor tells me, you are in love?"

Laurel flinched at her twin's quick change of mood. She was as flighty as a fairy.

Honor looked around the hall expectantly.

"But where is the Summer King? Did he not accompany you?"

Laurel couldn't hide her anguish.

Her sister was dismayed.

"Have you not forgiven him? Oh El! Was he not both wicked and blameless?"

"I . . . I can't forgive him. I won't. Not ever. And I can't stand the sight of him. Every time I look at him, I hear him laughing as he shoots the arrow. You may be happy, but if it wasn't for him you'd still be alive and living out your life with me."

Honor shook her head sadly.

"Alas that my joy must bring you pain."

Despite her words, Laurel saw with a pang that her twin didn't really understand. She was a fairy now, and felt no sorrow in the parting of death. Laurel was beginning to notice other differences; the faint shimmer of gold on her sister's skin, the fey look in her eyes.

Honor turned to Midir to take his arm, and together the royal couple glided over the floor. All the bright lords and ladies bowed low to the High King and High Queen of Faerie, and as they passed by, a beautiful voice sang out.

⟶ ⟵

Cónaímid i spreach solais
Mear mar eite fáinleoige,
Lá grianmhar is lá pianmhar.

Ansin titeann an contráth:
Agus eitlíonn an t-éan abhaile san oíche.

Sheol mé long dúghorm an stuimine oir
Thar sáile áiféalta réalta go brách,
Thrasnaigh mé imeall tine an chaomhnóra
Is ghaibh mé isteach sa Bhrionglóid.

As the words shape-shifted in Laurel's mind so that
she understood them, she realized it was Honor singing.

We live in a flicker of light
Swift as swallows' wings,
A day of sunshine and pain.

Then dusk falls:
And the bird flies home in the evening.

I have sailed the blue ship with the silver prow
Over the sea of eternal stars,
I have crossed the guardian's rim of fire
And passed into the Dreaming.

With the elegy still echoing in her mind, Laurel slipped

away from the ball and stepped out onto the terrace. She did not feel like dancing or feasting. The sadness enfolded her like a cloak.

The sun was rising on the horizon, tinting the sky a rosy gold. Midsummer's Eve was over and the dawn of the summer solstice had come. Behind her, the music and revelry grew mute. Only now did Laurel acknowledge that a full year had passed since her sister's death. There was no going back. Her twin would never return.

The days of quiet mourning had begun.

EPILOGUE

It was early morning. The promenade of Bray beach was deserted. A pale mist crept over the sea's surface as the sun began to warm the waters. The tide was receding. The sand was strewn with seaweed and torqued pieces of driftwood. As the waves retreated, pebbles clinked together with a musical rhythm. A lone heron stood in the shallows, its wings folded like an old man with his hands in his pockets, its feathers tinged with red. Letting out a squawk, it took to the air and flew toward Bray Head. The cluricaun? Laurel followed his flight till he disappeared beyond the cliffs.

Her way of looking at the world had changed forever. There was so much more to life than what met the eye. It was a truth she cherished, a consolation for all that she had lost and may yet lose. And though it inspired in her a longing for an existence beyond her, she accepted the longing itself as a reminder of the truth.

That morning, she had gone into her grandfather's library to place the golden feather in one of his books. She chose a collection of poetry by W. B. Yeats and found a page with a poem that she liked.

—⌀ ⌀—

Come away, O human child!
To the waters and the wild
With a faery, hand in hand,
For the world's more full of weeping than you
  can understand.

She was just about to close the book when she glanced over at the fireplace. There sat the cluricaun in his old red suit, puffing on his pipe.

"It was my Granda who first bound the Summer King, wasn't it?"

The cluricaun nodded.

"Is that why Honor and I were chosen for the mission?"

"Yes and no. Ye might call it the Faerie version of the oul Grandfather Paradox. Do ye know it?"

She didn't.

"Bit of a head stagger," he said. "If ye go back in time and kill your grandfather before he met your grandmother, then ye could never have been born, so therefore ye couldn't have gone back in time. Got that?"

"Almost," she admitted.

"Well, your mission and his is the same difference. But do ye really need to know the whole story? I never could agree with people that want every happening sorted out and explained. Where's the mystery in that? Where's the magic?"

Laurel recognized the shifty look in his eyes.

"I like things explained," she said evenly. "Just give me the facts."

The cluricaun wriggled in his chair.

"You've got to keep in mind, we were workin' in the dark. We knew the king had been banished for his crimes, but the who and the where were unbeknownst. We went lookin' for the human that did the job, and bejapers it took a while. 'Twas the golden feather tipped us off to your grandfather. But we were slow to cop on to Ian, more's the pity, and by the time we did, he had nicked the feather and scarpered for Achill. That was the Summer King's plan, ye see. His *scáth* was born near your Granda, and he had only to wait for the right time to act. Ian himself knew nothin' about the king, but was always under his sway and sufferin' because of it."

The little man paused as if expecting Laurel to say something about Ian, but she didn't. She would never be one who spoke freely about her personal life, especially the painful parts.

"To begin at the beginning," he resumed. "'Twas a dark day, that Midsummer's Eve, when the Queen of Clan Egli was murdered and the Temple of the Birds destroyed. It all happened so fast, Faerie was shook to the core. Finvarra, the High King at the time, went to Laheen in his eyrie and swore to punish the culprit.

"There was many in the Court wanted him kilt and be done with it, but Finvarra didn't like to lose the Ring of the Sun forever. He was never in a hurry to let go of a good thing. And here's the bit of the story that we only know now, since our new High King came into his own.

"'Twas agreed between Finvarra and Laheen that the Summer King would be imprisoned, and the last of the Fir-Fia-Caw would be his jailers. The Old Eagle gave Finvarra one of Ular's feathers to vanquish the king in her name. He also told Finvarra about a family on Achill who had the same claim against the Summer King, for his arrow would kill one of their own."

Laurel frowned, unsure of what she was hearing.

"Finvarra was pleased with the news. He was always a belt-and-braces man, and liked to get two for the price of one. To counter the power of the Summer King were two things to bind him: the Queen's feather and the kin-blood of the slain. On top of that, the job would be done by a mortal, in the high tradition of Faerie."

"Wait a minute," she interrupted, her mind spinning. "Are you saying they knew in the past that Honor would die in the future?"

The cluricaun nodded reluctantly.

Angry tears pricked Laurel's eyes. This was a betrayal she couldn't have expected.

"Why did Laheen let it happen?" she demanded. "Why didn't he stop the Summer King?"

The cluricaun heaved a deep sigh.

"Rare are the times the Old Ones intervene in the worlds, and when they do, 'tis only for the good of all. Yet it is told in the tale of the Doom of Clan Egli that when Ular came out of Faerie to be his bride, Laheen warned her that she would die one day at the hand of his enemy, and he bade her return to her homeland. But she who loved him chose her own destiny to be the Queen of Clan Egli and Mother of the Birds, and long and glorious was her reign till the hour of her death."

"At least she had a choice," Laurel said bitterly. "No one warned Honor!"

The little man's look was sympathetic, but he shook his head.

"That isn't true, *girseach*, and well you know it. Didn't Midir himself try to dissuade her from the path, though he knew nothing of her fate? One way or another, all are warned who enter the Perilous Realm."

She knew he was right, but she didn't want to admit it. She would have argued further if her grandfather hadn't walked into the room.

"Oh," he said, looking around. "You're alone. I thought I heard voices."

The cluricaun began making faces at Granda. Laurel's anger dissipated and she had to stifle a laugh.

Her grandfather spotted the golden feather jutting out from the book in her hand.

"You found it!"

"Yes, I did," she murmured, offering it to him.

He placed it reverently to his lips.

"Who gave it to you, Granda?" she asked, curious to see what he would say.

He frowned a moment, and looked a little lost.

"It was a long time ago . . ."

He moved toward the chair where the cluricaun was seated, and the little man disappeared with a last wink to Laurel. Sitting down, Granda gazed thoughtfully at the feather.

"I've never told anyone this before, but I've always believed that I was taken by the fairies when I was young. I don't have much to go on, only impressions and fleeting images, as if from an old story or an old dream. When I try to catch hold of it, it disappears like mist in the sunshine." He smiled a little sadly. "It was a beautiful story, a beautiful dream, and I have been chasing it all my life. That's why I chose, as a young man, to study folklore at the university and not law, as my father wished me to do."

He let out a deep sigh.

"It will come back to you one day," Laurel assured him quietly.

He looked at her fondly and nodded.

"As your grandmother would say, hope burns eternal in the human heart."

Laurel continued along the promenade, refreshed by the breezes that blew across the sea. Turning her face to the sky, she felt the light kiss of the sun. Soon she would leave Ireland, even as she had left Achill, and the shadow of many partings hung over her.

It was after she had said farewell to Honor that Laurel wandered into the palace gardens newly bright with morning. Stepping out of her golden slippers, she walked barefoot across the lawns toward the maze. The grass was cool and damp with dew. As she entered the green shadows of the labyrinth, she inhaled the perfume of leaves and flowers. Remembering the solution from the view above, she navigated the winding pathways till she reached the center. And there at the heart of the puzzle, in the gazebo made of living birch, he waited for her.

He wore a light-blue tunic trimmed with silver, and a dark-blue mantle pinned with a brooch in the shape of a flame. The raven-black hair fell to his shoulders, bound with a circlet of sapphires. The features were Ian's—the blue eyes, pale skin, and full red mouth—but the torment and anger were gone. His face was kingly and serene.

"Lady, art thou well?"

Torn by too many warring emotions, she could hardly speak. Her eyes rested on the brooch.

"You're the Summer King."

He took a moment to respond and when he did, he sounded as heavy-hearted as she.

"I am Ian but, yes, I am also the king. Yet his fiery nature which did such harm is bound inside me. I can contain it. I am stronger now . . . thanks to you."

She remained silent.

He pressed on.

"I wish you to know that I will remain in Hy Brasil. My people have welcomed the change in me. I will do my best to redeem my kingdom and to restore what I can to those I have wronged."

She couldn't stop herself.

"You're leaving our world?"

"I was never happy there. I did not belong. Strangely enough, or perhaps not so, I always felt that my real home, my true life, was elsewhere. There is nothing to hold me to the Earthworld."

She heard the edge in his voice, the unasked question, but she ignored it.

"What about your parents?" she said, instead.

"I brought only pain into their lives. They will recover from their loss and be all the happier for it."

She knew in her heart it was wrong. Her whole being cried out against it. But still she didn't speak.

The labyrinth was already dissolving around her when he bade her farewell.

And then they were no longer in the palace gardens on Hy Brasil.

They were in the sea beyond Achill Head.

It was a shock of murderous wet and cold, white foam and icy water. Laurel's instincts acted instantly to save her. Though her soaked jeans were weighing her down, she kicked off her shoes and thrashed against the waves to keep afloat.

Ian was nearby, flailing wildly.

The Lady of Doona was just beyond them. Gracie was spinning the wheel, shouting frantically to her passengers to keep their heads up. A freak wave had washed them overboard.

Now Laurel heard Ian repeat his last words, just before he sank.

"Fare thee well, beloved."

She tread the freezing water, hanging on by sheer will. Long moments to survive before Gracie could come. Moments that seemed to stretch forever. She knew what was happening. She understood what he was doing. He had to die in one world to live fully in the other.

The knowledge struck her heart like an arrow.

"NO!"

She dove beneath the water.

If I have not love, I am nothing.

Desperately she searched the shadowy depths. There, at last, she spied him. Sinking like a stone. Too far. Too deep.

She had to surface for breath, gasping wildly, sucking in as much air as possible.

Then she dove again.

Love is patient. Love is kind.

There he was, a blur in the darkness, falling downward. Though the Summer King knew how to swim, Ian was making no effort to save himself.

It bears all things.

Her lungs were bursting. Soon she would pass the point of no return, but she continued to swim downward. Now she reached out to grasp his hand. Their fingertips brushed.

He looked up in surprise.

Her body writhed with pain. Lights were exploding behind her eyes. She had come too far. She was drowning.

Love never fails.

He kicked his legs fiercely and caught her on his way

up, surging through the water with all the strength at his command. They broke the waves together.

Love is as strong as death.

After Gracie had hauled them into the boat, they huddled together, wrapped in blankets. Their teeth chattered, their lips were purple, their hair was flattened against their skulls.

"It was my right to go home," he murmured, though with no real force.

Her voice shook from the cold as she argued with him.

"Your kingdom can wait. You were born into this world. It's your duty to live here."

"Are we ever going to agree on anything?" he said, managing to grin.

She took his hands and held them tightly.

"Life isn't as magical here, and you're not the only one who feels like you don't belong, or that it's better somewhere else. But there *are* things worth living for. And the best part is you never know what's going to happen next."

She lifted his fingers to her lips.

The blue eyes of Faerie stared into hers.

"Eejit," he said softly.

They were kissing each other when Gracie stuck her head out of the wheelhouse.

"Keep it up! Heats the blood!"

Laurel grinned to herself as she left the promenade and crossed the road, walking toward the street where Ian lived. Her smile widened when she remembered how his mother looked that first day he returned; when her son lifted her up in a bear hug. Behind them, the minister's face had crumpled as if all his prayers had been answered.

The change in Laurel was obvious, too. Though still in mourning, she was lighter and happier, more at peace with herself.

Only Nannaflor expressed no surprise.

"I always said those two would be good for each other," she pointed out to everyone.

Laurel was still lost in her memories when she heard the motorcycle behind her.

As Ian drew up alongside, she saw, for a moment, a dark-blue chariot with fiery wings.

He removed his helmet and caught her around the waist to pull her close.

"I got fed up waiting for you," he said.

She laughed and kissed him. Then he handed her the spare helmet. Before she climbed on the bike, she asked the question she had been wondering about.

"Is your name 'Ian' in Hy Brasil? I mean, is it the Summer King's name?"

"Nah. That's my human name, the one my parents gave me."

"What's your other name then?"

Mischief flashed in his eyes.

"You wouldn't be able to pronounce it."

She gave him a little punch, then donned her helmet and sat behind him.

He kicked the bike into a roar, and they sped away.

As they turned the corner, onto the road that led up into the town, Laurel cast a last glance over the sea. Where the morning mist mingled with the sunlight, a vision shone on the waves. The White Lady upon her pale horse. Though she was far in the distance, on the rim of the horizon, Laurel could see her features. At first she thought she was looking at Honor's face. Then she realized she was looking at her own.

GLOSSARY
Key to Pronunciation
and Meaning of Irish Words
(plus a bit of Hebridean Gaelic)

a leanbh (aah laan-iv)—my child, little one (vocative)

A stór (aah store) – sweetheart. Literally, "treasure"

abú (aah-boo)—forever!

Agus fasann úlla agus géaga cumhra ar an chrann is ísle bláth. (aw-gus faw-sunn oo-laah aw-gus gay-gaah koo-raah air awn 'hrawn iss eesh-leh blaw)—And apples and fragrant blossoms grow on the low branch. A line from an anonymous love poem c. 1800, *"An Draighnéann Donn,"* The Blackbird. See *An Leabhar Mór, The Great Book of Gaelic* (Canongate Books, 2002).

An bhfuil Gaeilge agat? (awn will gwale-guh aah-gut?)— Do you speak Irish? Literally, "Do you have Irish?"

An grá a théid fán chroí, cha scaoiltear as é go brách. (awn graw aah hade fawn cree, haw squeel-tur awss ay goe brock)—When the heart finds what it loves, it will never lose it. A line from an anonymous love poem c. 1800 called *"Tá Mé i Mo Shuí,"* Sitting Up (All Night).

See *An Leabhar Mór, The Great Book of Gaelic* (Canongate Books, 2002).

An Réilt (awn rale-t)—The Star

An Sasanaigh sibh? (awn sass-a-nig shiv)—Are you English? (you, plural)

boctogai (bock-togue-ee)—the word used on the western coast of Donegal (and here moved a bit south) for fairies who live in the sea or in caves by the shore. They are known to be wilder and far less friendly to humans than their counterparts further inland.

Bruíon Amhra (bree-un ow-ra)— The Wonderful Strife, term used for Faerie warfare.

Bunadh na Farraige (bun-naah naah fair-uh-guh)—The Kindred of the Sea, i.e., sea fairies

Caisleán Riabhach (cawsh-lawn ree-a-vock)—anglicized to Castlerea, literally "Brindled Castle"

Ceol as binne de gach ceol. (key-ole awss bi-neh jeh gock key-ole)—Music sweeter than all music. A line from the poem *"A'Chomhachag"* by Dómhnall mac Fhionnlaigh Nan Dán, c. 1540–1610. See *An Leabhar Mór, The Great Book of Gaelic* (Canongate Books, 2002).

Cill Dara (kill darr-aah)—Anglicized to Kildare, literally "Church of the Oak Tree."

cluricaun—anglicized version of *clúrachán* (clew-raa-cawn), also *lucharachán* (lew-cur-aah-cawn)—literally, "puny creature, pigmy, dwarf." Belonging to the class of solitary fairies, cluricauns are distant cousins of leprechauns, but they are not shoemakers by trade, rather they are distillers of *poitín*. They hide barrels of whiskey the way leprechauns hide pots of gold. Preferring to dress in red as opposed to the leprechaun's green, cluricauns are known to be better-humored than leprechauns and friendlier to humans, perhaps because they are usually inebriated. See note concerning the *Fir Dhearga* and Santa Claus.

Cónaímid i spreach solais
Mear mar eite fáinleoige
Lá grianmhar is lá pianmhar.

Ansin titeann an contráth:
Agus eitlíonn an t-éan abhaile san oíche.

Sheol mé long dúghorm an stuimine óir
Thar sáile áiféalta réalta go brách,
Thrasnaigh mé imeall tine an chaomhnóra
Is ghaibh mé isteach sa Bhrionglóid.

(cawn-aah-midge jeh sprack saw-liss

marr mair etch-uh fown-loy-guh
law gree-un-varr iss law pee-un-varr.

awn-shinn titch-unn awn cawn-traw
aw-guss etch-leen awn chain aah-wallya sawn ee-huh

hy'ole may lawng doo-yorrum awn stuh-minn-uh orr
harr soil aah-fale-tuh rale-tuh goe brock
h'rass-nee may im-uh'l chinn awn c'weeve-norr-aah
iss yaw-iv may iss-chalk saah vreen-gloyd)

We live in a flicker of light
Swift as swallows' wings,
A day of sunshine and pain.

Then dusk falls:
And the bird flies home in the evening.

I have sailed the blue ship with the silver prow
Over the sea of eternal stars,
I have crossed the guardian's rim of fire
And passed into the Dreaming.*

*English poem by O.R. Melling, translated into Irish by
Findabhair ní Fhaoláin.

craic (krack)—Conversation, chat, but now generally
means "fun." Often used with *ceoil (kee-ole)*—
"music"—e.g. people go out for night of *craic agus*

ceoil—"fun and music." Note the difference an accent can make: *cráic* (crock) means "buttocks" or "anus"!

crannóg (krawn-ogue)—ancient fortified lake dwellings built on pilings to form a manmade island, literally "piece of wood, wooden pole"

curach (kurr-uck)—"currach" in Hiberno-English, a coastal rowing boat "as old as Ireland herself." With a frame constructed of wood and originally covered with animal skins, currachs are now covered with tarred canvas, giving them their distinctive black beetle look. They can vary in size from six feet to twenty-six feet and also in shape, each style having the name of the area in which they are built, e.g. the Achill currach or Kerry currach. According to ancient manuscripts, St. Brendan the Navigator sailed to North America in a large currach in the sixth century A.D. before the Vikings got there. In 1976–77, the Irish adventurer Tim Severin proved that this was possible when he sailed from Ireland to Newfoundland in a leather boat! See *The Brendan Voyage,* by Tim Severin.

eejit—Hiberno-English slang word for "idiot" (but less offensive and often affectionate)

Éist nóiméad. (aysht noe-made)—Listen a minute.

Fáinne na Gréine (fawnya na grane-aah)—Ring of the Sun

Fir Dhearga (feer yarr-i-guh)—Red Men or Red People, i.e., a particular clan of fairies who like to drink to excess, thus having red faces and red noses. Another name for a cluricaun. Note: the *Fir Dhearga* claim Santa Claus as their most famous son.

Fir-Fia-Caw (fur fee-aah caw)—author's anglicized version of *Fir Fiacha (Dubh)* (fur fee-aah caw doove), literally, "Raven Men" or "Raven People." Ruarc is Captain of the first troop of seven brothers, the other six being Fráecc, Duarcán, Affric, Feradác, Uillecc, and Ceartacc. The second troop of seven brothers is led by Cádac, the other six being Adarcc, Fecíne, Cellacc, Fiacc, Máedoc, and Corcc. Note: the word *fiacha* (fee-aah-caw) means "raven" either alone or with the added word *dubh* (doove or doo) meaning "black." *Fiacha* is also the Irish word for "hunter." Ravens are known to be the companions of golden eagles and wolves, with whom they may hunt.

Gairm slógaidh (geer-um slow-geh)—call to arms, hosting, mobilization

. *Gile na gile* (geela naah geela)—Brightness of brightness. The first line of an *aisling* (ashling) or "vision" poem by Aogán Ó Rathaille, c. 1675–1729.

girseach (geer-shuck)—young girl

Go cinnte (goe kinn-cheh)—Certainly! Indeed!

Go hálainn! (goe haw-leen)—Beautiful!

"Go mbhfearr léi lán loinge de Chloinn Conroi agus de Chloinn Mic an Allaidh ná lán loinge d'ór." (go marr lay lawn ling duh clinn cawn-ree awgg-is de clinn mick awn alley nawh lawn ling deh orr)—"I'd rather have a shipful of Conroys and McAnallys than a shipful of gold." (Words historically attributed to Grace O'Malley, c. 1530–1603.)

Gráinne na gCearrbhach (grawn-ya naah gair-vock) Grace of the Gamblers

Gránuaile (grawn-ya-wale)—shortened version of *Gráinne Uí Mhaille,* Grace O'Malley, literally "Grace, a female of the O'Malleys." Note: Grace is not an invention of the author, but a real historical figure. The usual dates given for her are c. 1530–1603.

Inisbófin (in-ish boe-finn)—Island of the White Cow

Leitir Bhreac (letcher vrack)—Anglicized to Letterfrack, literally, "Speckled Hillside."

Loch Béal Séad (lock bale shade)—Lake of the Jeweled Mouth

Mná-Fia-Caw (muh-naw fee-aah caw)—author's anglicized version of *Mná Fiacha (Dubh)* (muh-naw fee-aah caw doove), literally, "Raven Women." Aróc is Captain of the troop of seven sisters, the other six being Ceara, Fuince, Cearcc, Fiacca, Créde, and Duarcca. Note: the word *fiacha* (fee-aah-caw) means "raven" either alone or with the added word *dubh* (doove or doo) meaning "black." *Fiacha* is also the Irish word for "hunter." Ravens are known to be the companions of golden eagles and wolves, with whom they may hunt.

mo chara (mo harr-ah)—my friend, but there is also a sense of "dear one."

Na Daoine Maithe (na deeny maw-haw)—The Fairy Folk, literally "The Good People."

Na Daoine Sídhe (na deeny shee)—The Fairy Folk, literally "The People of the Fairy Mounds."

Ní cladhaire í. (nee kly-raah ee.)—She is no milksop.

Ní hea. (nee hah)—No.

Níl sé 'na lá, níl a ghrá
Níl sé 'na lá, na baol ar maidin
Níl sé 'na lá, níl a ghrá
*Solas ard atá sa ghealaigh.**

(neel shinn law, neel aah graw
neel shinn law, naa bwale air mawh-jinn

neel shinn law, neel aah graw
saw-lis ord aah-taw saa gy'alley)

It is not yet day, it's not, my love
It is not yet day, nor yet the morning
It is not yet day, it's not, my love
For the moon is shining brightly.

*Traditional, collected on Tory Island, off the north coast
of Donegal by members of Clannad.

Oró! sé do bheatha 'bhaile! (3x)
*Tá Gránuaile ag teacht thar sáile.**

(oh-roe! shay doe vaah-haa wawl-ya!
taw grawn-ya-wale egg chawk't harr soyle-ya)

Oho! head home for your life!
Gránuaile is coming over the sea.

*Though it is little known these days (even among the
Irish), this song was written by Padraic Pearse
(1879–1916), schoolteacher and leader of the Easter
Rising or Irish Rebellion in 1916. He was executed by the
British. The author has taken some liberties with the
song by replacing the last line of the chorus with a line
from one of the verses. Also *Gráinne Mhaol* has been
anglicized to the more commonly known Granuaile.

pisreog (pish-rogue) *or piseog* (pish-ogue)—a fairy charm or spell

Pog mo thóin (pogue moe hone)—Kiss my ass.

poitín (puh-cheen)—home-distilled (illicit) whiskey, poteen, i.e., Irish moonshine

Raidió na Gaeltachta (raah-dee-oh naah gwale-tawk-taw)—Irish-language radio station founded in 1972 to serve the Irish-speaking areas of Ireland, now listened to countrywide.

ruaille-buaille (rool-ya bool-ya)—uproar, commotion, tumult. In Hiberno-English becomes "roolie-boolie" or "roolye-boolye."

scáth (scaw)—shadow

Sídhe (shee)—plural word meaning "fairy folk" that can be used as a noun or adjective. It is understood to be related to the Old Irish word *síd* used for a mound or hill-fort, in which the fairy folk are said to dwell. *Sídhe* is a variant spelling of the more modern *sí*.

Slievemore (shleeve-more)—Anglicized version of *Sliabh Mór*, "Great Mountain."

súgán (shew-gawn) —straw rope. The *súgan* chair, made

Glossary

of wood with a straw rope seat, is a handcrafted piece of country furniture found all over Ireland in both Irish and Scots-Irish traditions.

Tá sí sa leabhar ag an bhfiach dubh. (taw shee saah l-ower egg awn vee-uck duv)—literally "She is in the book of the raven." An old way of saying "her days are numbered," or "her time is up."

Tánaiste (tawn-ish-tuh)—Tanist, second-in-command, heir presumptive; in modern Ireland this is the title of the Deputy Prime Minister.

Teach Faoi Thalamh (chock fwee haw-luv)—House Under Ground

Trian Láir (tree-in lawr)—middle of nowhere, literally "middle of a third"

Togaidh sinn ar fonn an ard,
Togaidh sinn ar fonn an ard
'S ged 'tha mi fada bhuat
Cha dhealaich sinn a'chaoidh*

(togue-ee sheen'yair fown awn aarrd
togue-ee sheen'yair fown awn aarrd
iss keh taw mee faa-taa woo-ah
gaw yaa-lee sheen'ya k'wee)

355

We will lift up our voices
We will lift up our voices
Although I am now so far from you
We will never sever.

Scots Gaelic—song by Celtic folk rock band Runrig, founded in the Scottish Outer Hebrides, with a Canadian from Cape Breton as lead singer.

Tulach Mhór (tuh-luck vorr)—anglicized to Tullamore, literally "Great Hill."

uisce beatha (ish-kaa baah-haa)—literally, "water of life," i.e., the best Irish whiskey!

Note on the reintroduction of the Golden Eagle to Ireland: A five-year project is underway "to re-establish a viable breeding population in the northwest of the Republic of Ireland" with young birds from Scotland. See www.goldeneagle.ie. *Not all that is gone is gone forever.*

Note on the Irish Language

The historical speech of the Irish people is a Goidelic Celtic language variously called Gaelic, Irish Gaelic (as opposed to Scots Gaelic), and Erse. In Ireland, it is simply called the Irish language or "Irish." For over two thousand years, Irish—Old, Middle, and Modern—was the language of Ireland, until the English conquest enforced its near eradication. Today it is the official first language of Eire, the Irish Republic. Recently it has been awarded official status in the Six Counties of Northern Ireland through the Good Friday Agreement.

As a native language or mother tongue, Irish is found only in a number of small communities called *Gaeltachtaí*, located chiefly on the west coast of Ireland. Sadly, these communities are declining due to economic factors, reduced rural population, social disintegration, intermarriage with non-native speakers, attrition, and the settling of non-native speakers in the areas. Some estimates put the demise of the *Gaeltachtaí* within the next few generations, a loss that would be of incalculable magnitude to Irish culture and society. It must be said, however, that native speakers ignore these rumors of their death with characteristic forbearance.

Meanwhile, the knowledge and use of the Irish language is increasing among the English-speaking population of the island. In the most recent census of 2002 (preliminary results), over a million people in the Republic and 140,000 in Northern Ireland reported having a reasonable proficiency in the language. Census figures for the use of Irish continually increase. Globally, study groups and language classes are popular not only among the Diaspora—those Irish and their descendants who have emigrated throughout the world—but also among non-Irish peoples such as the Japanese, Danish, French, and Germans. In the United States (*Na Stáit Aontaithe*), Irish language classes are available throughout the country, while the Internet lists countless sites that teach and encourage Irish.

Back home in Ireland, the grassroots phenomenon of *Gaelscoileanna*—primary and secondary schools teaching in Irish—is widespread and rapidly growing, despite tacit resistance from successive Irish governments. These schools guarantee new generations of Irish speakers whose second language is fluent Irish. The longstanding Irish-language radio station *Raidió na Gaeltachta* continues to broadcast from the viewpoint of native speakers, while the new television station *Teilifís na Gaeilge* (TG4) caters to both native and second-language speakers. Many institutions both private and public support the language, the most venerable being *Conradh na Gaeilge (www.cnag.ie)*.

There are several dialects within the Irish language which express regional differences among the provinces of Munster, Leinster, Connaught, and Ulster. Also extant is Shelta, the secret language of the Irish Travellers (nomadic people who live in caravan trailers) which weaves Romany words with Irish Gaelic.

In whatever form, long may the language survive. *Gaeilge abú!*

ABOUT THE AUTHOR

O.R. Melling was born in Ireland and grew up in Toronto with her seven sisters and two brothers. At eighteen, she hitchhiked across Canada to California, seeking adventure. A year later, she was off to Malaysia and Borneo on a youth-exchange program. That set her motto for life, "to travel hopefully." She has a B.A. in Philosophy and Celtic Studies and an M.A. in Medieval Irish History. To date, her books have been translated into Japanese, Chinese, Russian, Czech, and Slovenian. The next book in her *The Chronicles of Faerie* series, which can be read in any order, is *The Light-Bearer's Daughter*. She lives in her hometown of Bray in Ireland with her teenage daughter Findabhair. Visit her Web site at www.ormelling.com.

This book was designed by Jay Colvin and art directed by Becky Terhune. It is set in Horley Old Style MT, a Monotype font designed by the English type designer Robert Norton. The chapter heads are set in Mason, which was created by Jonathan Barnbrook based on ancient Greek and Roman stone carvings.